SLEIGHT of HAND

Karin Kallmaker
writing as
LAURA ADAMS

Bella
BOOKS

Ferndale, Michigan
2001

Bella Books, Inc.
P.O. Box 201007
Ferndale, MI 48220

Printed in the United States of America on acid-free paper
First Edition

Editor: Lila Empson
Cover designer: Bonnie Liss (Phoenix Graphics)

ISBN 0-9677753-7-X

For Maria, who encouraged this book
before I knew I could I write it.
To all the women who love
stories without boundaries.

Books by Laura Adams:

Christabel
Night Vision (Daughters of Pallas 1)
The Dawning (Daughters of Pallas 2)

Writing as Karin Kallmaker*:

Unforgettable
Watermark
Making Up for Lost Time
Embrace in Motion
Wild Things
Painted Moon
Car Pool
Paperback Romance
Touchwood
In Every Port

*Works writtten by Karin Kallmaker, as well as the Daughters of Pallas series and Christabel by Laura Adams, are published by and available from Naiad Press.

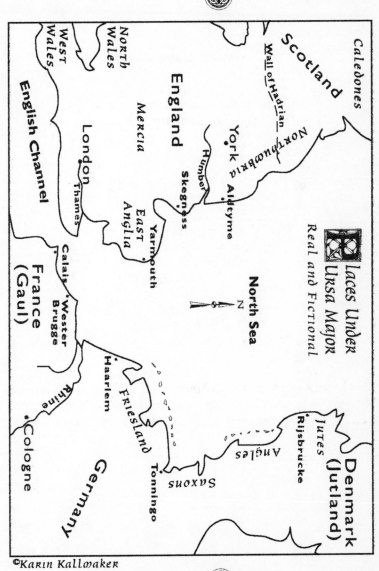

Places Under Ursa Major
Real and Fictional

©Karin Kallmaker

Tableau

"Child."

So much in a single word — admonition, understanding, a gentle reminder of who was who in the cottage where all of them, young and old, had spent most of their lives. A frigid wind rattled the thick windowpanes that were frosted with both a late winter fog and age.

Ursula Columbine was not drinking her tea. She held the thick ceramic mug to quell the urge to clap her hands over her ears and sing "Rule, Britannia" with all the volume of a Women's Institute Chorus. She was twenty-seven and could hardly argue her right to decide her life's path while reverting to childish behavior, even if they were still calling her "child."

As firmly and calmly as she had for the last hour, she said, "I'm in love and I'm going to her."

"You just think you're in love." Aunt Lillidd's tone allowed for no uncertainty in her evaluation.

Ursula wanted to remind Aunt Lill that her life as a celibate left her unqualified to judge affairs of body and heart. Still, she said nothing because she could not be swayed so it mattered naught what Aunt Lill had to say. Why argue when the outcome was certain? She would not change her mind.

It was Aunt Kaitlynn who put voice to Ursula's thoughts. "Oh, Lill, what would you know about it? That's not a criticism, dear, but you should stay within your field of expertise."

Aunt Lill sniffed. Beloved Aunt Kait, Ursula thought. She rested her arm on the mantel, letting the heat of the dancing flames soak into her bones. The cold and bitter winter was almost behind them. Crocuses would soon give way to daffodils.

"I, on the other hand," Aunt Kait went on, "have some small experience in these matters, and I have to tell you, Ursula dear, that you seem far more interested in the subject of love than your lover."

The tea mug sloshed on Ursula's smock as her hands jerked. She dabbed the spill with her sleeve and silently recited the first three stanzas of *Idylls of the King* while Aunt Kait covered in depth the loving, passionate quality that her own many relationships had never lacked. Aunt Kait concluded her lengthy list with, Ursula had to admit, the truthful assessment that she'd become an excellent judge of love, passion, and people.

She wanted to cry. She had thought that of her three aunts Kaitlynn would understand the call of the heart.

"And so I must say," Aunt Kait concluded, "that while you do seem to have a deep connection with Kelly — whom I like, dear, really I do — I think you're hasty in believing her to be your ultimate love."

Ursula smiled without bitterness. "How will we know who is right if I don't go to her?"

"Don't be cheeky." Aunt Lillidd could turn a roomful of schoolchildren to stone with that tone, but Ursula refused to let it have the same effect on her.

"I am going." Ursula gritted her teeth. They were making her feel seventeen, not twenty-seven. "I am not the only person who can convene a ten-point circle!"

"Of course not." Aunt Kait gently touched her shoulder. "But you are the best we have. Think what you will leave. Why can't she come to you?"

Ursula didn't want to leave them. She knew she had a place in the work the circle did. How could she explain that it wasn't enough, that it never had been? It would sound too convenient when they knew, just as she did, that she loved the circle. How could she say now that her happy life was also a drifting one? That it was a life chosen for her by others, out of love, but still not her choice? She hadn't suspected it was so until Kelly had walked into their little store. She belonged with Kelly and had known it instantly. The little time they had spent together before Kelly had gone home had only confirmed the feeling.

"She has a farm and a seed business that is booming. The Internet is a wonderful thing, so she says. She's as attached to her plants as you are, all of you." She'd explained this before. Kelly's similar interests had brought her into their herb store in the first place. She could not explain the inner warning bell that had chimed when she'd thought to ask Kelly if she would consider immigrating instead of the other way around. The journey was hers to undertake — all her instincts said so. "I love you, and I don't want to leave you, please believe that. Every day I'll wonder when I'll see you again."

"You can't walk away from your obligations," Aunt Justine pronounced.

It was too much. The younger woman faced her three judges, who had raised her from birth, bathed and purified her, fed her, loved her and made her one of them.

"Obligations?" Ursula set the mug on the mantel. "I have lived up to a lifetime of obligations —"

"Don't speak to us of lifetimes —"

"You have no idea what you're saying —"

"It's only the beginning, Ursula, dear —"

"Obligations that never ended and will never end." Ursula's voice was squeaky with anger. "I no longer believe that is my only purpose. There is something more, I know it. Maybe I have to go find it. Or maybe Kelly is my purpose and she found me. That was her part. Now I must do the rest."

"Your place is in the circle." Aunt Lill had that tone of having pronounced the final word.

3

Ursula tried to soften her words — there was no room in their lives for bitterness. "I was never happier than when I worked the circle with you. At least until I saw Kelly for the first time. Our circle has no room for one more — it has always been ten plus one. What do I tell her? Give up your life, move here with me, and be excluded from the focal point of my energy? Priscilla can replace me, but who would we throw out of the circle to make room for Kelly? It won't work, you know it won't." She looked at each of them in turn. "Maybe I am meant to start over. That is what my heart tells me to do."

"Your heart is in a flutter over a pretty girl." Aunt Justine wrinkled her nose over the dregs of her tea.

Ursula considered that Kelly wouldn't care for the adjective pretty, but remained silent until Aunt Justine looked up to see why she said nothing. "After all your hard work, Aunt, do you really think I am that shallow?"

"I wouldn't have thought so until now," Aunt Justine replied.

"Justine, Ursula doesn't deserve that. This seems black and white to us, but it can't to her."

"You coddle her, Kait, you always have."

"I am not five years old," Ursula snapped. "You can't talk about me as if I'm not here. I don't want to wait around all my life for some unknown thing to happen to me. Have you ever considered that maybe I'm wasting my life waiting when I ought to actually *do* something?"

"If you're going to act like a child —"

"I'm going!" Now Ursula was shouting, and her turmoil did not allow her to see that the other three women had drawn back a hairsbreadth. The small movement would have amazed her, for she had never seen any of them flinch at anything, at anytime. There was no mirror to tell her that her long, red braid glowed with an inner light or that the ends that hung loose below the braid's final tie stirred as if a breeze blew up from the cold floor. "I'm going. And unless you plan to force one of your special herbal brews on me, you can't stop me."

Silence followed. The three older witches regarded the youngest of them, and by virtue of their many years of living and working together and the precedence of age, Justine answered.

"You are right. You are old enough to stop yourself."

4

Ursula caught her retort before it spilled out. She calmed herself with a brief relaxing spell and found her balance again. Telling her that following her heart was not the adult thing to do, well, it wasn't going to work. She was going, as she had known all along she would. She would make the journey to Kelly, to a farm in Paradise, Pennsylvania, USA.

It was a long way from Aldtyme, a small Northumberland seaport, a very long way from all she had ever known. It would mean an airplane — a different kind of flying than that engendered by one of Aunt Lill's teas. She would miss Aldtyme and her aunts, but Kelly promised hills just as green in spring and people just as stubbornly set in their ways as the close-knit community that had made up Ursula's world until now. It would be enough like Northumberland to make the homesickness bearable, Ursula thought. And Kelly would be there. Love would be there.

"I'm going, then," was all she said.

The day after the vernal equinox, when spring began to brush the moors with the silvered purple of heather, she went.

It had happened a year ago. One year ago, today.

Autumn Bradley shrugged out of her long coat as she pondered the significance of the anniversary. The night air was cool but not so cool that her brisk pace hadn't worked up a sweat. Her pace did not slacken as she remembered hearing the music she remembered. She had been filled with memory for just a moment, and then she had fainted.

Her footsteps were light on the broken ground as she moved noiselessly into the train yard that separated the Las Vegas strip from a neighborhood far less resplendent. She paused, felt she was alone, and crossed the first line of huge storage containers.

She had never heard the music before, but she had remembered it. It had happened the day she turned twenty-six, that is if the tattered address card they'd found in her pocket so many years ago had been hers. The card had been dated March 21 and read in block letters, TO AUTUMN ON HER SEVENTEENTH BIRTHDAY. A clerk who issued identification cards for the State of Nevada had given her the last name Bradley.

If she was the Autumn who had turned seventeen that day ten years ago, she was now twenty-seven. If she was that Autumn, she had had a life before she'd been found muttering to herself in a casino bathroom. The music she had remembered one year ago had been completely new to her ears, so the knowing of it, the feeling of it in her nerves and bones, must come from Before. Before she was seventeen, when she must have known her name for certain.

It was the first thing she had remembered in the ten years since she'd been found. She wondered sometimes how many people thought of themselves as found, not born.

If she was not the Autumn who had turned seventeen that day, she was her own Autumn now, she told herself. She told herself that who she had been Before no longer mattered, but she didn't yet believe it. Still, though the first seventeen years of her life might be lost, the Autumn Bradley who had lived and survived the last ten years had done so with nothing but her wits and her quick fingers. It had been ten years of being on the edge of eviction, the edge of success, the edge of reality. Ten years of saying, "Pick a card, any card." She had survived.

Exactly one year ago, she had heard the music and remembered. Her mind had nimbly translated the Latin to English. Remembering every nuance and upward leaping melody had so stunned her mind that she had fainted.

When the store clerk had helped her up off the floor, she had refused an ambulance and bought the compact disc of *Chants for the Feast of St. Ursula* and a boom box to play it on. It was the first thing aside from groceries, and other necessities like sheets and clothing, that she had ever bought for herself.

All she knew of Saint Ursula, or of the composer Hildegard von Bingen, she learned from the CD liner notes. Saint Ursula had been the leader of a pilgrimage of Christian virgins — 11,000 by some accounts — who had been slaughtered near Cologne by invading Huns sometime in the fourth or fifth century A. D. Hildegard von Bingen was a twelfth-century abbess who had been a prophet, poet and scientist. In her spare time, she wrote, among many other works, the transcendentally beautiful polyphonic liturgy celebrating the Feast of Saint Ursula, the music that had, on her twenty-sixth birthday, made Autumn faint.

~ ~ ~ ~ ~

She passed the third row of containers and considered the clear space she had to cross. Though she made the crossing every night undetected, a natural caution always made her stop and listen. She still felt she was alone, so she trod quickly across the open space to the shadow of the next row of containers. Crossing through the train yard saved her about eight blocks of walking through a neighborhood far more dangerous than the train yard. She was eager to get home, too. It was the anniversary of her first emergent memory. It was her birthday. She would listen to the music again tonight, just as she did every night before she went to sleep. Something — after all these years — something might emerge again.

She considered that what she was feeling was hope. That alone was new. Her emotions were as locked up as her memories. Hope was something she had never felt before, and perhaps that was this year's gift. If so, it was highly questionable because she had always accepted what life had dealt her. To hope for something different was to acknowledge that something was wrong with the here and now. She had never known anything else, so, in spite of its limitations, her current life was all she had. To hope for something else would mean giving up the only thing that was truly hers. She had not known she was capable of that risk, and she never took chances unless she knew she would win.

She stopped to look up at the stars glittering brilliantly in the cool, desert sky. She didn't want her life to change. She shouldn't still be hoping someone would recognize her. She shouldn't be afraid that if she left Vegas the people who had loved her Before wouldn't know where to look. If anything changed she would have to experience not just hope, but self-pity and despair. So she didn't really want to be hoping something would happen today of all days, her birthday, and exactly one year since she had first remembered anything from Before.

But the hope was there. Okay, she thought. I'll just have to deal with it. She hummed a fragment of one of the chants. She did not know how, but her mind translated the Latin. As always, she made plural singular. It meant more somehow.

7

Most beautiful sight,
sweetest scent of desired delights,
I long ever after you in tearful exile.
When may I see you and be with you?
I am alone and you are in my mind . . .

Supposedly it was a plea from Ursula to Christ, assuring Christ of her intent to desert the bridegroom her father had chosen and be his bride instead, as a virgin nun. Autumn thought it seemed a little too physical for a mere religious plea, but since she knew no other religious music she could hardly judge. What she knew of music was what Vegas knew — the never-ending rotation of names on marquees. There had been a time when she'd gone to shows thinking she might find the enjoyment and escape that Las Vegas entertainment provided every night of the year, but none of the show business magic touched her. The Strip was always frenzied. It would be spring break in a few weeks and every marquee would blaze with new shows, new names, new acts, new dancers, and so on — new, new, new.

None of it had come to mean anything to her. Not the acclaimed divas or daring circuses, not the sex symbols, and not the has-beens who still found a stage. Certainly not the nearly naked women and men who paraded on the streets and stages in a cult of youth and beauty. Names on marquees might change, new casinos bolt up from the barren desert floor, but none of it touched her. The only performers she went to see now were illusionists and magicians, and that was just business. She always knew how they did their tricks, but occasionally she learned something she could use in her own meager act.

Suddenly she sensed she wasn't alone anymore. Autumn quickly hid her close-cropped white hair under her coat, and paused. Nothing stirred near her. In the near-total darkness ahead of her, however, four men were crossing between the trains, no more eager to be seen than she was. Thieves, she knew suddenly. Still, there was no telling what impulse would be aroused if they found a woman alone with them in an otherwise deserted train yard. She ought to have been frightened, she knew, but fear was another emotion she rarely experienced.

:We are alone.: She sent the thought winging toward the huddled

8

group and silently slipped between two cars, over the next rail and between two more after that. Every night there were predators between her midnight show at the decrepit House of Cards and her loft. They never found her.

Who am I, she wondered. Who am I to know how to walk safely through the dark? Who am I to plant a simple idea in someone else's brain to keep myself safe?

The train yard finally gave way to badly lit industrial buildings. After several blocks the occasional dwelling showed up, scattered between metalworks, cabinetmakers and auto-body repair shops. The area was beginning to attract the notice of the artsy crowd. Big loft buildings, low rents and Marge's Diner had all the makings an arts community needed.

She rounded the last corner before home and saw that the dog was still there. Ordinary and gray with white paws and ears, the mixed breed, medium-sized mutt watched her come around the corner as if it had known she was approaching. Autumn had to pass it to get home. Every night for the past week the dog had watched her go home.

She had not had a pet in these last ten years and didn't want one now. The dog didn't bark as she passed, but when she was almost out of earshot it whimpered needfully. Not loudly, but just loud enough.

She was already turning and already berating herself for the impulse.

"Nowhere to go, huh?"

The dog's tail thumped enthusiastically on the broken sidewalk. Its eyes held such joy at her attention that Autumn felt blinded for a moment. The sensation passed and the dog was just a dog that wanted a meal and a soft place to sleep. The streets were broken and cold. Hell.

"Well, come on, then." She had not known she had a compassionate impulse in her.

The dog trotted toward her and then walked sedately at her side. And that was the second time Autumn remembered something, but this time she did not faint. This dog was too young to have known her Before, but she had walked this way, with a dog trotting at her side, in her past. Her single, carefully guarded hope had been rewarded. The memory was a gift indeed. Whether the dog was a gift remained to be seen. She imagined her landlord would have something to say about a canine tenant.

She fed the dog — a her, she discovered — some leftover hotdogs, slightly stale pretzels and all the fresh water she wanted, then offered her an old rug near the window. The dog settled with a sigh that could have been happiness or relief. The dog looked at her. She looked at the dog. There was something to be said, but Autumn didn't know what.

Belatedly she remembered to turn on the CD. The moment the first chant began, the dog was on her feet again. She circled Autumn three times, then sat down. So Autumn sat down, her back to the dog's, and wondered who she was that she knew this was the right thing to do.

When the CD was over the dog trotted back to the rug and Autumn ignored the first glimmerings of sunrise. She slept more deeply than she ever remembered doing before, and slept feeling protected in a way she couldn't even describe. It was a new but remembered sensation.

Part One:

The Blade

And so it came to pass that the dagger outlasted
the sheath, its home, and
sought a new place to rest the many years.
— Honore de Blois, "The Lament of Annlynn"

One

How could she have been so stupid? Autumn checked her wallet one more time, but the contents — lack of — hadn't changed.

She'd already broken into her emergency twenty. There was nothing but an old "inspected by" slip of paper in the worn creases.

The white ball circling the numbered slots was dizzying. She had no stake to play the roulette tables now. Her emergency twenty, played properly, had been going to get some groceries, dog food, new shoes she could no longer put off acquiring, and pay her back rent. She was even more broke than she thought. Summer had seemed to arrive early this year, and the record temperatures had used up the last of the House of Cards' antiquated air conditioning. No air conditioning, no customers. No customers, no two-drink minimum. For Autumn, it had meant no shows and no income for the six weeks it had taken for the club owner to raise the cash for repairs. Tonight the club reopened, but she couldn't wait the week it would take for cash to start flowing to her again.

I should have acted then, she thought. She'd had the cash. If she'd played the tables six weeks ago she could have given the club owner the money for the air conditioning. But that would have meant explaining how she had come by the money and why she was willing to pay to keep performing there. The former question she didn't want to answer, and the latter she had no idea how to explain. So she'd waited until her cash had just about run out before she'd gone to the tables, only to discover her cash wasn't almost gone, it was completely gone. She had some coins, but fifty-three cents wouldn't get her anywhere.

Summer wasn't even half over, and an itch between Autumn's shoulder blades made her think the worst hadn't even happened yet.

She knew her face was grim as she abandoned the betting area. Since when was a twenty-dollar bill the difference between flush and broke? She tried to remember a time when things had been any different and came up as empty as her wallet.

Her stomach was already in knots. You can't be sick, she told herself sternly. Why she should have scruples she didn't know. Nobody had scruples in Vegas. What she was about to do was done thousands of times a day by many of the same people, who lived quite well on the proceeds.

There — the fool was even counting it in plain sight. The ruddy-faced tourist pocketed his wallet with half the wad of bills he'd been counting and put the rest of the bills in the hip pocket of his shorts where he was assuming it was safe.

His assumption was wrong.

She didn't take it all. She took the smallest number of bills she could manage during the split-second bump and pat-down. Ruddy Face enjoyed the pat down so much he grabbed her ass, which made her momentarily sorry she hadn't taken more.

She leaned against the bathroom stall door and swallowed her nausea. The revulsion she felt was the strongest emotion she ever experienced. Most of the time she floated in passive, bland contempt for herself and anyone else who lived in or chose to visit Las Vegas. Kindness, affection, passion — they were seas on the moon for all she knew of them. Early in the spring she'd had a brief acquaintance with hope, but that had been short-lived.

She'd netted a twenty and three fives for her trouble. Any other pickpocket would have taken the wallet and the roll of cash.

She wiped her mouth and forehead with toilet paper and didn't fight the voice that answered her.

You are not a pickpocket.

Then what the hell am I? Autumn asked the question every day — every hour. There was never an answer. The voice only told her what she was not. The voice had always been a part of her, for as long as she remembered. She had lived ten years being told by some inner voice what she was not, but never what she was.

She let herself out of the stall and washed her hands. She dabbed the moist paper towel to her still sweating brow. The face of a stranger stared back at her.

What am I? Who am I?

"It doesn't matter," she muttered at her reflection. "As long as you can turn thirty-five bucks into seven or eight hundred." The lumpy woman at the next basin glanced at her and edged away. Autumn knew how her all-black attire and white hair, cut a quarter-inch all over her head, stood out on the Fourth of July when everyone seemed draped in red, white and blue. She smoothed her hair needlessly and glanced at the woman again. "How's the weather in Cleveland?"

Lumpy gaped. "How did you know —"

Autumn was already at the exit. She shrugged. "Lucky guess."

She might not remember a thing before her seventeenth birthday, but luck was still with her.

"How much did you get?"

The laconic voice stopped her for a moment, then she continued toward the roulette tables. Evidently her luck was changing.

Detective Staghorn caught up to her easily. He was big and long-legged and a class-one pest. He was also *crooked*, a word synonymous with cop in Vegas. "You can talk to me now or at the station, you know."

He'd seen nothing. She was too good at what she did for him to have actually seen her lift the bills from Ruddy Face's pocket. Still, she slowed her pace. "I don't know what you're talking about."

"Wanna go look at the security tape?"

"All you're going to see is me minding my own business and some tourist playing grab-ass like I'm for sale."

Staghorn gave her ass a long look. "I hope you got at least fifty. It would be a fair price."

"I don't know what you're talking about," Autumn repeated. Contempt was easy to feel when Las Vegas seemed full of Staghorns. She signaled the croupier and put down the twenty. Without hesitation she put all the chips on red.

"Of course you don't." He was standing too close, and the mix of failing antiperspirant and sticky hair gel turned her stomach. "Master illusionist like you wouldn't have any idea what to do with her hands inside a man's jacket."

"If I were a master illusionist I wouldn't be talking to you." The little white ball landed neatly on red sixteen. She let it ride.

Staghorn smacked his lips to say she'd spoken the truth. Even in good times, her shows at the broken-down House of Cards barely kept her in food.

"Tell me." His smile was nasty. "Are those fingers of yours as talented inside a man's pants?"

"Please." She filled the word with the scorn of royalty.

"Maybe you just need practice with men. Thinking of your fingers busy in a woman's pants, now that gets me going, too."

"You redefine the word *crude*," Autumn snapped. Red nineteen. She pretended to be uncertain when she moved her winnings to black.

"That is, if you're into women. Considering how long I've had my eye on you and all those nights you've arrived home alone, I have no idea what floats your boat."

Autumn clamped down on her growing tension. For some time she'd had the feeling of something outside her loft — sometimes at the window, or just out of sight across the street. Sometimes Scylla would growl at the door. If the explanation was Staghorn, she was in trouble. It never paid to piss off a cop.

Black ten. She moved the eighty dollars in chips to red again. Twenty-five, nine, thirty-four, all red. She split the over six hundred bucks between even money on black and a much riskier bet on black twenty, straight up. She knew the ball would land on black four and she would lose the straight-up bet — she did it to distract the

16

croupier from her run of luck. It didn't pay to win too much in one place if you wanted not to be noticed. She got the loss back on her even-money bet and quit the table with all her six hundred and forty in winnings and yet looking like she'd just lost a big bet.

She ignored Staghorn and wondered if she could find Ruddy Face in order to slip the thirty-five bucks she'd lifted back into his pocket. It would calm the sick feeling still lingering in her stomach. She could hardly do that with Staghorn watching. Maybe the sick feeling was Staghorn, who was dogging her heels all the way to the cashier.

Runs of luck like she always had led to being asked to never play tables in the casinos that noticed, and she relied too much on gambling for income to risk a *persona non grata* label. That she wasn't cheating was irrelevant. She was winning without losing, and that wasn't permitted in a town built by losers. It was why she deliberately lost her straight-up bets in roulette. Even-money bets were far less noticeable.

One more casino and she'd have what she needed to face her landlord again and provide some food for Scylla, who didn't mind table scraps but was much more grateful for Science Diet. Gambling had always paid the rent, but having to use someone else's money to get going — it battered what little self-esteem she had. Ten years on the circuit and she had no savings, no buffer at all. It made her prey to the Staghorns of the world.

She waited in line at the cashier and forgot Staghorn was lingering nearby. Picking pockets again — she felt like she had when the Vegas social-welfare system had let go of her, after she'd been found. She'd tried waiting tables, but her customer-service skills were less than lousy. She was too quick to treat people like the fools they were. Her last waitressing job had had a running card game in the back — that was when she realized she had a gift. She knew the cards as they were dealt, and practicing with a deck at home had yielded instant results — and not just dealing. She found she could imitate any card trick she watched someone else do. Before long she was coming up with her own.

She'd tried to use her gift to win at the poker tables, but it had made her ill. The more she'd told herself she could cheat at cards the louder the voice had told her she was not a cheat. She found she was a terrible liar. The truth just wouldn't go unsaid. She was stuck with a moral code that she had no idea how she'd developed, and yet also with a gift that just cried out for her to break the rules.

After that she'd tried dealing cards, but her skill at sleight of hand had made her first employer too nervous. The pit boss had asked her one day if she knew how to deal off the bottom. Could she just say no? Of course not. The truth would not go unspoken. She'd not only said yes, she'd found herself demonstrating just how easy it was.

She'd learned afterward that it was that easy for her. She also learned that if one casino lets a dealer go, none would hire that dealer for any reason.

She could have gone to Reno, to one of the few independents, but that would have meant leaving the only place she'd ever known, the only place where anyone who might know who she was would come to look for her. In those early years she'd cared about someone coming to look for her. Ten-plus years later it was obvious no one was going to. She was alone, unable even to connect physically or emotionally with other people. Something separated her, kept her from caring or needing or wanting. It was probably the same thing that had taken her memory away.

She thought suddenly of Scylla. There was Scylla. A more well-behaved, pleasing, loving dog was hard to imagine. She connected with Scylla, and that was the only soft spot she had.

She was at the front of the cashier line at last. The cashier handed over six C-notes and two twenties. Before she could pocket it, a large hand closed over hers.

"I'll take this as an advance on what you scored that I am so nicely not running you in for." Staghorn sucked on his teeth, and she hated the sound of it. Her six hundred and forty dollars disappeared into his shirt pocket. "I never saw anything so smooth. We could have a nice partnership."

Autumn clenched her hands. Anything to get rid of Staghorn for now until she could think what to do. How had she gotten on Staghorn's skewer?

"Good girl," he purred. "You think about what I said. About partnership — and those talented fingers of yours." He sucked his teeth again, the avaricious sound of which nearly cost her what was left of the meager dinner in her stomach.

Though inside she was reeling, she walked steadily through the sweltering dusk to the next faux opulent casino. In spite of the lavish, outrageously improbable exteriors, all casinos were the same on the inside. She no longer heard the endless bedlam of bells, music and the clack of slot machines. She got chips for two of the three fives Staghorn didn't know she had left. The bastard. Black, red, red, black, black, black and on to the next casino. She did not look around to see if Staghorn was following her. She couldn't show him fear.

Sloppy tourists and overdressed working girls clogged the entrance to Caesar's. She forced her way through, aware that she was the only one wearing a jacket of any kind. A three-quarter-length black leather jacket over tight black cotton-and-spandex bodywear was her daily attire. She liked her stage persona and never wore anything else when she was in the casinos. She presented the same face to the world no matter what. Staghorn would not see anything different no matter how hard he looked. She would not show him a vulnerable side.

Red, black, red, black, red, red, black. The croupier was noticing — he was paid to notice. She deliberately lost a straight-up bet and cashed out again, six hundred and forty dollars to the good.

It was after eleven. She had what she needed and her workday was just beginning. Her throat ached with cigarette smoke, and she had a midnight show at the House of Cards ahead of her. Not having time for one of the many cheap buffets that kept her and Scylla alive, she spent six bucks on a burger and Coke and walked out to the moonlit but still baking streets. Fourth of July fireworks displays over the Strip were winding down, but the sidewalks were still crowded with tourists gawking at laser lighting and gaudy fountains.

She reached the House of Cards just before midnight and quickly set up the small amount of staging she needed. The rent was due, and she could pay it, and last month's, too.

She signaled the club owner, and the curtains parted.

Sucker.

Fear was gone — contempt was back. Autumn had the out-of-towner hooked, and he didn't even know it yet. His wallet was up one sleeve, and she was wearing his watch.

19

"How did you do that? How'd you do it?"

Autumn shrugged. "You don't believe in magic?"

"I know it's a trick of some kind."

"No, this is a trick." She held up the wrist with his watch on it. "You're five minutes fast, though."

The small audience snickered with appreciation. She slipped the watch off and let him snatch it from her fingertips. Mr. Tight Collar was the worst audience sucker she'd played in a while — no sense of humor. She wasn't often wrong when she picked her pigeons.

Tight Collar looked down at the paper he'd written a name on, watched her tear the paper into pieces, and throw the paper away. Now the paper was back in one piece, complete with creases that looked like they had once been torn. "Tell me how you did it."

"Magic, I told you. You believe me, right?" She appealed to the bleary woman who had been seated at the table with him. Tipsy Missus looked about four deep in the two-drink minimum.

"Looked like magic to me," she slurred.

"You're sweet," Autumn said. "I'd like to buy you a drink." She whipped Tight Collar's wallet out of her sleeve so quickly it looked like it appeared from nowhere. "Hey, waiter, here, put it on one of these credit cards."

There was laughter and applause while Tight Collar blustered and grabbed at his wallet. He stuffed it into his pocket and glared at her. Autumn was sure he thought he'd retrieved all his belongings.

She flicked his Discover card into view between her index and middle finger. He yelped and snatched it. American Express. Snatch. Library card. Snatch. Driver's license. Snatch.

The audience was howling at that point. At least her hard work was pleasing them. Tight Collar dropped all the loot he'd been gathering onto Tipsy Missus and looked like he was going to take a swing at her.

"Cute kids." Photographs were a little harder to handle because they flexed more, but she managed to flip out the next one. Just as he reached for it she took in the cheesecake pose and complete lack of resemblance to Tipsy Missus and flicked it back into her sleeve, producing another photo in its place. Fear that Tipsy Missus would see it accounted for his panic. Cheating bastard.

"Okay, here're the rest." Autumn favored him with a congenial stage smile that was wasted on him. She'd even put the mistress's photo on the bottom of the stack, but he would just think that was dumb luck. "Thanks for being such a good sport." She headed for the two steps to the small stage. "How about a hand for my victim?" A twenty dropped out of her coat and she knew without looking that Tight Collar had jumped on it like a bear on a fish.

The audience kept laughing as a few more bills floated down. She'd only taken three or four, and one of them was hers. Never let it be said that Autumn Bradley took more than she gave back. She could hardly afford the money, but it was a defense to say she always gave more back than she took if anyone accused her of stealing. Which sometimes they did. If Tight Collar made trouble later, she'd tell Tipsy Missus to check his photo collection.

Card tricks were her specialty, but she was equally skilled at manipulations — coins appearing from nowhere, balls or dice seeming to multiply or vanish, and other minor sleight-of-hand tricks. Sometimes she played it so her marks were utterly absorbed in what her hands were doing. They would look out at the roaring audience, perplexed at what was so funny, never seeing that the disappearing balls were simply being tossed aside. That was how fast her fingers were; that was how intimate her "magic" was. In larger rooms she always lost the fringes. She needed people up close to trick them.

She stuck with it, year after year, because all she wanted was to know who she was. Being good at magic and mind tricks was the only insight she had into that question. She wanted an epiphany of some sort that would tell her who she was and why she was here.

She set up the next trick with her usual panache. Why bother about the past, she told herself. She fanned out the deck on the small table and glanced around for her next pigeon. You're probably an escaped mental case and your purpose in life is to be empty.

You are not an escaped mental case. Your purpose in life is not to be empty.

She caught herself before her wandering mind affected the act. She quickly chose Flowery Blouse at table three and asked her to "Pick a card, any card."

She always closed with handcuff escapes. Because of the small venue and the closeness of the tables, the simple act of removing locked handcuffs from her wrists, and then the wrists of volunteers, always drew amazed response. There were no half-naked showgirls, shimmering mirrors or hungry lions to distract them. The cuffs would fall off right before their eyes, sometimes within inches, at the lightest touch of Autumn's fingertips.

Leather Babe, whom Autumn chose because she looked as if she knew her way around handcuffs for recreational purposes, was delighted. Cynical amusement replaced Autumn's habitual contempt — that was quite a range of emotion for her in one night. She let Leather once again test the cuffs and spin the ratchets through, then Autumn cuffed her loosely and let her try to work her way out. Leather only succeeded in clicking the ratchets tighter.

Autumn said aloud, "Given the leather bodysuit, I thought for sure you'd know how to get out of cuffs — you know, for when the key goes missing." The audience laughed, but Leather's blue-now-green eyes were not as amused as the smile she wore. Autumn found she had to blink to break her gaze. Leather was just another sucker, in spite of the way she carried herself, Autumn told herself. She thought she could show you up and she couldn't. *C'est la vie, Leather Babe.*

Autumn put an index finger on the keyhole of each cuff and closed her eyes. They were trick cuffs, and simple to open if you knew how. The locks popped and the cuffs clanked loudly to the floor.

"There are people I know who would love to be able to do that!" Leather Babe had decided to be a good sport, so Autumn gave her a rare smile. Leather arched one eyebrow and lips that seemed suddenly full and alluring curved into a suggestive smile. "Do you give private lessons?"

Autumn caught her breath. It would never do to let the audience see her flustered, but flustered she was. The sensation in her stomach was utterly foreign and terrifying because she seemed to have no control over it. "My secrets are my own," she managed, which was what she always said when someone asked for lessons. This woman was suggesting something far more intense than lessons.

"Why don't we try *my* cuffs?"

The familiar and detested voice added to Autumn's consternation. It was Staghorn, the bastard. He had his police cuffs dangling from one hand and his badge in the other.

The audience good-naturedly egged him on. Leather backed away a few feet, her presence suddenly neutral to Autumn's nerves. Never let a heckler get the upper hand, Autumn thought belatedly. Leather had thrown off her pacing, and now Staghorn was actually on the stage and reaching for her wrists.

Possibilities for graceful escape were dwindling, but as he snapped them on — too tightly, the rat snake bastard — she knew this was probably not going to end well for her. She had labored for such a long time for such a small reputation, and Staghorn was going to ruin what there was of it. She suddenly knew his goal was to make her dependent on him for a living as a pickpocket.

An anticipatory silence fell over the room. Autumn did not notice that Leather stepped closer to witness what did or did not happen.

"Are you sure you want people to know how lousy Vegas P.D.'s cuffs are?" It was a feeble try, but all Autumn could think of.

"I can handle it." Staghorn was smug. She wanted to boot his face around the room. Anger, again.

She flicked her wrists so her thumbtips were on the keyholes. They weren't trick cuffs, she reminded herself. This wasn't going to work. She closed her eyes.

Open, damn it! It was just a thought, a plea of desperation. Then she felt the weights fall from her wrists and heard the hard thunk as the twin pieces of metal hit the stage floor.

The audience went crazy. She clung to a nonchalant air in spite of the fury in Staghorn's eyes. She jumped, though, when Leather Babe whispered in her ear, "Well done!"

Staghorn bent to pick up his cuffs, then caught her completely off guard as he grabbed her arms and spun her around to cuff her hands behind her back. He used Leather as a wall to twist Autumn's arms as he did it so that her elbows were together and fingers splayed apart. He was good at it. She was caught before she could utter more than, "What the hell?"

She was only on her feet because Leather was holding her up. Autumn's cheek was against Leather's breast, and she again felt a terrifying swell of foreign emotion. "You can do this," Leather whispered.

Leather helped her get her balance back, then stepped away. The audience was beginning to figure out something was amiss. She saw the club owner hovering at the side of the stage, looking for a sign from her that things were okay. She nodded slightly and added another emotion to the night's list — she was not just angry, she was enraged. Usually she didn't bother enough with people to get more than cranky.

She looked Staghorn up and down, not bothering to hide her contempt. "I don't know what your game is, but this is my stage." *Open*, she thought. She couldn't even touch the locks this time, and they were not trick cuffs. *Open*.

And the cuffs dropped to the floor.

Staghorn's eyes were dark with an emotion Autumn didn't want to name. The crowd was cheering, and Leather had left the stage. I am nobody's tool, she thought. I never have been, I never will be.

You are nobody's tool, her voice answered, for the first time telling her what she was instead of what she was not.

Staghorn slammed out of the room ahead of the rest of the audience. She was clearing up her stage gear when she sensed another presence at the side stage. Her skin felt as if it were rippling. It was a pleasing sensation, but the lack of control was not. She tried to find a smile for Leather Babe, who had encouraged her to beat Staghorn's little game, but her stage persona was exhausted. Smiles never came easily to her and were even harder to come by when she was tired.

"How come you're not playing the big clubs?" Leather's chestnut-blond hair was tightly coiled into a type of braid Autumn hadn't seen before, and it hung all the way down to a curvaceous bottom. It made Leather's eyes look enormous. Those blue-now-green eyes were watching Autumn put the cards and other paraphernalia away.

Autumn knew she looked into the fathomless blue-green too long before answering. Her palms were damp. She almost felt ill. "First of all, mounting a production like that takes money. Second of all, you have to have a different kind of talent than what I've got. Large audiences take an incredible amount of showmanship to manage, and I spend all my energy on what I'm doing."

"Mirrors and glitz are hardly your style, that's true." She glanced around the cheaply painted black background spangled with silver stars. "You do have a talent though, and isn't talent supposed to be enough?"

Autumn shrugged. "I've seen shows where the maestro's only talent was strutting a bare chest and hiring buxom assistants. Otherwise, it was all black-on-black curtains and pushing the right button." She snapped the packing case closed and set the locks, then began pushing it backstage. She didn't protest when Leather put one shoulder to it as well.

Their faces were inches apart. Leather wore a faint perfume, an earthy scent that tickled Autumn's nostrils. It mingled with the soft leather that molded her breasts. Autumn could still feel the sensation of them under her cheek. She thought fleetingly that she'd never considered wanting a woman, but then she had never considered wanting a man either. Wanting was not something she experienced. There was habitual contempt, and more rarely a faint amusement or frustration. Tonight there had been anger and a near-blinding rage. And this.

Leather was kissing her now, and Autumn felt naked with desire and terror. Her tight black shirt felt like it was on fire. She opened to Leather's exploration of her mouth and the something in her that was always rigid, always on guard, it didn't yield, but the tide of emotion ignored the guards and she was lost. Leather's perfume was intoxicating. It was as if Autumn had never known caution or restraint.

She forgot to breathe, forgot to blink. She felt as if she were wavering on the edge of a precipice that had always been at her feet yet she'd never seen before. Something — just a flicker, as insubstantial as a mote of dust — moved inside her, and she remembered being in a woman's arms before.

It hadn't been like this. She had not felt afraid and lost and overwhelmed. She had not — the memory was slipping away and so was all the fear. She was aching with the pressure of Leather's kiss, and when their mouths finally parted she groaned with loss.

"I wouldn't have believed it," Leather whispered, and she kissed Autumn again.

~ ~ ~ ~ ~

They were in Leather's car, a low, sleek sports car as violently red as Leather's lips. Autumn was forgetting something, she knew that much, but she gave shaky directions to her loft and trembled inside for what they were going to do when they got there. Academically, she knew what it was. Sex was commerce in Las Vegas, and it was everywhere. She had moved through it like a sleepwalker, untouched by both cheap and profound beauty, equally unmoved by subtle or profane cues.

"I don't even know your name," she managed.

Leather turned right at the light Autumn indicated and accelerated hard. The warm desert air whipped past Autumn's ears. "Rueda."

Autumn didn't say, "How unusual," but Rueda smiled as if she knew Autumn was thinking it.

In all the years Autumn had lived in the furnished loft over her landlord's woodworking shop, the only person who had been inside had been Ed, and then only when the rent was past due. He'd visited just that morning, sorry to do so, but rent was rent. Autumn knew she should feel self-conscious about the dirty dishes piled up, the mattress on cinder blocks with less than fresh sheets, but those impulses were little used and did not bother her now.

What she should have remembered, and did not, was that the dog she had named Scylla was waiting for her at the edge of the train yard, just as she had waited every night for the last two and a half months.

"Let it out," Rueda was telling her. Autumn wanted to scream with the pleasure of Rueda's fingers. She felt alive — finally alive, not sleepwalking through the days and nights, wondering who she was and when she would remember.

She did remember this, and it was exquisite. Rueda's leather peeled away, and Autumn tasted the skin underneath, every sensation new and old. Soft, alluring breasts, the heat and wet of desire. She felt as if she was being baptized to a religion of ecstasy, one that sang true in her bones and her heart and her soul because it was what she was, a part at least, a glorious, wrenching, wild part. She was alive. And so she screamed when sensation was too much to bear and did not hear Rueda's throaty laugh of victory.

A mile away, on the other side of a dark train yard, a gray, mixed-breed dog was waiting patiently. Suddenly its ears swiveled back and tail went down, then it leapt toward home with a howl that might have been a warning or a lament.

Autumn clawed her way up from the depths she had traversed, aware of Rueda straddling her. She smiled and ran her hands over the strong thighs and wondered how she could propose returning all the sensation Rueda had given her.

"There's no need," Rueda whispered. She bent to kiss Autumn affectionately on the nose. "Though I can assure you that I wish there was enough time." Her smile was unsettlingly triumphant. "But I would like to try one more thing before the moon sets. A little extra fireworks." She withdrew a small black pouch from the satchel she had carried into the house.

Autumn was too replete with satisfaction to do more than watch curiously. And so she was unprepared for Rueda's sudden move to hold the open pouch under her nose.

Immobility seared through her nerves. Her breath rattled in her ears as if she were under water. From a great distance she heard Rueda say, "And now we'll use my cuffs."

They were not cuffs, they were manacles. Autumn knew they were old, very old, and the metal burned her wrists with cold. Rueda said something, it might have been Latin, when she locked each of Autumn's wrists and Autumn had a muddled vision of Rueda's hair wound around her head like a crown. She glowed under her skin like the moonlight through the thin blinds. From the bag, now that Autumn's hands were bound above her head, Rueda drew a black and pitted dagger.

Autumn wanted to scream again, but her throat was closed. She could hardly breathe, and she was utterly helpless. *Open,* she pleaded. *Open, please.* The manacles remained shut.

"That won't work now." Leather spoke as if to a small child. "It was very good of you to demonstrate, however. I was able to prepare for it."

Autumn's vision was fading in and out, light and dark. She hoped she would suffocate before whatever Rueda intended to do with the dagger was begun. She couldn't face this — she wasn't that strong.

You are that strong. The voice was there, that useless, stupid voice, telling her for the second time in all these years what she was instead of what she was not.

Who was she that she should have to face this? What had she done to deserve death this way?

Rueda straddled Autumn again. She raised the dagger, and cold light seemed to dance on its sharp tip. "You came willingly to this bed. You even wanted me," she said as if they were continuing an ordinary conversation. "I think that's what I've been doing wrong."

Pain exploded in every cell of Autumn's body, and in the last beat of her heart she was floating above the pain, looking down at the blade trembling inside her chest and hearing Rueda's laughter on the hot wind.

Two

Did all journeys begin with not leaving? Ursula Columbine ignored the jostling of the overexcited man behind her in the queue for the gate and ticketing counter. "I'm sorry, but what does *overbooked* mean?"

"It means we're screwed," the man snapped. "I demand compensation," he snarled at the uniformed woman behind the counter.

"I'm doing the best I can," the woman said coolly. Her nametag said she was Elsa Goodings.

"Ms. Goodings," Ursula said calmly, "I've never flown before, and I'm very confused. I know I'm going to get where I'm going, but how?"

Ms. Goodings's prim smile warmed a little. "I know it's frustrating. You see, we can't afford to have empty seats. So we sell more tickets than we have seats, so if people don't show up we'll still have someone to pay the fare. It's one of the ways we keep our prices down."

"And the people who show up last because they actually work for a living get screwed out of their seat." The man's nasal American accent grated on Ursula like a saw on wood.

"But I didn't get here last," Ursula said to Ms. Goodings. "I've been here nearly four hours. I went to the counter at the very front of the terminal and they gave me this." She gave her ticket packet to Ms. Goodings. The clerk at the main counter had said she was all checked in and didn't have to get to the gate until thirty minutes before departure. Ursula had taken advantage of the free time to walk the airport and look at everything. She'd seen more people in those few hours than she had in her entire life. When she'd come to the gate there had been a long line, but since she was already checked in she had waited near the Jetway. Then they had announced the flight was full and anyone who had not yet checked in at the desk would not get on the plane.

"Oh dear," Ms. Goodings said. "No one told me there'd been an early check-in, and I've promised the first ten standbys already. Oh my, I am so sorry." She began frantically pecking at her keyboard.

The man was shaking his head. "Nothing but mistakes. You wonder how they get a plane in the air."

"It's not your fault," Ursula said to Ms. Goodings. "I just don't know what to do now."

"You scream loud." The man seemed intent on making a scene.

Ursula studied his face for a moment, trying to empathize with his frustration. "What good would that do me? I might feel better, but she won't feel better, and then my feeling better will wear off because I still wouldn't have a seat on this flight. So I'll actually feel worse because I made her feel bad and didn't make myself feel better in the end. So I might as well keep my temper, which actually makes me feel better at the outset."

The man blinked. "I-I, I guess so."

Ms. Goodings had pretty eyes, Ursula thought, especially when she was trying not to laugh. "There you are, Ms. Columbine. You can board at any time."

"But the flight is full." Ursula looked at Ms. Goodings in awe. "How did you manage it?"

"You were here first so I was able to switch things around a bit. Have a pleasant journey. I hope I'll see you again on British Airways."

She thanked Ms. Goodings profusely and hardly heard the American meekly asking for whatever arrangement Ursula had just managed. Then she was swept into the queue for the Jetway. She stumbled when a suitcase nudged her in the knees. The fellow next to her caught her before she fell.

"Thank you," she stammered. She was not used to everyone trying to go everywhere all at once regardless of the laws of physics.

"Don't mention it. Are you traveling alone?" Another American, though his accent was slower and less nasal.

"Yes," she said, before she remembered Merwyn Dee's warnings to her just this morning about foreign men. To Merwyn anyone not from their corner of Northumberland was foreign.

"I'd take good care of you. It's a long flight. We could really get to know each other."

His tone seemed overly familiar, but Ursula met his gaze to take his real measure. He winked at her. Aunt Justine would call that saucy, but there was nothing in him that frightened her. "Thank you for your kindness," she said gently.

He colored slightly, and his bravado faded. "They want your ticket," he said finally.

"Oh, sorry." Ursula realized she was holding up the line.

The steward tore one of her tickets out of her packet and said 'Welcome aboard," in a tired, automatic voice. He glanced at her, then looked into her eyes. His face lit up with a genuine smile. "Have a pleasant flight."

She crossed the plane's threshold and sniffed the pungent mix of disinfectant and fuel. She showed the flight attendant her ticket. "I'm not sure where."

"Row two, on the left, window seat," the woman said. She gestured vaguely.

"Thank you," Ursula said. She took a moment to make eye contact — she'd not yet met so many people that day that she wanted to avoid it. It seemed everyone around her was avoiding actually looking at each other, as if they no longer had room in themselves for remembering eyes. Ursula hoped she would never travel so much or so far that she would tire of the moment of meeting a new person.

The flight attendant's professional distance seemed to dissolve as their gaze met. Her nametag said she was Jenna Beaudelaire. "You're welcome. Right over here. Is that your only bag?" Jenna seemed startled.

"Yes," Ursula said. Several boxes of books and one box of clothes had been sent to Kelly's address last week by parcel service. She carried only a few books, her identification papers, some last minute gifts that she'd received as she'd left Aldtyme that morning, and a change of clothes. A family with several small bags and diaper supplies pushed past them. "I guess this is traveling light."

"It'll fit nicely right there." Jenna pointed at the space under the seat in front of hers. "Is this your first flight?"

Ursula nodded. She was not frightened, but she was excited in a way that made her stomach feel odd. She knew Kelly would be waiting for her. Her pulse suddenly pounded. There had hardly been enough privacy or opportunity to satisfy what they had both wanted. It had only been a beginning. Belatedly she realized Jenna was still lingering. "I'm not nervous, though. A bit excited."

Jenna lightly touched her shoulder. "It'll be fine." She demonstrated how to make the roomy seat recline into a comfortable sleeping position. It was far more luxurious than Ursula had expected. "If you want anything at all, or have questions about what's happening aboard, just push this button and I'll be right with you. In a few minutes, I'll be back with some juice so you can settle in."

"Thank you." Everyone was being so nice, really. After Merwyn Dee's dire predictions about the surliness of city folk, especially in crowded Newcastle, it was a welcome surprise.

She watched a few more passengers file down the aisle nearest her, noting that they looked enviously at her roomy seat. They proceeded through a curtain to the rear. She craned her neck and saw much less comfortable and far more crowded seating stretching the length of the aircraft.

32

She was in first class. She pushed the button, and Jenna was there almost immediately. "There seems to be some mistake. I don't have a first-class ticket."

Jenna put her index finger over her lips. "Mum's the word. I understand there was a problem with your boarding pass, and the people at the gate can fix it this way. You got the last empty seat."

"Ms. Goodings was very nice," Ursula volunteered.

"A compliment instead of a complaint — thank you," Jenna said. "Relax and enjoy it. Not bad for a first time."

An hour later, with the plane gliding gracefully over a bank of white clouds, Jenna's words came back to Ursula. Not bad for a first time. She found the sensation of flight pleasing and reclined her seat to rest. She'd been up at four A.M. and had left the only home she'd ever known as the winter sun rose. It had been bitterly cold and, though she'd begged, her aunts had refused to let her walk alone to Merwyn Dee's. Lillidd went before her while Justine and Kaitlynn came behind, just as they had always entered the circle.

Lights had been on in cottages, which was strange for so early. Doors were open, even, letting out precious heat. "We'll miss you," someone called.

Ursula recognized Priscilla Muldoon's voice, and she raised a hand in her direction. She'd said a formal good-bye and given the kiss of peace last night to the others in the working circle, when she'd officially ceded her place to Priscilla. She'd walked the interlaced path for the last time, at least here. She and Priscilla had a special bond from a Midsummer's Night working nearly ten years earlier. It had been so easy and fun with Priscilla. So fevered and hurried with Kelly.

The town shops had been open early, and she'd quickly been laden with a small box of clotted creams, a tin of biscuits, two drop scones already split, buttered, and smeared with orange marmalade, and a fresh, still-hot pasty. Merwyn Dee's old lorry was cold for the first hour, and the hot pasty had warmed her hands. The tea towel it had been wrapped in had dried tears that sprang up every time she thought of her three aunts waving good-bye through tears of their own, wondering if they would ever see her in the flesh again.

She'd split the pasty with Merwyn and wondered how long it would be before she had another like it. They didn't eat much mutton in America, Kelly said, so it could be a long time. It had been a thoughtful gift. Everyone had been so kind, although she was leaving all of them, perhaps forever.

Perhaps forever.

As the distance between her and England grew, Ursula felt she might never get back. She rolled over so her sudden tears would be a secret between her and the wall. She might never see her beloved aunts again. She was homesick for them already.

She remembered, then, the scones. She dried her eyes and sat up. The scones were cold, but they melted in her mouth. She wanted tea and more preserves, to be a child again when an extra lump of sugar in the tea and a fresh biscuit made the world a perfect place. She wanted home. Kelly would become home, she told herself. Kelly is your home now.

"How are you faring?" Jenna offered a cup of freshly brewed tea.

"I'm fine. Thank you." She sipped the tea and hoped her recent tears didn't show.

"Would you like some lunch now? You could start with a salad and cheese."

Merwyn Dee had said they'd probably feed her nothing but juice and peanuts, so she'd been glad of the scones. "I think I like first class." Ursula smiled at Jenna because she knew Jenna would smile back. Jenna did, and Ursula felt better.

"Like I said, not bad for a first time. I'll start your salad, then."

Not bad for a first time, Ursula echoed. She looked out the window and had to close her eyes. She wanted to visualize the memory perfectly. Kelly had said just those words after they'd first made love. It was time to think about Kelly and not so much about home. Kelly will become home, she repeated to herself.

It had been a day like any other, very late fall with winter taking grasp. Aunt Kait had been baking bread while Aunt Justine measured dried herbs and slipped them in packets for sale. Aunt Lillidd separated seeds for next year's planting and wrapped them for storage.

Her task that morning had been inventory, something they all hated. The shop bell had tinkled, and she had turned from counting packets of dried marjoram to see a broad-shouldered woman closing the door. Broad-shouldered and tall, with short hair the color of late summer wheat.

She hadn't been able to breathe — even now Ursula remembered the sensation. The shop suddenly glowed with the light of a full working, or at least it had seemed to her. She had struggled to find words to greet this newcomer, unable to overcome the shocked awareness that her life had just changed forever.

Her offer of assistance finally passed her lips and she met the toffee-colored gaze with an intense sensation of joy. Kelly Dove, who was visiting from Pennsylvania USA, wanted to know where the best walking was.

"It depends what you're looking for," Ursula had answered.

Kelly hadn't answered right away. Then she abruptly inhaled as if she'd forgotten to breathe. "Vegetation and trees. Wild herbs I can perhaps take a few clippings from. I run a seed farm at home for herbs. It's a hobby I love, comparing varieties of the same species from different parts of the world. It gives me an excuse to travel all sorts of places."

"I'd walk the rim of the moor," Ursula told her. "The variety between moor and forest is interesting, and the largest plant diversity is there."

"I don't suppose — I was hoping to hire a guide. Someone in another shop said I might find somebody willing here."

Ursula considered that she was willing. Willing for more than she could consider without blushing. She knew that even if Kelly hadn't asked for a guide she would have found a way to spend more time in her company. Her blood was singing. She knew her cheeks were stained with color.

Aunt Kait had come out from the kitchen and said, "Why don't you go with her, Ursula? Let me put together a lunch for both of you so you can make the best of the light."

Just like that it was settled. Ursula had refused any form of payment, saying any excuse to escape her taskmaster aunts was a welcome one. Kelly's eyes glinted with ready laughter and something more, something that made Ursula breathless for the first few minutes of their walk.

They'd tramped up the hill behind the village to the flat of the moor, then across the tufts of brittle heather to the edge of the forest near the sea cliffs. They'd looked down at the gray ocean and Ursula had had the first wave of déjà vu, as if she and Kelly had stood on the cliff before. It was most unsettling because the flash of memory had been of them both as adults and yet she knew she had never seen Kelly before today. She would not have forgotten someone with the light Kelly carried with her.

As they walked the feeling grew and her memory-vision gained color and sound. The forest and its creatures were virtually unchanged. They, on the other hand, seemed to be wearing more cumbersome clothing and their words were garbled. They would sound almost familiar but then utterly foreign.

They reached an outcrop of rock and, rather than walk around, Kelly climbed them. It was easy for her long, well-muscled legs. Ursula could make the same quick scramble upward but took the hand Kelly offered because she had done so in the memory-vision. She took it because, here and now, she wanted to touch Kelly.

Kelly had almost lost her grasp for a moment, then hauled Ursula upward with an impressive display of steady strength. Ursula's body was shuddering with awareness — the momentary clasp of their fingers had unfolded the rest of her memory, of another time, another life, when they had completed each other. It was only a flash, but she had seen Kelly in a thick gray robe tied with deep red cording that blew into view when her long cloak was opened by the wind. A flash, then it was gone. It was enough.

She looked into Kelly's eyes more deeply than before — they were a lovely golden brown, like a fawn's first coat. She knew those eyes, knew she had looked into them, just this way, long ago. The cold seemed to make the air between them crackle.

Kelly finally said, with uncertainty welling in her eyes, "I don't — I don't believe this."

"I believe enough for both of us," Ursula said. She drew Kelly into the sheltering privacy of the trees. She brushed Kelly's short hair behind her ears, then gently cupped the back of her neck. The kiss had felt like journey's end and beginning at the same time, and Kelly's moan of surprise and desire had stirred Ursula's pulse to a higher point. She slipped her fingers inside the collar of Kelly's shirt and began to unfasten her anorak with her other hand. Here, now. It was needful.

Kelly's touch was at first timid, as if she did not quite know what to do. But when Ursula guided her hands under the thick woolen sweater, the shock of warm skin to her cold fingers seemed to wake Kelly from a long dream.

Kelly had kissed her harder then, grasped her waist and kissed her with a pent-up passion that had startled Ursula, then aroused her further. She guided one of Kelly's hands to the waistband of her old trews, inviting an exploration in which she intended to hold back nothing.

It was not the easy dance of Midsummer's Night, not the quick and casual coupling that shared life and light. Their mutual need was too undeniable for that. Kelly was breathing hard in her ear and held Ursula tight when her knees buckled. Without stopping her sensuous attention, Kelly lowered Ursula to the mossy ground, then kissed her again. Ursula held nothing back, she never did, it wasn't her way. She needed, she said so, and Kelly knew what to do. Kelly knew what she wanted, and Ursula joyously gave back the passion Kelly had given her.

They had lain quietly on the cold earth for a few minutes, hands wet and legs tangled. Ursula blinked away her tears and looked into the warm brown of Kelly's eyes, surprised to find tears there as well. Kelly did not seem a woman to cry.

"Not bad for a first time." Kelly had laughed in her ear, and even on an airplane, several months later, Ursula could feel the warmth of it. Their walk on the moor had become a search for hiding places, looking for any screened privacy just long enough to touch and please each other again, to wonder aloud why it felt so right, why they felt they had known each other all their lives. Ursula did not share with Kelly her intuition that they had known each other in an earlier time. She did not know if Kelly was ready to believe or if Kelly even needed to believe.

Two days later Kelly had gone home, but not before asking Ursula to come with her. Ursula had asked for some time to decide because her life in Aldtyme, as simple as it appeared, was deeply connected to many people. It was her decision to make, but could not be made in a moment. After that first week without Kelly, Ursula had found herself thinking about not if she could say good-bye to this person or that, but how and how soon.

In another six hours or so she would see Kelly again. Her voice on a long-distance call had not been enough. Her short, almost terse letters had not been enough, even though Ursula knew how to read between lines. She saw the desire and love in every word. She'd argued with her aunts, known she was right, and now she was finishing the journey that had begun with that first kiss.

She relived the kiss until Jenna brought her lunch. After that she put herself to sleep, and the memory of the kiss was still there. Journey's end. Journey's beginning. Could it matter when Kelly was there?

She changed planes in New York, after going through customs and receiving several pamphlets about her visa and noncitizen status. She hadn't given citizenship a thought and wondered if not being one would limit her ability to stay for a very long time. Americans were in even more of a hurry than Brits — she felt pummeled by the time she found the next queue. The flight on the smaller aircraft was also overbooked, but she was one of the last to get a seat. The offer of money to wait for a later flight wasn't inducement enough to delay seeing Kelly for even a few more hours.

The time in the air from New York to Philadelphia was short, but as cramped and uncomfortable as she'd been led to expect all air travel to be. Heavy rain delayed their departure for an extra hour. She watched drops pelt the small window and wished she weren't thirsty. The stale air gave her a headache.

It took effort to shut out the man in the next seat reciting a tedious rundown of plots from recent episodes of an American television program. His traveling companion only grunted in reply. Takeoff and touchdown were both bumpy and Ursula dearly wished she had saved the scones. A taste of home would have been helped enormously.

They weren't even at the gate when everyone stood up and began hoisting their luggage onto their shoulders and standing in the aisle. Bags and computer cases were everywhere, but no one could get out of the plane yet.

Ursula stood up after a minute because everyone else had done so, even though the purpose of it wasn't clear. She bumped her head on the overhead compartment and scrabbled at her bag under the seat. Hunching over was uncomfortable. She looked around. There was enough space for her to stand in the aisle if the man next to her would lean back. "Excuse me," she said. She gestured at the empty space. "Might I step over there?"

"Lady, we'll be moving in a min —" His eyes were the same color as a rich, dark cup of tea. "I mean, sure."

He leaned back, and Ursula slipped past him. "That's much more comfortable, thank you."

"You're welcome." His expression was bemused.

A waft of damp but fresh air announced the opening of the door, and Ursula's spirits lifted.

Off the plane at last. Up the Jetway. Kelly would be there. Would be there. Her heart was pounding in anticipation of the moment of light, seeing Kelly's light and letting it warm her again.

Journey's end. Journey's end in Kelly's arms.

She burst into the terminal and knew immediately which way to look. Kelly was to her left, just beyond the row of empty wheelchairs. Journey's end.

She belonged with Kelly. Had left the only world she knew to be here. Journey's end. Her hair seemed to float behind her as she half ran toward the glow of Kelly and the joy of her arms.

Kelly finally saw her and let out a whoop worthy of the *bane sidhe*. Ursula started to cry, and she let herself be hugged fiercely, protectively.

"I can't believe I'm here," she managed.

Journey's end.

"I can't believe it either." Kelly squeezed her again.

Journey's beginning.

She belonged with Kelly. She could feel it. It ran deep in her bones, the ephemeral connection of spirit strengthened by lengths and lengths of strong chain, forged over years, over centuries. She felt it even more strongly now, away from the Aldtyme circle. With just Kelly calling to her heart she felt the click of their beings. She cried because she had been right about that. She'd been right to come. It was right to be here.

She cried because, just for a moment, at her journey's end, she had also known she had come home to the wrong woman.

~ ~ ~ ~ ~

It was early for oranges in Aldtyme, but not in Pennsylvania. The small market Kelly pulled into had oranges heaped in a cart just inside the door. Ursula inhaled the bright scent and picked one up reverently. "Can I get some of these?"

"Sure, anything you want. I just need fresh milk, and I wanted to give you a chance to get anything you're partial to. Like coffee or tea — I didn't know what you'd prefer. You must be feeling homesick already."

Kelly was perceptive. Ursula had told her all about the plane flight, only omitting that flash of prescience that had said her journey was only beginning, the confusing flash that had told her she belonged with Kelly, but Kelly was not the woman she was traveling to. "We haven't seen oranges for several months at home, but I couldn't — strawberries? Already?"

"Get some," Kelly said. "Get whatever you like, really. The farmers' market won't have them."

Ursula gazed around the produce section. Kelly had called the grocery store small, but its produce section was twice that of the market in Hornsea. It was almost . . . obscene. Not just the mounds of oranges or even something as rare as strawberries in March. There were melons of every variety, blueberries and kiwi fruit. Peppers, loads of them. Bananas, even peaches and plums and papaya, mango — fruit so exotic she'd only read about it. The second day of spring and an entire summer's bounty was available. She laughed and rolled an orange between her hands.

The woman next to her, who was picking out oranges, glanced her way. The woman was older, but not as old as her aunts, and had eyes an unusual shade of gray. "I'm just laughing at myself," Ursula explained. "I was thinking I needed to stock up and start canning, and it's only the very beginning of spring. Are there always strawberries, all year round?"

"It *is* wonderful to have them, isn't it?" The woman had seemed annoyed a moment ago, but now she was animated. "Course they're better later in the season when they're local grown, but this will chase away the last of winter."

Ursula inhaled the scent of the oranges. "So will these oranges."

"Oranges are Florida sunshine," the woman volunteered.

"The sign says these are from South America."

She shrugged. "Sunshine is sunshine. Are you from England?"

"The accent gives me away, doesn't it?" She started to peel the orange but stopped at the woman's raised eyebrows. "Is that not permitted?"

"Not usually, but what's an orange?"

"I would pay for it, of course. Perhaps just one slice."

The woman's eyes crinkled, like a kindly Mrs. Claus. "One slice couldn't hurt."

She broke open the fragrant fruit and peeled away one section. It burst in her mouth like liquid sunshine. She could feel it in her blood, all the way in her toes. "I think this may be the best orange I've ever had."

She did not see that the ends of her red hair that hung free from the braiding were floating as if a cold breeze had come up from the floor, nor did she see that heads had turned to find the sudden source of warm light. Ursula opened her eyes. "I shall have to get a bag of these."

The woman had stepped back slightly. "Enjoy your stay in America," she said, and she meant it. She was smiling, not quite frightened, but uneasy, and Ursula had no idea why.

"Shoplifting already?" Kelly arrived with a cart containing milk, a box of Milky Way bars and a loaf of bread.

"It'll be okay, won't it? I only had one slice."

"Eat the whole thing. We'll tell the cashier. I wouldn't want to compromise your honor for an orange."

Ursula filled a bag and then liberally helped herself to other fruit and vegetables. When she couldn't reach the cucumber she wanted, a long arm reached around her and offered it to her. She thanked the man and wondered why he was blinking, like someone who had just stepped out of a dark room.

The girl at the checkout stand was very sweet. She bagged their groceries while Kelly swiped a credit card through a machine, a process that was new to Ursula. She glanced around and didn't see cash anywhere. So this was life away from Aldtyme.

They ran through the rain with the cart and piled the groceries behind the passenger seat of Kelly's big Explorer. Once inside they kissed as they had in the airport parking lot. "I'm so glad you're here," Kelly said again.

"So am I. Everyone told me Americans were perpetually in a bad mood, but I think Americans are very friendly. Present company included."

Kelly laughed and started the car. "It all depends. I've been shopping at that market for five years, and that's the first time anyone has ever bagged the groceries for me."

"Why did they this time?" Ursula peeled another orange. It smelled fabulous. She offered a slice to Kelly.

"Gee, I don't know. It wouldn't have anything to do with a five-foot-ten, roses-and-cream-skinned Englishwoman with thick red hair all the way down to her butt." She bit into the orange and put the car in reverse. "That tastes great, thanks."

"Because of me? Why? Because of the accent? I'm just a country girl. I felt horribly out of fashion."

Kelly put the car back in park and turned off the engine. Her mouth tasted of oranges, and the sweet assault caught Ursula by surprise. Kelly's lips were at her throat, oh, she remembered now, how easily Kelly moved her. This was not the wrong woman, everything was right.

"I would give up the world for you," Kelly whispered. "I'd have moved to England, to Aldtyme, in a second. You had only to ask me."

"It wasn't right," Ursula said. "I had to come to you." Kelly's hands cupped her face, and Ursula felt a delicious lightheadedness. "I want to go home with you."

Kelly kissed her again, then said raggedly, "Okay."

Kelly maneuvered the oversize vehicle through crowded streets until they came to a thruway. They were up to speed in a moment.

Ursula had to stretch to put her hand on Kelly's leg. "This car is very big."

"You wouldn't regret it if we got in the backseat."

Ursula blushed. "How far is it to home?"

"About an hour in the rain."

"An hour." Ursula laughed. "I guess we'll have to settle for talking then. We didn't do enough of that in Aldtyme. We have a lot to learn about each other."

"Are you scared? You've come so far."

"A little, but not of you." I'm frightened of myself, she wanted to say. "I know this was the right thing to do. You're not a stranger to me, though I know so little about you. I'm just realizing how little."

Kelly cleared her throat. "You should know the most important thing already."

"What's that?"

"I love you. I still love you."

"I love you, too." Ursula had a sense of echoes, as if they'd had this conversation many times. In the echoes, Kelly meant one thing and she meant another. Not this time, she told herself. That moment of thinking there was someone else she was supposed to find — that was just nerves. You love her, you know you do.

Later the love was there. They were alone in Kelly's farmhouse, far away from the rest of the world, naked to each other as they had never had the chance to be in Aldtyme. The rolling hills were less forested than Ursula was used to, but they were drenched with spring rain and carpeted with green, like the hills of home. Kelly swore they would be as green as Ireland by April and glorious with grain and vegetables by July. They had passed a horse-drawn carriage along the way, its simple black exterior marred by a reflective orange triangle on the back. Kelly was respectful, especially after she had passed the buggy, saying she never wanted to think she'd kicked up mud into a horse's nose.

Ursula felt as if she'd left Aldtyme to step forward in time, to the age of airplanes and oranges in March, but now she was back where she belonged, where she could smell rain and earth and feel the pulse of nature.

The love was there, in their own world, with no one but Kelly to hear her private pleading when Kelly took her. There was no one but Ursula to hear Kelly crying an end to loneliness and longing when Ursula's mouth drank what it craved.

They heard each other, and it wasn't the first time they had shared a bed. Ursula knew it but could not bring herself to ask Kelly if she felt that peculiar echo of sensation. They had been this to each other before.

"Please, please," Kelly said. "I have to. One more time."

"Yes, be . . . darling." Ursula wanted Kelly inside her again. The first time had been for love and desire born of that love, but now she needed to chase away the sudden sureness of another woman somewhere, another woman who was her journey's end. Kelly was deep inside her where the sensation was piercing and overwhelming. She had been about to call Kelly "beloved," but that wasn't right. She wrapped her legs around Kelly and fought a part of her she'd never experienced before, a part that wanted to hold something back from this moment, as if that part of her belonged to someone else. She focused on the fullness of Kelly's fingers inside her and overcame the resistance. Holding back wasn't her way, and it would not become her way with Kelly. It could not.

It could not because they had been this to each other before. At the height of Kelly's lovemaking, the moment when Ursula felt her spirit undone and naked, at the moment when their mouths gasped and opened to each other again to taste the perfect moment, to hold time fast between their suspended bodies, at that moment Ursula knew it all. She loved Kelly and Kelly loved her. She had been right to make the journey. But it was not journey's end. There *was* someone else and the way she loved Kelly, and yet wanted to hold something back, told her so.

The future had a past, but it was clouded to her. The future was also built on the present. In the present her body was trembling with sated desire and wet with the aftermath of a passion that touched her most secret places, places she had kept to herself and the circle. Kelly was in the circle she had come here to build. She would always give Kelly entrance to that place, and yet she knew, with bittersweet certainty, it was not what Kelly wanted of her.

She knew all this and wondered how she knew, not surprised given the way her aunts had raised her, but still, she wondered how she knew. She'd had none of Aunt Lill's tea, only the ecstasy of Kelly's fingers and mouth, and now the gentle whisper of Kelly's sleeping breath at her ear.

She was tired and ought to sleep. There was one last thing to try, however, and she settled into a light trance, intending to go no deeper than was safe with no one to monitor her. Many years of practice helped her reach her still point quickly. She continued breathing deeply until her fingertips tingled with the surfeit of oxygen.

The arc of light took shape and she breathed it in, firmly anchoring her spirit in her nearly sleeping body. Another breath and her spirit became elongated as it stretched toward the familiar river. The gate of her consciousness was before her, and she effortlessly passed through, opening a tunnel in the river of chaotic energy that roiled beyond all gates. The stretching of her mind took energy and she had little to spare, but she knew her aunts were waiting for a sign.

She turned her tunnel east, confident she could find the Aldtyme gate no matter where in the world she was. In an instant of thought she was at the Aldtyme gate and then she was through it. She would always have entry here. *:I'm safe.:*

Aunt Kait was on vigil. All around her were the pulses of light and affection that had been a part of every day of Ursula's life. *:We knew you were, child, but it is good to see you. You're tired. Don't linger.:*

:Kiss them both for me.: In a flash of thought Ursula sent other messages, giving thanks for the gifts and sending greetings from the other side of the ocean. It was a long way for her mind to go, but she would be able to undertake such a journey on her own whenever she got homesick. She would be able to keep in ready contact with her aunts. She would know how everyone in Aldtyme was faring, and she would know in a matter of moments. It was better than a phone call and more of her old home than she had hoped for, much more.

She felt her tunnel collapsing on itself as she slid down the long arc toward natural sleep. One more look around, she thought, to get a sense of this place.

The area where Kelly lived was lightly populated, but less than an hour's drive to the east were densely populated areas with noise and endless light. She wandered a little, turning north and south. The dense population generated a lot of random energy she had to shut out, and she knew she was draining herself as she strengthened the walls of the tunnel that held the chaos at bay. The densely packed cities gave way to the dark sea and the long way to Europe. She knew that way now. A quick search to the west, then sleep.

She skimmed over the still densely populated areas, knowing she didn't have the resources to stop any one place to look for other gates. She was used to finding ocean by now, used to the dark gap between England and Ireland, but this westward journey went on and on, through vast open spaces and the cacophony of harried populations. She traveled a long way and felt the strain of the day taking its toll.

There was yet more land to the west, but she was tiring. Desert, a wasteland of salt, deep waters, so beautiful, and it went on and on. She had come too far, she knew that suddenly, and she tried to slow down. The river of energy she plumbed threatened to breach her thinning tunnel walls, the walls of her mind. Instead of deliberate perception of what she saw around her, she was getting random snatches of thought and music, the bedlam of ringing bells, the honking of cars. It was all crashing in on her. She had come too far.

It took what will she had left to turn back. It took so much effort, and she was so very tired. Just as she was able to visualize returning east, she caught the faint twining of women's voices. The haunting voices drew her in. She held her position, moving neither east nor west, and listened. Voices soared in a transcendent love, upward arcing, searching, trying to end a profound emptiness.

O pulcherrima forma,
o suavissimus odor desiderabilium deliciarum
semper suspiramus post te in lacrimabili exilio.
Quando te videamus et tecum maneamus?
Nos sumus in mundo, et tu in mente nostra . . .

The lyric soprano sang of desired delights longed for, and other voices supported her lament, voices sharp and pure in harmonies that seared through the darkness. The harmonies were looking for an ending, a beginning, a way to fill the emptiness.

The harmonies found her, and she felt pierced by their purity. She had come too far and could not get back. Her command of Latin was weak, but she thought part was a question. She wanted to answer their plea. *When may I see you and be with you?* "I am here," she whispered. "I am here."

Kelly stirred. "Are you having trouble sleeping?"

Ursula could not make a reply — she was stretched too far. The music was drawing her in. She tried to speak, but her lips would not obey. She had overextended herself without a monitor, like some

46

neophyte and not the practiced adept she was. Any of her aunts, anyone in her old circle, would have known what to do now, but Kelly had no idea.

Kelly kissed her shoulder, then lazily stroked Ursula's ribs. She slid back into sleep.

Ursula tried to use Kelly as her anchor, to leave the music behind. It wouldn't work, but she tried anyway. *When may I see you and be with you?*

Kelly rolled over, and Ursula had the sudden sense of Kelly's spirit, its steadiness and constancy. Kelly was a woman of rock, set deep in herself and her world. In her own bed, Kelly's sleeping self was like a beacon of safety. In the state of unprotected sleep, with Ursula's own magic filling the room, Kelly glowed like a flare. She was an anchor of some magnitude, a quality she might never know she possessed.

Ursula could show her. Would show her, if she survived her reckless journey. She wasn't breathing now and hadn't been for at least a minute. It was so far to travel and the music was still calling her in the other direction.

She told herself Kelly was the anchor and she was not tired. She could feel her body shifting from sleep to unconsciousness. Aunt Kait was too far away in the other direction, and there was still too far to go.

A flutter of wings and a shock of wailing guitar tore the binding harmonies out of Ursula's thoughts. The thread of her mind that carried Ursula through the night began to wind itself toward home, but a spiral gate of black emptiness opened in the heart of the river. It beckoned to her and it terrified her, by the mother, by all the gods, she would not go into that place, not again, never again.

She was stretched too far. She saw the dagger in the heart of the spiraling darkness. The razor-sharp edge glinted toward the thread of her mind that bound her to her body.

Inside she was screaming for help, but her lips never moved.

The guitar pierced the landscape of her mind again, lancing fire behind her eyes. The dark spiral shattered, and the dagger disappeared. A voice brittle with fury shouted, "I am so fucking tired of this!"

Ursula was hurling through the night again, to the east, but she had no strength left to hold to the thread. She would hurl this way

47

forever until the walls of her self-made tunnel evaporated and she spun without control into the river of energy and chaos. It would tear her to pieces, and what was left of her the dark spiral would find. She was lost.

Kelly rose from the land under her, naked, strong and unrelenting, like a mountain of granite that would never be worn away. "Come back to me."

It was simply said. Aunt Lillidd would have used verse, Aunt Justine an ancient command. Aunt Kait would have found a gentle, coaxing appeal to the child in Ursula who would always come home.

Kelly's words, spoken without training or true awareness of what she did, had a well of deep love behind them. She would always ask Ursula to come back. She was the anchor. Ursula's spirit dropped like a stone into her body, and she convulsed against Kelly, willing her heart to beat again.

Kelly was holding her as she choked in air. "Was it a nightmare? What can I do?"

"Just hold me," Ursula gasped. She shivered with shock. "Don't worry, I'm home."

"You'll get used to it, I know you will."

"It's okay," Ursula mumbled. "I'm fine now. I love you . . . I do . . ." Home in Kelly's arms.

She had to rest now. She invoked the spell under her breath and felt lassitude sweep over her. Just before she fell into badly needed sleep she had a vision of a mountain of granite breaking in two, a dagger and Kelly dying for love. She plummeted into her first night of unrestful slumber and would not awaken refreshed.

Three

There was a commotion outside. A flicker of curiosity immediately drew Autumn through the roof and into the sky. She looked down on the building where she was dying and saw the dog trying to tear the heavy front door down with her claws. Splinters flew through the air. But it would be too late, Autumn thought. There was so much blood.

The thought took her back inside and she looked at her blood seeping into the mattress. Rueda was reverently cleaning the scarred and pitted dagger. Satisfied with its condition, she touched the blade to her lips.

"Fiat na lux na ma lux," she murmured.

In less than a heartbeat, if Autumn's heart had still been moving, Rueda was gone and every trace of her — clothes, satchel, dagger, car — was gone as well. Autumn floated down to her ruined body. Only Rueda's scent remained. The part of her that was still a stage magician thought Rueda's disappearance was a neat trick. Part of her was frightened. Part of her was already dead.

Scylla's yelps and howls split the night. With less purpose Autumn went outside again. The light in her landlord's house was on and the back door open. There was Ed and his baseball bat. He shouted at Scylla to shut up, but Scylla did not stop her relentless attack on the door.

"Blasted dog," he swore, but he was coming to investigate. He was a practical man in a world that had dealt harshly with him, but he wasn't uncaring. He limped up the steps until he could look in a window without coming too close to the enraged Scylla. He was too slow and would be too late.

The blinds were closed, and he wasted no time calling out to Autumn. If she was there and able, she would have let Scylla in by now. More lights came on as the baseball bat shattered the glass and the blinds were torn from their anchors.

Then, plainly over Scylla's panting and exhausted howling, Ed said, "Good God in heaven."

The baseball bat finished the door and Autumn sailed back inside with man and dog. The dog sank down, tail tucked, ears back, and shivered as if with shock. Autumn could see the bloody outline of Scylla's paw prints on the cheap linoleum. She wanted to say, "Good dog," but she was dead.

Nine-one-one would not be fast enough. Autumn knew this because she was already dead. Ed was praying over her. He was a good man under the pain, but it would not be enough. Later there was oxygen being forced into her lungs, and it was not enough.

When the tunnel opened she wanted to laugh. After all this, was everything a cliché? She floated into the tunnel, and then it closed behind her. Where was the bright light? Where were the family and friends who had gone on ahead, welcoming her to the afterlife?

It occurred to her then that because she could not remember any family or friends, knew no one who had died, that there might be no one to take her to where she was supposed to go. This insubstantial gray fog might be all there was for someone like her, a sometime pickpocket.

You are not a pickpocket.

Oh shut the fuck up, she told the voice. It doesn't matter now.

It seemed to be a lifetime before the fog lifted. She had felt as if she was drifting upward, but that had changed. The tunnel was bending toward a silver lake so still it mirrored the stars. She skipped the surface like a child's stone, and each contact with the quicksilver coolness brought memory.

She was clambering into a swaying crow's nest. She looked down at the ship's deck so far away. A man she loved raised his hat in the air, and she drew her bow.

She ran to the embrace of a red-haired woman whose laughter was rich and easy. They rolled together in sweet clover, unmindful of the offended bees.

The red-haired woman was pushing her away. Making her go. Had paid a terrible price for freedom Autumn did not want. She could hardly see for tears. She ran through cruel trees that scratched her cheeks while a wolf crashed through the bushes next to her. Rueda had taken her dagger, and so she drew an arrow, the only weapon she had.

Grey-robed women moved slowly through the stone halls, candles bringing light to darkness. Their voices lifted in a song of praise: *When can we see you and be with you?*

She listened to a lamenting pipe that echoed off hills and ponds in a world that seemed to be holding its breath. The pipe became a voice: *When can I see you and be with you?*

She skipped the silver lake for the last time, the chant echoing off the walls of the tunnel that now bore her upward. Through the glasslike walls of the tunnel she could see the earth below her. She wanted to take the time to admire a view only astronauts saw, but then she remembered she was dead.

She thought bitterly, "You would think, being dead and all, I'd remember who I was."

Laughter made her look up. The features were ethereally beautiful with translucent skin Autumn knew would be soft and warm to the touch. The red hair was unbound, long and fine and would feel like warm silk against her face. They had rolled together in clover, been pledged together, but when? The lips were curved in

51

a laughing welcome, and Autumn knew their texture and taste. Those sparkling black eyes knew her, searched her every feature with hunger. Autumn would have caught her breath had she been breathing. The woman was a Presence that made Autumn feel she was experiencing something unintended for the living. Then she remembered she was not among the living anymore.

Laughter faded from the bright black eyes, slowly replaced by an expression that made Autumn's nerves tingle. Had it not been for Rueda's seduction she would not have recognized the expression or her own response.

"Please." She had never asked for help in her life, not even at the beginning, when they'd found her in the casino bathroom. "I want to know. Who am I?"

"Beloved." It was a whisper, but each syllable pulsed through the tunnel with white light.

The sensation of soaring upward had stopped. Autumn thought irrelevantly, "What goes up must come down." She started to slip feetfirst and scrabbled from some sort of purchase on the tunnel's glasslike surface.

"Beloved . . ."

"Help me!"

"Beloved . . ." The red-haired woman closed her black eyes for a moment.

Autumn slipped a few inches. She knew she had left her body far behind, but when the black eyes snapped open the light within them lanced through her body with a flash of intense pain followed by welcome euphoria. She was suddenly falling headfirst, with nothing to grasp, nothing to slow her down. Her scream resounded through her body, and the glass shimmered with the echo.

She tried to look ahead, behind, anything to get a sense of where she was going and how fast. She was drawn to light, to a sea of lights circling a stage. A guitar riff threatened to shatter the glass that held Autumn, and she saw the audience flicking lighters as the wild-eyed performer with magenta- streaked hair brought her guitar to a wailing, piercing finale. For a moment the guitarist seemed to be robed and caressing some sort of ancient guitar in a candlelit sanctuary, then that impression was gone with the scream of amplifiers. *When can I see you and be with you?*

"I'm here," Autumn tried to tell her.

"That's all!" The guitarist shouted at the crowd with her fist raised. She looked heavenward suddenly and shouted, "I'm done with it!"

"Help me!" Autumn was passing it all by.

The guitarist brandished her fist again. "Fuck you all!"

The crowd's cheering pushed Autumn farther away. She glimpsed gray-robed figures walking an interlacing path to light white tapers. A white-robed woman offered the contents of a chalice to a kneeling row of gray-robed nuns. Then she was coughing at the lingering smoke from fireworks. For a moment she was inside a car and she saw the beautiful red-haired woman crying her need for release into the ear of another woman whose face Autumn could not see. Her thighs were wet with desire and her black eyes were wet with tears.

Autumn tried to touch her, to feel the satin of her skin one last time.

"Please!" One hand raised toward her for one strained moment, then it seemed as if wings fluttered between them, dark wings of a predatory bird. The raised hand dropped to her lover's back, leaving scratches as ecstasy and grief warred in her face.

She heard Scylla's sharp bark, just once. She stretched toward that commanding bark. The tunnel arced downward and she was going to slam into something at the bottom. If there was a bottom. Of course there would be a bottom, she thought, and it would be cement. That was how her luck had been today.

She was falling too fast to do anything about the paramedics. They were packing up their gear with a uniformed police officer watching and she screamed again, trying to warn them that her falling body would kill them, too. Ed, thank goodness, stood a little bit away. Falling objects had damaged him enough.

The tunnel's walls were hot with her speed and she felt her skin burning. Pain was coming back.

Her lungs ached for air. The glass walls were turning to liquid, melting to nothing.

At the last was a searing flash of light that blinded her and took her voice. She lay there, trying to breathe in just a little air.

Whatever sound she made was enough. Scylla was nuzzling her face, licking her eyes. Autumn hated that. Her firm command to stop was a wheeze.

The paramedics froze, then Ed's jubilant, "She ain't dead yet!" goaded them into renewed action.

Oxygen. She had never felt anything so wonderful as the oxygen in her lungs and the air outside as they carried her down the steps to the waiting ambulance — it was cool and refreshing to skin still burning from the speed of her fall. Scylla danced alongside, whimpers of happiness coming to Autumn like music.

They were closing the door. She heard Ed tell one of the paramedics that he would take the dog to the vet for her torn paws. A dog like that, Ed was saying, you take good care of.

When she first woke up, she didn't remember what had happened. The doctor told her she would and then, after a while, she did. She told the police what she knew, which wasn't much, and they went away, which was what she wanted.

She slept and dreamed, but the visions were as insubstantial as mist. Flashes of sound, the mingling of voices, that was all. She slept for what seemed like centuries. When she woke up again, the first thing she thought was, "You are Autumn."

There were no additional memories from Before, but she no longer felt any doubt. She was Autumn, and what she knew was that Rueda had known that, too. She longed to fathom what Rueda had done, but for the moment, weak and in pain, it was enough to know Rueda had done it for a specific reason. Rueda had killed her because she was Autumn.

"You're lookin' a pint low."

Autumn still had the sensation of reaching up from a pit whenever she awakened from her frequent dozes. The painkillers, she supposed.

"Did I wake you? The nurses said you were awake."

She met Ed's concerned gaze with a faint smile. She'd been

dead, and now she smiled more than she ever had before. "I wasn't exactly asleep. Drugs."

"I know all about that." Ed eased his big frame into the uncomfortable chair at the foot of the bed and let his four-footed cane stand as if at attention next to him. "Now this is the voice of experience, darlin'. You take all the drugs they'll give you, you eat everything they bring you and you get the hell out of here the soonest you can. Hospitals'll kill you if you give them the chance."

Autumn chuckled — and amazed herself. Chuckle? Smile? Feel indulgently sentimental? She was Autumn, she told herself, and the Autumn Bradley she had been for the last ten years did not chuckle. She tried to summon a distant amusement, but failed utterly. She grinned. "Why, Ed, I didn't know you cared."

His round face crinkled into lines of humor that seemed as infrequently used as her own. "I didn't know either. You're the best damned tenant I've ever had —"

"When I can pay the rent."

"'Sides that. No drugs, no music — just that chanty stuff that doesn't bother me. No pets until you brought home that dog, but she doesn't dig holes or bark. Just saves your life."

"A dog like that you take care of." She laughed again and was exhausted.

Ed saw her change of expression and got slowly to his feet. "I'm tiring you out. I just wanted to tell you everything is all cleaned up. You can come home whenever you want. The neighbors chipped in and got you a new bed —"

"That wasn't necessary," Autumn began weakly.

"Terrible thing to happen, we all feel real bad about it. And Scylla's okay, just fine. You ever need to find a home for her, she's got one, I tell you." Ed's voice came to Autumn from far away. "I told her how much I hate the alarm clock, and she wakes me every morning now, just before it goes off, and I swear, I swear she smiles at me . . ."

Autumn slept again, and her dreams were full of fog and music.

It was two days before she got out of bed and two more before she could manage the six or seven steps to the bathroom by herself.

She completed the trip for the morning, including swishing some toothpaste in her mouth, and headed back to bed only to find Detective Staghorn sitting on the hard chair and sifting through her things.

"Get out," she snapped. In a rush all the distant contempt and condescension came back. It was as if until this moment she'd forgotten the Staghorns of the world existed.

Staghorn let a hospital magazine fall back on the table. There was nothing of value in the bedside drawer, so Autumn wasn't surprised to see everything was still there.

"You know what I think?"

"I don't care. Go or I'll call a nurse."

"And I'll get out my badge."

"And I'll pass out. I'm not that far from it, you bastard." Autumn eased herself onto the bed. The stitches that ran the length of her sternum were starting to itch. The bottle of Vitamin E lotion was nearby, but she was not about to undo the hospital gown any further than it already was.

"You just rest your cute little ass and listen, then."

She stretched out in bed and tried not to show any additional weakness. She now remembered how he had tried to embarrass her during her show, his crude suggestions and illegal partnership proposal. She'd trusted Rueda in part because she'd helped Autumn get the best of Staghorn. She didn't want to listen to him, but caution said she should know his mind to better defend herself. So she closed her eyes as if going to sleep, but she didn't ring the call button as she had threatened.

He smacked his lips. Even with her eyes closed she could see his narrow, conniving eyes and long, quivering chin. Add whiskers and the ferret was complete.

"The bombshell you left with that night — never seen her before and never since, and a body like that I don't forget. I'll bet she had a nice time rolling around in bed with you. You didn't tell that to the detectives, now did you? And you didn't tell them a fellow officer could ID her. I wonder why?"

She had forgotten about Staghorn at the club until she'd discovered him here. All she had remembered was Rueda, the way she smelled, the feel of her fingers. She was not going to tell some disinterested cops about the sex. They'd taken one look at her short-cropped white hair and assumed she was some Goth idiot who had gotten more than she could handle in some cult thing.

Why bother to enlighten them? She was not going to tell them about how the thought of Rueda made her feel. She was not going to tell anyone that reliving that night had become a habit and that she was even learning to stop the flow of memory just before Rueda reached for the drug that had paralyzed her. She would forget about that part.

You will remember.

Well, holy crap. The voice was back. She'd even forgotten about the voice. No wonder she had been smiling and laughing with Ed — she'd forgotten that her life was a pit. It was all coming back now.

She kept her breathing steady.

"So I think somehow I must have given you the wrong idea. You don't need to be afraid of me."

Sleep, she thought. Leave the ugliness behind. Sleep.

You will remember.

The voice would not let her sleep. She remembered, was caught again between ecstasy and horror. She should hate Rueda, should want revenge, should feel something other than ... desire. It was sick, wanting to see the woman again. She fucked you over but good, Autumn thought. She made you like being killed because of what she did first.

She remembered then, Rueda saying something about having done it wrong in the past. What wrong? Trying to kill her? Was Rueda from Before? But Autumn bore no scars from some previous attack.

"Don't pretend you're sleeping. Even looking like a vampire's had you, you're damned attractive. I could be the best friend you ever had." She hated his voice — oily and smug.

Autumn did nothing to give away her awareness of his continued presence until she felt his hand on her thigh.

The speed of her reaction surprised both of them. She was weak, but the reflexes came from somewhere. She seized his near arm and pulled him onto the bed.

He had enough time to say, "Okay, babe, let's get to it," before he felt the barrel of his own gun in his gut.

She did not know how, but she knew the heft of the weapon, what it would take to flip off the safety, the pressure it would take to fire. She felt her eyes go dead as she met his bloodshot gaze. Her voice was level and betrayed nothing other than deadly intent. "Touch me again and I will kill you."

He was far stronger than she was but still had to struggle a few seconds before he was out of her grasp. He stumbled off the bed to his feet.

She flipped his badge on the floor, grateful to know she'd lost none of the dexterity in her fingers. "That's what I think of that. Now get out or I'll call a real cop."

He patted his holster and discovered the gun had been returned. He mocked her bravado with a hateful smile, and his eyes were as cold as hers were. "You're mine and you don't know it, bitch. I'll keep explaining it until you finally understand."

She pressed the call button. Staghorn left as the nurse's footsteps approached.

Exhaustion and a painkiller carried her to unconsciousness.

A black magician's box painted with silver moons and stars rose out of her oblivion, and she dreamed she stood before it. The box was as tall as she was, and when she opened the door there was just enough room inside for one person. She rapped her knuckles on the back wall with a flourish, then shut the door firmly. Spreading her arms, she stepped back. Light sprang out of her stillness, flowed from her fingertips. The door flew open. The back of the box was a vast spiral of light.

She stepped into the spiral and tumbled away. The caw of seabirds caught her ear, and she flipped through another spiral to jolt to her feet. Someone else's feet. She was looking through someone else's eyes. Or were they her eyes? Someone else's hands were wrapped around a ship's wheel. No, they were her hands. She knew her own hands. They were her hands. Before her was the rail of an ancient sailing ship, dotted with sextants and coils of thick hemp rope. Riggings stretched from behind her to the top of the large, primary sail. Above that a curious topsail fluttered just below the crow's nest.

The tiny foredeck and nearly square sail off the bow were like nothing she had ever seen before. The sea was a deep gray-green, rolling with the gentle wind as they headed north. Sharp cliffs and desolate moors rose to port. She knew it all, loved it all.

Tain's voice floated down from the crow's nest. "Captain, the Bay of Humber to port!" Tain immediately lapsed into his forlorn song about the wild green hills of home and the cruel lure of the sea. Tain was eager to see his home again, but Autumn knew in a day he'd be wanting to cast off. Not one of the crew, not Tain, not her father, not herself, would trade the sea for anything.

There was a rustle of parchment behind her and her father announced, "This time tomorrow, then. We could be in harbor at midday and gone by sunset. I hope the fare is worth it."

"It should be. And we'll get top trade for the cargo we do have," she said with confidence. "If everything is coming overland because of the pirates, our grain will be the freshest they've seen in a while. Those dogs didn't get the figs, either."

Autumn glanced over her shoulder to see Ed hunched over a small table covered by a large parchment that looked like a map. The edge closest was hand-penned in elaborate letters with, "Heire Be Dragyns."

"We'll still have trouble filling the hold to feed ourselves without a fare." Her father sighed. "Eyes front if you want the tiller."

Autumn went back to casting her gaze over the gentle sea. No longboats in sight. "It's not your fault that we had to give most to that motherless son." If the gods had given her the power, she'd have burned that empty-hearted dog and his swift-moving longboat with her eyes. Angle pirates were all dogs. They'd stood into shore to water at a fast-flowing stream and been surprised by the half-dozen longboats. It could have been worse. The pirates had not found the secret hold where Autumn had been hiding with their best cargo.

Part of Autumn knew all of this was a dream. Yet her nose was filled with the sharp tang of salted hemp and cool, moist air. The fear she'd felt when the pirates had boarded them was still churning in her blood. If they'd found her she'd be in a slave market by now, or dead by her own hand using the dagger in her boot. A vivid dream, then, as clear in her memory as Rueda, as her voyage through the tunnel when she died, as clear as the red-haired woman who had sent her back to life.

Ed grunted. "Not my fault, but we might be hungry. We may have to go south and do some short runs."

The crew, like Autumn and Ed, loved longer voyages. Ferrying from Mythe to Calais was tedious. Give them a cargo well valued in Ajaccio, Genoa or Naples, a long run with the wind full in their sails, ending in the warm, jeweled seas of the Mediterranean.

But Italy was no more. Rome had fallen to the Vandals and the marauding Goths and Huns had ridden down from Germania and into Gaul. The order of an empire that had made her father a wealthy man at one time had all been swept away. Corrupt ports charged arrival and departure taxes and confiscated cargo without warrant. Then there were the pirates that raided unchecked along the coast of Northumbria and Mercia. The Romans had abandoned their hold on Britannia nearly thirty years ago, leaving the wall of their emperor unwatched. Those Roman lords who had stayed to keep the land they'd fought three centuries to tame were on their own, as much at the mercy of Angle and Jute pirates as a lone trader, no matter how gallant the ship.

Autumn wished they hadn't come north. The chance at a wealthy passenger did not make up for the risk of pirates. But they'd had no idea the pirates had grown so bold.

For a moment Autumn heard the squeak of nurse's shoes on linoleum, then it faded to the slap of the water against the hull. She found the idea that Ed was her father absurd. His roots were African and hers, with nearly white hair and pale skin, far to the north.

She took after her mother. Edrigo had often told her so. This is a dream, she told herself, but the distinction was getting harder to maintain.

Tain, almost as much father to her as Ed, had ended his song. "Edrigo! We should have our journey wine now so we'll be sober when we land!"

The crew cheered the idea. Tain swung out on the riggings. "We'll land sober, but we'll not be that for long!"

Autumn's agreement died in her throat. Her dream self was chanting good-humoredly for wine too, but her watching eyes saw the rigging sag as if she had known it was going to unexpectedly give an inch or two, as if she had seen it before. An errant wave lurched the deck — it happened many times every hour. But this time Tain's fingers slipped; she had known they would. The collective gasp from the crew seemed to hold him up for just a moment.

Like a flutter of ravens over Autumn's shoulder, Tain's shadow plummeted over her, meeting his body with a sickening crunch on the deck. She screamed but couldn't leave the tiller. Her father's training made her stay, and it was the hardest thing she had done in her young life. She didn't hear Tain's dying words to her father, but later the ship's mate told her he'd spoken only of the many long years of love he'd shared with the captain and the devoted affection he had for the captain's daughter. Then he'd appealed to Mithras for a safe journey.

It was a bad dream now. Autumn wanted out. She couldn't look at Edrigo's face, Ed's face, terrible with grief and angry at the gods. One of her fathers was dead. Never again would he ease the boredom of a becalmed sea by teaching her quick-fingered tricks with coins and dice. The dagger wound was throbbing, and she woke up what seemed a million years later with the same heavy grief and the sound of a slamming gate ringing in her ears. The smell of antiseptic replaced brine and timber. The beeping of monitors drowned out the lonely echo of a wolf's mournful howl.

Three days later, when she left the hospital, she signed a paper saying she'd pay them a pittance a month for the rest of her life. No insurance, no assets — they were writing her off the moment she left. She was perhaps lucky they hadn't known she was uninsured until after they'd stitched her up and put her in intensive care.

She went home in a cab, not wanting to bother Ed and his ancient Dodge. She could not shake the image of him as her father in the dream, and it had made it hard to look at him when he had visited her again. She got out stiffly and was surprised by the cabby's assistance. Everyone had been nice to her, and kindness still startled her, after ten years of doing everything for herself. What had changed? Them or her?

She felt the tautness of the stitches and knew the scars would never fade. She knew who had changed.

A bolt of gray lightning shot from Ed's opening door and barreled down on her with an ecstatic yelp.

Autumn gasped, "Scylla, no," and feared for her stitches as well as for the cab driver, who had put up a warning hand.

Scylla stopped in her tracks, then trotted sedately to her side. The ferociously wagging tail was the only thing not under control. The happy welcome made Autumn feel better already.

Ed had been as good as his word — the blood-soaked mattress was gone and a new mattress was in its place, on a real bed frame, made up with new green jersey linens. Ed paid the taxi driver with some of the cash Autumn had told him earlier to find in her jacket. He handed the rest to her.

"This is too much," Autumn said. "You did take the rent out of it, didn't you?"

Ed shrugged. "I thought you might need it while you're laid up. You're good for it."

She was touched more than she could say. She'd hardly said more than "here's the rent" to Ed since she'd found the loft, and that had been at least eight years ago.

Something foreign was unfurling inside her, and the last time that had happened hadn't ended well at all. She had a sudden headache.

"You'll be wanting to sleep," Ed said. "Marge from the diner put some grub in the fridge for you, so don't worry about the market. It's a mite better than rations. There's even a big wedge of fresh peach pie. Under the sink is plenty of feed for Scylla. You need anything, you just send Scylla to get me. You send Scylla to see me any time." He scratched Scylla's ruff fondly, and Scylla gave him a gaze of pure adoration.

"Thank you." It seemed inadequate, but she touched his beefy hand and for a moment he was Edrigo from her dream, worried about the cargo and then racked with grief — then the dream image was gone.

As Autumn settled into the wonderfully comfortable bed, Scylla favored her with a long, resentful stare.

"I know, I forgot to get you," Autumn said sleepily. "I won't ever forget again."

The last thing Autumn saw before she slept was Scylla's watchful eyes.

Then Autumn was caught in the vapor of dream. She opened the door of the box and stepped through the spiral gate.

Four

The air inside the barn was heavy with scents so intense that Ursula sneezed every time she carried in a tray of bulbs or seeds. Kelly had filled the larger of her two barns with hanging bunches of drying potpourri plants and herbs. Wooden scaffolds and long lattices on pulleys allowed for maximum use of the space and resulted in a dense mixture of pungent spices. It was particularly sharp now with summer savory and thyme. Ursula put down the tray of hollyhock seeds and dabbed at her nose with the inside of her T-shirt.

Everything she did on the farm was like home, even sneezing. Every day of the past three months had been a blissful ritual of watering, fertilizing, harvesting and wondering at the miracle of it all. Kelly had long established herself locally as the best source for both seeds for a variety of tomatoes, as well as bulbs in the garlic and shallot families. Her Web site business had grown sufficiently to keep her debt-free and able to hire extra hands during the heaviest planting and harvest schedules.

Ursula left the thick air of the barn for the humid breezes that eddied around the sorting tables. The brick-red awning kept the sun at bay, but she still wore a straw hat with a brim so broad it shaded her shoulders. Her days were perfect. They were all she could have hoped for.

Her nights were perfect as well, that is, until Kelly went to sleep. Not for the first time she wondered if her unguarded foray past the gate that very first night had set things permanently awry. When Kelly slept, Ursula felt an irresistible compulsion to go beyond the gate to search for the source of the music that had called her so powerfully that first night. She would cast west as she had that first night, and every journey until last night she had been turned back by her own fear.

At first it was fear of finding the source of the music she had heard that first night. She could still hear it, deep in her bones. When Kelly slept the music became louder. It was hard to fall asleep with the memory of it playing in her head. Every instinct told her the music was a bridge to that other woman, the one she knew existed and yet refused to believe in. Believing two conflicting things at the same time was taxing, and so was the guilt she felt every time she told Kelly how much she loved her.

It wasn't a lie. But it wasn't the truth.

Hills golden with grain and clustered with dark green conifers and oaks stretched as far as she could see. It was easy to picture herself in an Andrew Wyeth painting, surrounded by a sea of summer grasses. Only narrow roads, a distant barn or farmhouse, and an occasional silo broke a landscape that probably had not changed in hundreds of years. She felt the richness of the soil under her feet and heard the endless buzz of insects. Birds took wing in lazy circles in a cloudless sky of soft blue.

She loved this place. Paradise was aptly named. Hourly reminders of nature's cycle and the gift of life surrounded and nourished her. She never wanted to leave, yet she knew she would give it all up to find the source of the music and the woman to whom she believed the music would lead her. Her certainty that she could and would walk away from this happiness terrified her. What kind of person was she that she could so easily throw away love in return for a mystery she couldn't begin to comprehend?

Even after she'd made her nightly journey past the gate, she could not fall asleep without asking herself why she found herself in this position. Why did she have to choose between this sweet life with a loving woman and an unknown future that so far had brought her nothing but heartache? What kind of choice was that? What had she done to be tested this way?

She had never been happier and unhappier in her life. She hadn't asked to know her happiness was founded on true love that was yet somehow a lie. At times it seemed utterly unfair. Why should she have to live with a shadow on her love for Kelly?

She wanted to ask her aunts the answer, but her stubborn pride didn't want to admit she needed their help. She didn't want answers or solutions. She wanted to love Kelly and stay here for the rest of her life. Every chirp of crickets while she lay awake at night told her time was passing. She was running out of days.

Irritated at her inability to let her turmoil go for more than a few minutes at a time, she knocked dirt off the clumps of shallots and sorted them for sale at the farmers' market, their own use, and for storage as next season's bulbs. Kelly was in the tomato garden picking a half-bushel of her famous Carnival beefsteak tomatoes to take as an offering at her aunt's Fourth of July picnic later in the day. Soon she would be back and would kiss Ursula as she always did when they had been parted. Ursula would lose herself in the kiss as if it was the last they would share.

Every kiss might be the last. The feeling was inescapable and had been for many weeks. These idyllic months were going to end. She was going to find the music and the woman, and when she did she would break Kelly's heart. Her own heartbreak she could bear, but she would never get over hurting Kelly.

So she went beyond the gate every night, and felt every time she was betraying Kelly. She felt guilty for not having told Kelly about her esoteric life, especially when it was so clear to her that Kelly had a talent she had never explored. She should be helping Kelly explore it, helping Kelly build and use her own gate. She ought to be raising her own circle for their protection, but if she did that, Kelly would learn how bittersweet Ursula's joy had become. Kelly would see how the music called to Ursula like siren song.

Each night she was also increasingly afraid. There was something else beyond the gate, to the west. At first her own fears had kept her from reaching to the source of the music, but that had changed since summer solstice. She never had a problem traveling east, directly to the Aldtyme gate and into the Aldtyme circle. On the solstice she had especially made the journey to partake vicariously in the ritual of thanks for the ripening fields and coming harvest. It was the first time since she was thirteen that she did not actively participate in the ritual of the day. She could have made the simplest of efforts — lighting a candle — but was too afraid Kelly would ask its significance.

She had left the Aldtyme circle that night and journeyed to the west, feeling both homesick and cowardly. Distracted, she had almost not seen the dark spiral and dagger rising between her and the music. Sickly green light danced the length of the blade as the tip descended toward her. She had quickly roused herself from her trance and reinforced her gate as she fought down her terror. Every night since then music had swelled and called to her and it had become clear that the darkness deliberately blocked the way.

Last night had been the worst of all. She had just cleared the gate to find the darkness waiting. She hadn't even been able to turn east to Aldtyme. It was as if the darkness knew where to find her now. She almost fancied she could feel it pressing against the gate now, even though she was not in trance.

A light breeze cooled the perspiration on her face, and she consciously directed her senses to the physical world that sustained her. The wind was heavy with the scent of tilled, moist soil. Ursula loved the smell — it was life. This place had a light of its own, like Aldtyme did, but it was not enough. It was past time to get help. Last night the darkness had touched her, a terrible caress, and she had been forced back through her gate, slamming it behind her just in time. She would see if she could slip past the darkness in a few days and get to Aldtyme, to her aunts. She'd waited too long to ask for their help.

She stripped off her gloves and was momentarily stunned by the sight of her hands. They seemed almost like claws. She had lost weight, but how much she wasn't sure. She hadn't thought it unhealthy, but as she gazed at her bony hands she had to face facts. She was living on less than three hours of sleep most nights. Though she ate vast quantities of healthy and not-so-healthy food — Kelly was fond of pizza and burgers — she was losing weight. She put her hands on her hips and was startled by the sharpness of the bones. The skin over her ribs seemed paper thin.

She loved Kelly and she loved this place, and yet she felt as if she were being steadily drained by its perfection.

She showered and changed her clothes before Kelly came in from the garden. The quick glance in the full-length mirror as she stepped into her best slacks was frightening. Her features were gaunt and her skin was sallow. Her eyes seemed only slightly less dull than her hair. If she had to confront the darkness lurking on the other side of the gate — so close she could feel it now in spite of her efforts to turn down her awareness — she had no reserves. She would have to do it alone if she ever wanted to travel beyond the gate again. Or she could tell Kelly the whole truth and ask for her help. Or she could go back to Aldtyme where she had always been safe. Either way, she would break Kelly's heart.

"Those pants look good on you." Kelly said from the doorway.

"Thanks. I got the next batch of shallots sorted, by the way."

"Great." Kelly stopped to nuzzle her neck on the way to the shower. "We don't have to leave for an hour or so, you know. It's a national holiday — let's celebrate."

She let Kelly circle her hips with her hands and pull her close. She hoped Kelly didn't feel her thinness. "I thought that's what the fireworks were for later."

"Why wait for the fireworks when we can make our own?"

"My love, don't take this the wrong way, but today, just today, a nap sounds better than sex."

Kelly's expression was wounded for just a moment, then she said gently, "You do look like you could use a rest. You work too hard."

Ursula couldn't explain that she'd worked harder in Aldtyme. The hours of sleep she did manage would have helped more if she hadn't heard the distant twining of a mournful chant. *When can we see you and be with you?* The women were calling to her, but she did not know why. Between her and their twining voices was a darkness that would consume her and she did not know why.

~ ~ ~ ~ ~

Kelly's aunt lived just north of Allentown next to a baseball park that always hosted fireworks on the Fourth of July. They'd have great seats for the show after an afternoon and evening of burned hotdogs and burgers and the conversation of the rest of Kelly's extended family. Her mother had died when Kelly was seventeen, and she had never known her father. Ursula understood perfectly how important extended ties were. She had never known her own parents.

"They're not too bad," Kelly was saying. "I just learned not to argue with them about Rush Limbaugh. Aunt Mona will like you and it's her house. I know Aunt Mary and Uncle Floyd will be there, they always are. I don't know about their daughter Liz, though. I hope so. She's a closet case or my gaydar is defective."

Ursula was learning the slang of American gayspeak. She stretched, feeling much better for the short nap she'd had in the car. She wished she hadn't had to put herself out with a quick spell, but she had more than replenished the energy the spell had taken. The time would come too soon when she would have to tell Kelly why her sleep was so easily disturbed. "What would happen if she showed up?"

"She'd meet you." Kelly looked over at her with a smile.

"What would that achieve?"

Kelly shrugged. "You bring out the best in people. There's something about you. I don't think anyone could lie to you and get away with it."

Ursula found the button to raise the seat back. "Aunt Lillidd tried to get me into teaching just because, as you said, kids seem unable to lie to me. But I wanted to work in the garden too much for university."

"For which I am eternally grateful. What if you had been teaching the day I walked into the shop?"

"I shudder to think." Ursula patted the knee closest to her. She would still be in Aldtyme, perhaps, and not knowing that a darkness looked for her, nor that somewhere a woman waited to be found. But she would also not feel the nourishment of Kelly's light.

Kelly turned off the thruway and circled around a crowded

business district that gave way to the baseball park. "Anyway, I hope Liz is here. You won't make her nearly as nervous as I do."

"I still don't get it."

"Guilt by association. You look far less like a dyke than I do."

Ursula pondered the mystery of that while Kelly parked the Explorer in the block behind her aunt's house. They carried the heavy basket of tomatoes between them through the hot afternoon. The muggy heat was a shock after the chill of the car's air conditioning.

"Let's just go around the back," Kelly said. "I'll bet there's no one to answer the door." She lifted the gate latch and Ursula followed after her.

Just before they came into sight of the backyard, Kelly turned. "If anyone starts saying stupid things, just walk away."

"It's my preferred method of combat," Ursula said.

"Sure it is," Kelly answered. "You don't like to argue, oh no. There's my aunt."

Aunt Mona was welcoming and seemed utterly charming in that open way Ursula was finding in many Americans. Kelly had told her the Amish farmers who bought seed from her were dour, but she'd found them more than companionable. Ursula soon had a can of pop in one hand and a plate of snacks in the other. Mona's husband, Stan, wore a barbecue apron and hat and took delight in announcing whenever something new had been put "on the barbie."

They both sat down on the grass in the shade of a beach umbrella to eat and chat. Ursula bit into a slice of sharp-tasting sausage and turned to Kelly. "What's this? It's delicious."

"That would be Lebanon bologna, made in Lebanon, Pennsylvania."

"It's yummy." Her tongue discerned a complex blend of herbs and pungent seasonings. "I don't think I've ever tasted anything quite like it."

Uncle Stan chimed in, "When Mona and I visited London I definitely came away thinking that the best cooks came to the colonies."

Ursula laughed. "I have three lion aunts who would take exception to that. They're marvelous cooks. But I will admit that when British food isn't made well it quickly can get nasty. There are few things as unpleasant as badly made bubble and squeak, for instance."

Kelly gave a mock shudder. "I think I had it only made badly, then. It's not something I'd ever order again."

"What part of England are you from, Ursula?" Mary, one of Mona's half-sisters, had eyes very like Kelly's — bright and golden.

"Aldtyme is in Northumberland, that's in the northeast, a bit below Hadrian's Wall." Mary looked as if she was trying to picture a map of the island. "The wall is just south of the Scottish border. Aldtyme is on the coast. Just inland you'll find York and Leeds."

"Oh, okay. I can picture that. I've always wanted to tour England." Mary sighed. "All that history. Just to see the city gates at York or to walk the fields at Lewes and Runnymede."

"There's plenty of history here." Mary's husband, Floyd, seemed intent on discouraging foreign travel.

"Oh, Floyd, you know perfectly well that a lot of our history started there. We had a revolution because of what happened at Runnymede Meadow. It would be thrilling to see."

Ursula guessed that Mary would be a long time getting to England if Floyd had no interest. "If you actually want to see the Magna Carta you have to go to London."

"Well, if there are a lot of women like you over there, I might make the trip sooner rather than later." Floyd winked at her.

"Women like me?" Ursula smiled because she could tell he meant no offense. "How'd you mean?"

"Yeah, Floyd, what exactly do you mean? Women like Ursula?" Kelly lifted the end of Ursula's thick braid from where it pooled around Ursula's bottom on the blanket. She twined it lovingly around one finger.

Floyd blinked at Kelly for a moment, then burst into a raucous laugh. "Dang me if I hadn't forgotten she was one of you!"

Everyone in earshot started to laugh, and Ursula controlled her own blush. She wasn't sure she got the joke, but that was probably for the best.

A newcomer joined them in the shade on the blanket. Kelly, who had been laughing with everyone else, broke off to say, "Hey, Liz."

"Hey. What's the joke?"

Liz had gentle brown-gray eyes, much like Kelly's but misty where Kelly's were bright. She met Ursula's gaze without flinching, though her pupils widened for just a moment. She was the first American Ursula had met who seemed to take her measure with a brief, studied meeting of gazes. Liz's eyes flicked to her braid and then to the end where Kelly was twisting it around her finger.

Kelly said nonchalantly, "Your dad was flirting with Ursula. He forgot she was my girlfriend."

Liz lost some of her color, and Ursula could see she was momentarily afraid. Then Liz swallowed hard and made a visible effort to relax.

"I'm Ursula," she said to Liz as she held out her hand.

"Nice to meet you," Liz said. She lifted her chin as if in defiance of her own fears and briefly touched her fingertips to Ursula's.

The fleeting touch was enough. Ursula bit back a gasp of both surprise and dismay, then she felt horribly faint.

"Are you all right, babe?" Kelly's voice came from far away.

She couldn't answer for a moment. The world steadied again and she managed, "I'm fine. Just the heat, probably."

A few seconds later Floyd was proffering a cold bottle of water to hold against her wrists. "Redheads and sun don't mix," he said. "That umbrella still lets some through."

Ursula let Kelly cradle her head on one shoulder for a moment. "Thank you. It's better already."

"Are you sure?"

She sat up with an effort and found her voice. "I'm fine, really."

"You're white as a ghost," Kelly said.

"I'm always white as a ghost. I'm English."

Kelly's eyes said she knew Ursula was being evasive. "You're absolutely sure you're okay?" Her gaze flickered over Ursula's body and then slowly came back to meet Ursula's gaze with concern.

"Yes." Ursula took a long draft from the water bottle. It did taste wonderful. "I probably am a little dehydrated." That was enough truth to satisfy Kelly in public, but Ursula knew when they were alone there would be more questions. Questions she did not yet want to answer. Questions about why she slept so poorly and was losing weight. Questions about why the summer heat affected her strongly enough to make her feel so faint.

How could she answer that it wasn't the heat, that it had been the brief contact with Liz? How could she say that without telling Kelly the rest? How would Kelly feel when Ursula told her that when she had touched Liz she heard music resonating between them? How could she then not tell Kelly about the Aldtyme circle? How would Kelly react when Ursula told her she was a witch, an adept? How could she explain that she'd let the last two and a half months go by without saying a word about any of it?

If she explained all that, how could she hold back her certainty of another woman surrounded by the music that also swirled in Liz? *Quando te videamus et tecum maneamus? When can we see you and be with you?*

That Liz knew the music too — Ursula could not even begin to grasp the significance. How could she explain any of it to Kelly when she understood so little herself?

There were forces at work that were much, much bigger than she, and beyond the ken and control of her meager talents. Aunt Justine would say it was a test of her soul, but why now, and why so much at Kelly's expense? She missed her aunts desperately and knew she had waited too long to ask their aid. She would pay for her pride — that was the nature of pride.

Liz was answering her parents' general questions about how she was doing, her job, and such. Ursula looked at her and wondered why she carried the music inside her.

When can we see you and be with you? She wondered what the music was, and what it meant. She could try to find out through Liz, but suddenly was afraid of the answer. The music was a bridge to the other woman. She loved Kelly.

When can we see you and be with you? She did not want to find the other woman, not today. Not tomorrow. Maybe not ever. Not in this life, she thought.

She shivered as if she'd made her own prophecy and knew that Kelly saw the goose flesh dusting her arms. Kelly would have so many questions when they were alone.

Homemade ice cream, thick with fresh peaches, was dished out to a long line of kids and adults alike. The festivities in the ballpark just over the back fence were underway. The contest between two local softball teams was over and the music preparing them for the fireworks had taken a decidedly patriotic turn. "God Bless America" was "God Save the Queen" in Ursula's ears, and the familiar anthem was suddenly poignant. She wanted Aunt Lillidd's interpretation of her jumbled dreams and Aunt Justine's translation of the words to the chant. She craved a huge stack of Aunt Kait's shortbread and strawberries.

Ursula excused herself to the bathroom for a moment of privacy. Kelly had not left her side since the incident with Liz. It was part worry and part something else. Suspicion, Ursula thought. *She suspects I'm not telling her something. She's noticed that I don't look well.* For the first time in her relationship with Kelly, Ursula dreaded being alone with her.

Not good, she told herself. Not good at all. She finished in the bathroom and made a pit stop at the ice chest in the kitchen for more soda. On the way through the back porch she nearly stumbled into Liz but caught herself just in time. Thank goodness, she thought. She doubted she could touch her again and stay on her feet.

"Hi," Liz said.

"Hullo."

The silence became awkward as it was obvious Liz wanted to say something and couldn't. Ursula studied Liz's misty eyes and saw the uncertainty, fear and hope swirling in them. Finally, when it was clear Liz's courage had failed her, Ursula said, "What is it?"

"It's a long drive back for you guys," Liz said in a rush. "We have a spare room. There'll be drunk drivers on the road, too. It'd be safer."

The choice was before her. Ursula knew that if she spent more time with Liz she'd have to ask her about the music. Kelly would suspect even more strongly that Ursula had a secret. Nothing good could come of it, she told herself.

Then Liz said quietly, "I'd like you to meet my roommate. My . . . girlfriend."

Ursula knew she could not say no, not when Liz had just trusted her with a precious secret. By all the gods, she thought, I have to do this. She wasn't prepared. She had wanted to put it off forever, but the cup was before her. "I'll ask Kelly, but I think yes, we'd love to."

The first flares of fireworks illuminated Liz's brilliant smile. "I like the way you do your hair," Liz said. "That braid is unusual."

Ursula touched the Norn braid and took comfort. The braiding was an ancient style and not without its own source of power. Her hair had been divided into three parts, and each braided tightly. The resulting strands were then intertwined again to form a single, heavy braid. One of her preparations to become the center of the Aldtyme circle had been the ritual braiding of her hair, and it had not been unbraided since. "Thank you. It's a lot of work to keep tidy."

"I know," Liz said oddly, then another burst of fireworks made them hurry outside.

Kelly took the cold soda Ursula had brought her and clearly wanted to kiss her by way of thanks, but resisted the impulse. Ursula was thirsty for the kiss. She needed to remember how deeply she loved Kelly and how true the feeling was. Something would change tonight, but that was later. Right now she wanted to be held and kissed, but there were too many people around.

Ursula settled as closely to Kelly as possible, letting her hair drape over Kelly's lap. After the concussion of the next burst of fireworks faded, she said into Kelly's ear. "We've been invited to stay the night at Liz's."

Kelly looked at her with raised eyebrows. Ursula leaned close again. "To meet her girlfriend."

"Fabulous! That's great. I just knew it!"

"You were right," Ursula said. She wanted to be kissed. She could not lean away. She only had to journey a matter of inches to feel the warmth of Kelly's lips on hers, to feel again the passion Kelly always engendered. The inches seemed like an ocean.

"Oh, baby, not here," Kelly whispered. "Don't look at me like that. I'll forget where we are."

With difficulty Ursula raised her gaze from Kelly's lips to her eyes. She knew her desire was naked, and she felt Kelly catch her breath. "I know." She swallowed hard. "I know."

Kelly got directions from Liz, and they took their leave of Aunt Mona a few minutes after Liz left. Ursula hurried to where Kelly had parked the car, divinely grateful that for a while she would not need to make pleasantries. Every passing minute had seemed more oppressive. The air was like lead on her body, threatening to force the breath out of her, and yet her body ached to be in Kelly's arms for even a few minutes. She had dreaded being alone with Kelly, but now she hungered for it.

It was longer than a few minutes, and the Explorer's backseat was every bit as roomy as Kelly had implied. Ursula knew she had never begged so piteously for Kelly to be inside her, begging all the while Kelly fumbled with her belt and zipper.

"Yes, baby, whatever you need," Kelly whispered and then her mouth found the breasts Ursula hurriedly bared and offered. Kelly was deep in her now, and still Ursula begged. She arched her back and closed her eyes. The gate was before her, it was opening, and the woman who soared through — by the mother, by all the gods, her heart sang.

It was Her and she reached toward Ursula. Ursula strained to touch her once again, it had been so long. She could clearly see only the woman's eyes, eyes of deep green, oceans-deep. "Please!"

The darkness interceded. It came between them with malevolent intent and Ursula could do nothing to stop it. She was naked with desire and utterly defenseless.

Then Kelly was covering her completely with her body, shielding her from the darkness. The gate slammed shut. The woman — Her — she was gone.

Ursula left nail marks on Kelly's back, overwrought with passion and grief. Both their mouths were bruised from the force of their kisses.

There could be no one else. "I love you," she gasped. It was truth and an utter lie.

Kelly answered and Ursula did not hear the tears in Kelly's voice. But she felt them later, against her thighs, and could not stop her own. She had never loved Kelly more. When they cuddled in exhausted silence, Ursula finally wondered why Kelly was crying.

But she could not ask. Questions would only lead to heartbreak now.

Liz's lover was the Reverend Taylor Saint Claire, and the moment Ursula looked into Taylor's eyes she knew something of great moment was about to happen to her. Taylor carried the same glow with her that Kelly did. She could now see that Liz did too, but at a much more subdued level.

Liz had stopped talking with an expectant air, but they just stood there, she and Taylor, staring into each other's eyes. Taylor was not the woman she was journeying to, Ursula knew that, but she was someone in this puzzle. Then she realized Taylor wore her thick black hair in a Norn braid.

Kelly finally said, "Do you know each other or something?"

"Or something," Ursula murmured.

Taylor held out one hand. Ursula swallowed hard before firmly grasping it.

The music was inside her, all around her, echoing through her blood. *Quando te videamus et tecum maneamus? When can we see you and be with you?* She staggered but knew Kelly would catch her. Kelly would always be there to catch her.

Taylor caught herself on the door jamb, but did not let go of Ursula's hand or break their locked gaze. The music soared to its loneliest heights, and Ursula saw Taylor in a white robe offering a chalice to gray-robed women who knelt to sip. *Our exile is tearful and we long ever for you. When can we see you and be with you?*

Ursula was finally able to gasp out, "Tell me!"

Taylor never blinked. "Ask me again!" She squeezed Ursula's hand harder.

"Tell me, please!"

"Let go of her," Kelly snapped. She started to pull Ursula's hand out of Taylor's grasp.

"No, Kelly, don't —"

:Ask again!:

The intensity of the command was inside her head, like when she conversed with her aunts in the circle. There was no circle here, only Taylor's unrelenting hold on her hand. *:The music, please tell me!:*

Taylor let go and they staggered apart. Ursula would have gone to her knees, but Kelly picked her up in her arms and headed for the nearest couch. She set Ursula down carefully, then rounded on Taylor. "What the hell did you do to her?"

Ursula managed to grab one of Kelly's hands. "It's okay."

"It's not okay!"

Liz stepped between the two women. "Taylor would never hurt anyone, Kelly."

"Then what the hell just happened?"

"I don't know," Liz answered with conviction. "I don't know, but I trust Taylor with everything."

Ursula knew Liz truly meant everything. Taylor was the center of a circle, just as Ursula herself had been in Aldtyme. Liz was a part of that circle and had more than once trusted everything to Taylor during each level of initiation. Ursula had developed similar trust in her aunts and the others of the Aldtyme circle.

"Good for you, but I want to know what just happened."

"Kelly, I'm okay. It was a shock."

"I was harsh," Taylor said finally. "I'm sorry. I — you took me completely by surprise. I didn't have any shields up."

"Me, neither." Ursula had rarely had need of personal shields, though she knew what to do with them. The Aldtyme circle had always been there to shield her — all of them — from reactions like she'd just experienced, the unexpected brushing of minds. Still, she ought to have raised shields to protect herself, just like she ought to have done many things to better cope with what had happened and was going to happen to her. Not protecting herself wouldn't stop the future from coming; it would only make the future hurt more when it happened. "Though I don't think it would have helped." She managed to sit up.

"Why am I the only one who doesn't know what's going on?" Kelly plopped down next to Ursula as if she could not have stood up another moment. Ursula wanted to reach for her hand, but she couldn't bear the possibility that Kelly would recoil from her touch.

Taylor looked the same question at Ursula, and Ursula felt a foreign sense of shame. Kelly deserved to know, and yet Ursula hadn't told her. She hadn't wanted to hurt Kelly, not for Kelly's sake, but because she didn't want the guilt. She'd been foolish and headstrong and selfish. "She doesn't know," she said to Taylor. "It's my fault."

Kelly looked at her then with the first ache of betrayal, and it cut Ursula like a knife. Kelly's defenses were completely down, and Ursula thought irrationally of a kicked puppy. "What haven't you told me?"

The first question — it would lead to so many more. Ursula tried to answer but could not speak for tears.

She woke to a darkened room and the awareness of Kelly not far away. She was both calm and comforted, yet her despair and fear were still within her, but as if behind a bolted door. Taylor's handiwork, she suspected. She turned over on the couch to see Kelly curled up in an oversize comfy chair. Quiet footfalls in the next room made her go in search of explanations.

Taylor was putting the kettle on. She wore an old plaid bathrobe, and her long Norn braid hung down her back. "Would you like some tea?"

"Yes, thank you." Ursula sat down in the indicated chair and wondered what to say. They were peers of a sort, but she felt much more like the student.

"Do you feel better?" Taylor set mugs down on the table with an assortment of teas.

"As a matter of fact, I do. I don't know why I was so hysterical. I mean, I know why, but —"

"It wasn't like you."

Ursula nodded and reached for the tin of Earl Grey. "It's been coming on for a while." Taylor's spell to calm her would easily come unraveled.

Taylor didn't say anything until she had poured boiling water into the mugs and returned the kettle to the stove. "Kelly told me you left Aldtyme in England to come and live with her."

"Aldtyme was my old circle."

"Why didn't you begin working with one when you got here? Without the respite it gives you, you're like a magnet for all sorts of negativity."

"I intended to. I was going to look for others. It only takes four plus one to get going." Ursula shook her head to stop her babbling. Taylor knew how many it took. "I intended to do it every day. But it would have meant explaining it to Kelly."

Taylor frowned. "She had a right to know. She belongs in a circle. She's not as sensitive as Liz, but what she lacks there she makes up for with strength of will. Any circle would jump at her for anchor."

"I know." Ursula dunked her tea bag absentmindedly. "Believe me, I know."

Taylor shrugged eloquently. "I don't understand why you didn't do it. You're falling apart because you don't have a circle to replenish yourself."

"No one told me this could happen. I've never heard of it happening to anyone else. If I'd known I might have acted differently."

"Not everyone has something hunting them on the other side of the gate."

Tea sloshed out of the mug onto Ursula's hand. She mopped up with the tea towel Taylor handed her. "You sensed that?"

"I would think every talent in this area senses it. Kelly does. I see it in the lines around her eyes. They match yours."

Ursula was shaken by a wave of guilt. She had not noticed Kelly's stress. She was a trained adept and ought to have been looking out for the untrained person. It was one of her most sacred oaths. "If I . . . help her . . . she'll lose me."

"That's usually not the way it works. It's usually the reverse."

"Don't you think I know that?" Guilt made it seem momentarily reasonable to be angry with Taylor, as if the truth was Taylor's fault. "To be in love with someone who has similar gifts is a precious thing. We could be even closer than we are. You and Liz obviously share it. Don't you think I long for that, too?" Ursula felt the edge of hysteria creeping into her voice.

Taylor touched her gently, index and thumb splayed in precise placement. "Peace."

The spell helped. "Thank you," Ursula said shakily. She gathered her wits as best she could. "I apologize. You shouldn't have to do that for me. And thank you for what you already did to make me feel better."

"My defenses here are good. I strengthened them to protect us all. The darkness hasn't found my gate, and I'd rather it didn't." Taylor shrugged. "Look, I want to help. I don't know why we both got such a jolt when we touched. That has never happened to me before." She let one hand fall across the table, palm up, fingers curling as they relaxed.

Ursula took a deep breath. Taylor was offering a closeness that could explain much, but it required complete trust. She was afraid of the explanations, deeply afraid, because she already knew part of the answer would hurt Kelly. Kelly was already hurting, Ursula told herself. She's hurting and doesn't know why. She deserves answers no matter what they cost you.

She had to take twice as many deep breaths as normal to find her still place. She had only done this within the Aldtyme circle, during a working ritual or when she traveled beyond the gate. Her aunts were the only people she knew who could do this whenever they wished, which put Taylor's decades-younger powers on a par with her aunts'. That reality was just plain intimidating. She let the fear run its course and waited for her heart to slow again. Then she laid her hand, palm down, on Taylor's.

They found rapport immediately.

Ursula became more profoundly aware of the natural shielding of Taylor's home. She sensed Liz's and Kelly's peaceful rest as a result.

:Let me help.: Taylor was a glow of comforting light behind Ursula's closed eyes.

:You never told me about the music.:

:You first.:

It only took a few moments. She showed Taylor the magic of Kelly walking into their shop and then all the rest: her leave taking from Aldtyme, all the days and weeks of turning soil, fertilizing, planting, sifting chaff for seeds, all the familiar tasks she had delighted in doing with Kelly. She showed Taylor the love and the sex and the pleasure of each other, then guided Taylor through everything one more time, only this time she shared the prescient awareness that she had come all this way to find the wrong woman waiting for her. She loved Kelly and yet knew she would love someone else, too. She showed Taylor the woman's eyes as she had seen them earlier tonight, while she had lain in Kelly's arms.

:I'm sorry.: Taylor's sympathy was unrestrained, but Ursula

knew Taylor could not possibly understand the bitterness of loving someone and knowing it would end. *:You can't protect her forever. You need a circle, and so does she.:*

:When I show her the circle she'll know everything. I have been so careless and selfish. I have never acted this way before, and I'm going to pay for it with potent coin. Kelly shouldn't have to pay. But she will anyway. I did not ask for this, and yet I've behaved so badly.:

Taylor made no answer for a long while. They rested after the intimacy of Ursula's sharing, and Ursula became dimly aware of the music, those longing voices, calling to her.

Their minds merged on the music. Taylor flowed through her memory of the first moment she had heard it, stretched so far from her body, far to the west, past desert and salt. In the early hours of every morning, when she should have been most deeply asleep, the music intruded enough to wake her.

Taylor was humming some of it. Taylor knew it. Ursula ceded the lead to Taylor, who swept her up into the glory of the full performance of the chant, a complete liturgy of longing, lament and praise. A chant for the feast of a saint, for the feast of Saint Ursula. A soloist sang of *virginum collegit* then the choir responded with upward leaping delight. *Ursule, Ursule.*

:In a fruit-laden garden and splendor of flowers, she gathered a throng of virgins about her.: Taylor translated the Latin with ease. *:Were you named for the saint?:*

:I don't think so. My aunts named me for the constellation. Ursa Major. It never sets in our part of the world.:

:Who are your parents?:

:I never knew my parents. I was a foundling.:

Taylor shuddered and broke contact. She put her hands over her eyes. "That's not a phrase you hear too much these days."

The abrupt break between them left Ursula with a pain between her temples. "Someone left me on my aunts' doorstep, and they took me in without hesitation."

Taylor was biting her lower lip. The nervous gesture seemed out of character. "I have to think about this. There are people I need to talk to."

"In your circle?" Though she felt completely drained, Ursula ran a quick spell to ease the pain a little and was surprised to find that it worked.

Taylor's expression turned slightly bitter. "I don't have a circle at the moment."

"What?" Taylor had an astonishing amount of power at her disposal and without a circle?

"I also don't have a parish. Both parts of my life want me to choose one over the other."

Ursula understood Taylor's plight. Though nothing in their work in the circles was contrary to Christian teaching, and on more esoteric levels actually blended with it perfectly, witches were witches in the eyes of most Christians. "I'm so sorry."

"I always knew I'd have to choose, sooner or later. I just thought I'd have a sign which calling was the higher one for me." Her sharp blue eyes fixed on Ursula. "The way is mysterious, and answers come when least expected."

"You sound like my Aunt Justine."

Taylor's calm cracked at the edges. "How many aunts do you have?"

Ursula knew the question was not idle curiosity. "Three. Justine, Lillidd and Kaitlynn."

Taylor bit down on her lip so hard Ursula thought she would draw blood. But all she said was, "We need some sleep."

Her self-esteem might be in tatters and her mind awash with guilt and regret, but Ursula knew that the many threads of her life all joined at this moment. She could have taken any road and ended up here. She should not have fought it so. "Like the river, tomorrow cometh, and we have work to do."

Sleep was elusive, even under Taylor's protection. She knew the gnawing darkness lurked on the other side of the gate, and she dared not take the risk. Kelly shifted in her sleep as if her dreams were unpleasant, and Ursula pushed away the guilt that reached for her again. Time for that later. Time for sleep now. She said the three words and closed her eyes. In the moment before sleep she unwillingly remembered the line of the chant that Taylor had whispered before she went to her own bed.

"Iste sanguis nos tangit, nunc omnes gaudeamus," she had sung lowly. "The blood of Ursule is upon us, now let us all rejoice."

Ursula dreamed she went beyond the gate. She dreamed that in the arc of tunnel light she followed the music to Aldtyme, where she had never heard it before and yet, in her dream, she discovered that she had.

Part Two:

The Garden of Fruit

Ripe. Heavy. My hands full.
You.
A dripping honeycomb.
— Hilary Blanc, "Splendor of Flowers"

Five

Edrigo had never allowed anyone else to bring the ship to dock, and the day after Tain's death was no different. Autumn watched his steady hands and marveled that a night of wine and grieving didn't show. She felt the loss of Tain like an open wound. He should have been telling a bawdy joke to pass the tense minutes as they edged to the dock. He should have had a rope to hand, his lithe body poised for the jump to the wooden planks. Much of what she knew she had learned from him.

Tears threatened again. Her own loss was nothing compared to the pain that Edrigo must feel. Tain had been there, always there, it seemed. Her fathers shared more than a bed — *had* shared, she reminded herself. No one had ever died on the *Verdant Bough*. Autumn wanted to ask the Sea Mother why Tain, why not someone else? Not fair, she answered herself. Would you pass your pain to someone else when you are strong enough to bear it?

Edrigo was also strong enough, it seemed. The *Verdant Bough* nudged the dock gently, and the experienced crew had her tied fast in a matter of moments. Her father signaled brusquely and Autumn jolted into action. She should have been up already.

She took care on the riggings because she knew Edrigo would be watching. How could he not watch? She paused where Tain had slipped and checked the knots for herself. They were fine. It had been an accident. All that love gone in a stupid accident. Sometimes she thought there were no gods.

She hauled herself into the crow's nest and looked down on the dock. They'd seen no sign of another ship, and so there was a good chance they were the first to answer the posted notice they'd seen in Calais asking for passage from Aldtyme to Rijsbrucke on the middle coast of Jutland. Rijsbrucke had been in the hands of the Angles until the Jutes had captured it several decades ago. The promise of gold had caught Edrigo's eye. It was an unusual journey, and not without risk, but if safely done the reward would be enough to dry-dock the *Bough* for repairs. Perhaps enough to buy a longboat for protection.

The dock at Aldtyme was quiet. Autumn had expected that, but it was unsettling. She was used to the splendid confusion of harbors. The inn before the city gates appeared to be closed, though it was already midmorning. That, too, was strange.

She scanned the horizon of the little town behind the fortress walls and spotted a large white cross affixed to the fortress keep itself. The Christians were making inroads here, just as they had seen in Gaul. Stories of birth without intercourse and rebirth from death sounded to Autumn like the tales sailors the world over liked to tell, with parts here and there changed to make them a continuous story of one god instead of many.

Every year it seemed the White Christ's holy days were celebrated closer to and more grandly than festival days as old as the sun, that witnessed the precise turning of the stars. To a sailor there was really only one truth and one way: The sea was truth, and the stars were the way to travel with truth. Had Tain made his final journey yet? She wondered what kind of truth he had learned along the way.

She blinked away tears. There was time for grieving when they were at sea again.

A contingent of what looked to be merchants were waiting at the foot of the gangplank, and her father strode ably down to meet them. Autumn's vantage point let her see that a well-matched pair of bays supporting a draped horsechair waited in the shade of the dock's only trees. She could see a train of pack animals laden with traveling trunks as well. It seemed the arrival of the *Verdant Bough* had been anticipated. The fare was theirs if they passed inspection. Why would they not? The *Verdant Bough* was in good repair and well crewed. Its modified Roman corbita design made it faster than most merchant vessels. They were new to this harbor, but a ship's reputation always arrived before the ship did. All sailors talked about in taverns was women, their own ship, and ships they had done business with. The *Verdant Bough* had been running the known seas for over thirty years.

Directly behind the horsechair was a flock of gray-veiled attendants that looked like Christian acolytes. Behind them the packhorses shuffled their hooves on the hard-packed earth. The sun was surprisingly warm for this early in the spring, but the animals did not seem distressed.

She couldn't hear what was said, of course, but nothing seemed amiss. Harbor merchants were slowly opening their shops, and Autumn caught a whiff of cooking meat. The door of the inn opened and several men issued forth to stand in watchful attention. Autumn's heart stopped for a moment, then she whispered one word to the crewman clinging to the riggings below her. "Saxons."

The message was passed on down the riggings to the ship's mate, who sent the cabin boy down the gangplank to her father's side. There was brief exchange, then her father returned to pleasantries and barter with the merchants. Autumn saw that Edrigo was now on his guard. Saxons in Aldtyme? They had firm hold of East Anglia to the south and part of Mercia, but here in Northumbria? She glanced up to the walls of Aldtyme's fortress. A Roman noble had posted the request for a ship, but who was really the ruler here now?

The message was sent up to her that they were getting top prices for their meager cargo. That was good news, then.

The cargo negotiations were concluded in short order. The

merchants stepped back to allow another man to step forward. His demeanor until then had been self-effacing, and Autumn saw that was why she had noticed him earlier. The herald had deliberately not called attention to himself to take her father's measure as he dealt with the merchants. Autumn was not used to missing such a clue to dockside behavior. Whoever this personage was, wanting passage on their ship, they were ably represented.

She also saw that the Saxons had moved closer. Although their goal seemed to be eavesdropping, she sent the message, "'Ware the Saxons."

More pleasantries. Edrigo bowed several times and gestured at their handsome vessel several more. He was inviting an inspection. The herald was no doubt asking about safety. She strung her bow and waited for her cue. It was her turn to demonstrate the *Verdant Bough*'s capabilities.

An imperious command issued from the horsechair, and the entire contingent — gods, what a lot of packing chests — moved forward. The herald was trying to stop their progress, but the commanding voice from inside the horsechair spoke again.

The dock grew even quieter and Autumn could finally hear the herald's raised voice. "But your ladyship, I must be assured of your safety! Your father and husband-to-be insist upon it!"

The horsechair came to a stop directly behind the herald. It was a graceless piece of work, a narrow wooden box with a heavy curtain over the small window at about the height where the occupant could look out. The curtain was lifted for a moment, then fell back into place.

A woman of rank traveling by hired ship? Had her father no vessels? Autumn realized that was one thing that had been bothering her — there were no other vessels in harbor, not even fishing boats. The folk of Aldtyme must rely on fishing to live, and it was hard to believe the fishing boats were all out at once. She sent the question, "Where are the other vessels," down to her father, and nocked an arrow to her sturdy yew bow.

"There is no safer vessel than the *Verdant Bough*," her father proclaimed. He thrust the sea cap he'd been holding into the air.

Autumn didn't hesitate.

In less time than the beat of a gull's wings the cap was pinned to the horsechair just below the window, pinned very neatly by Autumn's green-fletched arrow.

"Nice shot," the crewman below commented nonchalantly.

There was a stifled scream from inside the horsechair, and the herald's outrage was heard from one end of the dock to the other. "How dare you endanger her ladyship!"

"I have the best archers on the seas," Edrigo said calmly. "You asked for assurance of safety."

The horsechair door was thrust open, and a crimson-veiled woman half as wide as she was tall slid unceremoniously out of its dark recesses to the dock. "This will not do!"

"Your ladyship," Edrigo began.

"There must be another ship," the woman said imperiously. "This will not do!" Her shrill voice cut the air like birds fighting over prey. They were going all the way to Jutland with that voice? Autumn found herself hoping the deal would fall through. The crimson-veiled woman was betrothed? For all her energy, she looked old enough to be Edrigo's mother.

"You will be well protected —"

"We need an honest vessel, not a pirate!" Crimson Veil snatched the arrow out of the door.

"We are not pirates, but must defend ourselves from them," Edrigo said coldly. He glanced at the herald. "We have traveled a long way on the promise of taking a passenger to Jutland. You'll not find any other ship on the way. You might want to tell me why. And why no other vessel is in port."

The herald faltered. "We've had to devote all our vessels to protecting our fishing boats. Pirates —"

"I've met them," Edrigo said. "They seemed uncommonly bold."

"Our new allies are hunting them overland."

Allies. All the gods, Autumn thought. Saxons were no one's allies except at the highest possible price. Suddenly it all became clear. They were taking a bride to Jutland — one of the prices of the alliance? No Saxon lord could possibly value the woman in the horsechair that much. She was past childbearing and no great wealth could be eked from this place.

Her nimble mind carefully considered the puzzle. She studied the half-dozen gray-veiled attendants behind the horsechair and saw that two were probably as old as Crimson Veil, but the other four were much younger, taller, all slender with hands tucked piously inside their sleeves. The bride was one of those, she'd wager. Crimson Veil's masquerade allowed the bride anonymity while the ship was evaluated.

She sent her suspicions down to her father, who was detailing for the herald the number and quality of their archers. If they had not been caught completely off their guard, the Angle pirates would not have even come close to the *Verdant Bough*'s rails.

Crimson Veil was complaining that the ship was too small. Edrigo reminded her that no other ship was likely to come at all. Autumn noticed one of the Saxons gesturing brusquely at the herald, who nervously turned back to Edrigo. The Saxons wanted the bride on the sea.

Crimson Veil had pitched her voice so the Saxons could hear. "You know we are all committed to a life of service to Christ our Lord, and if we are to be turned from our path we could at least be conveyed to our fate by a Christian captain. Cynan of Jutland would at least know he comes between his bride and our Savior, the Savior who gave Constantine victory over the infidels."

The Saxons moved nervously, but the one in charge gestured again. Fear of this new god they called the son of the one god would not stop them from seeing their lord's bride on her way to his side.

Crimson Voice had not stopped. "To be conveyed to such a heathen place by pagan men with no sense of honor —"

Edrigo bridled. "My lady, you impugn my daughter and my crew with such —"

"Your daughter is on that ship?" Crimson Veil took a deep breath as if to launch into an assault on such an obvious lie.

"She is. I consider her safety and honor in all things," her father said firmly.

"I would see this . . . daughter."

There was nothing for it. Edrigo shrugged and gestured. Autumn threw her leg over the side of the crow's nest and started her descent, aware that every eye on the dock was following her movements.

"*That* is your daughter? She takes after her mother, then?"

There was crude laughter from some of the men on the dock, but it was nothing Autumn had not heard before. Her skin was as pale as Edrigo's was dark, which led to base speculations as to her real role on board. She thought suddenly of Tain and felt guilty for not having consciously mourned him these last few hours. It was too soon to let go grieving just because life went on. She set foot to the deck in good time, lifted her chin with pride, and strode to the top of the gangplank.

"That half-naked savage is *your* daughter?"

Autumn flushed. Half-naked indeed. So her hair and face weren't covered. That wasn't half-naked. Still, as she stepped down the gangplank she was aware of her sunburned nose and short, windblown hair. She stayed Scylla with a gesture. Better to keep the large creature out of sight for now.

"Your ladyship, my daughter, Autumn. She is her mother's daughter in looks, but my daughter in all else."

Autumn did not think a curtsey would impress anyone, especially since she had no idea how to go about it wearing thick woolen leggings and deck boots. Instead she inclined her head in respect and tried to look harmless. She belatedly realized her bow and quiver still dangled from her shoulder. The dagger in her boot seemed enormous.

"No, no," the woman said. "I don't think —"

"Enough." The cool voice stopped the woman instantly. "Enough, my dear aunt. The *Verdant Bough* will suit our needs."

One of the gray-veiled figures stepped forward. This would be the real bride, Autumn thought. "I am sorry for any insult you may have received, Captain. My protectors can be fierce." The slender figure extended her hand, and Edrigo formally bowed over it.

She turned to the herald, who nervously cleared his throat. "I present the Lady Ursula, fostered daughter of the noble Cressius, lord of lower Northumbria." The herald did not choose to hear the Saxons' audible snickers. A lord in name only, it seemed.

"Your ladyship," Autumn murmured. Her foster father had sold her for aid from the Saxons against whom? The Angles, probably. She felt sorry for the girl, who had probably had no choice in the matter. Belatedly she remembered her courtesy. "We are honored."

"That is your arrow?" Ursula held out one delicately boned hand and Crimson Veil gave it to her. "That was finely done. I will feel safe in your company, I am certain." She handed the arrow to Autumn, who slipped it into her quiver. Black eyes glinted with warmth above the gray veil.

"You shall have my cabin," Edrigo said. "If I may, how many are there?"

"We are three plus myself and used to sharing small quarters on this journey. Do not over concern yourself with our comfort."

"I will see to everything before you sail," Crimson Veil insisted, not without a sour look at the herald.

"I have no doubt of that, Aunt Lillidd," Ursula answered. "Captain?" She lifted one fragile hand and allowed Edrigo to assist her halfway up the gangplank. Then she stopped. "I would speak."

The merchants had left their stores, and more people flowed from the fortress gates to the dock. The Lady Ursula's leave-taking was obviously an event everyone wanted to witness. Were they eager or reluctant to see her go?

Ursula unveiled her face and Autumn's own reaction answered her question. The dock fell into complete silence. Even the water slapping against the *Verdant Bough* seemed muted.

It was a face as delicately formed as eggshell, with the red of sunrise in her cheeks. Reddish lashes and brows framed brightly glinting black eyes. She was no older than Autumn was, and she seemed utterly unaware of the effect her beauty had on those around her.

Autumn belatedly realized that everyone in the vicinity had gone to one knee. She followed suit, noticing that all caps had been removed and that those without caps tugged forelocks in respect. Even the Saxons bowed before her.

Ursula removed the rest of her veil, revealing thick, glorious red hair braided past her hips in a manner Autumn had never seen before. With a sense of profound shock, Autumn realized she was imagining holding that hair against her mouth, breathing in this beauty that was not meant for her.

"I would not leave you," Ursula said. Her voice carried over the silence of the dock. "All of you know what service I would have chosen, but what will be done is done with joy. We savor the old with the new wine, in the turning of the years. What is old is still with us, but we turn our face to the new. I will miss you. Our exile begins with tears, and we will long for home. I will always wonder when I can see you and be with you again."

The herald next to Autumn murmured, "Ursel." He was weeping. The word sounded like a Saxon version of Ursula, and Autumn remembered that many of these people would share ancestors with the invaders who now threatened their shores. The name was whispered around the dock and Ursula briefly closed her depthless black eyes. "I hear you. I will remember."

They weren't the words Autumn would have expected from a doomed Christian bride, pledged to a barbarian Saxon. They sounded more like a priestess's pledge to her adherents. Ursula was an enigma, Autumn thought, then she looked at Ursula's face again and felt a shivering weakness.

Ursula turned to walk up the gangplank, offering her hands up to the ship's mate who gently assisted her onto the main deck. The rest of the ladies followed except for Lillidd, who began arguing vociferously with Edrigo.

Autumn conquered her weakness to follow the other women up the steep gangplank. Her legs quivered, but she made it up on her own. Edrigo had told her she'd first climbed the gangplank unassisted when she was two and had not needed help since. She would not start now. Ursula was looking about her with interest and Autumn was rendered breathless by her innocence. She did not seem to see that every man on the deck, even those who chose men to bed, watched her every move.

Autumn was abruptly ashamed of herself. The men were at least looking at Ursula in reverence and awe, as if she was pure water after a lifetime of thirst. Her own feelings were much more base. Worship of another sort was in her mind, made her arms ache for loneliness and her heart beat like the drums of Tingeltangel. She tried to remind herself it wasn't a sacred orgy she should be thinking of. They would be at sea on Midsummer's Night, and there would be no bonfire bed for her and Ursula. These women were used to servants who pampered their every whim. No doubt she would hate them all by sunset.

Then Ursula looked at her. Black eyes met deep green and Ursula seemed to catch her breath.

One of the three other younger women stepped between them. "Perhaps you could show us to the cabin?"

"Thank you, Killera," Ursula murmured. "An excellent idea."

Her father's cabin had never seemed so small. The cabin boy had quickly cleared it of her father's most obvious belongings, and the six women glanced about.

"We have sufficient cots," Autumn offered quickly. Her voice sounded strange in her ears. "We'll do our best to make you comfortable."

"Is it always this stale?" The tallest of the women dropped into the only chair.

"Once we're at sea the air is fresh and clean, but it can be cold."

Ursula laughed gently. "Be thankful we're not nuns yet," she said. She untied her robe to reveal a simple garment of soft, finely spun wool. "That's a great deal better. If it gets much hotter I shall want an outfit like yours."

Autumn gestured at her thick shirt. "It hardly befits a nun."

Ursula's vivid red lips curved in another smile. "As I said, we're not nuns yet."

The other women began to laugh as if tension had been lifted. Autumn knew she should not be staring at Ursula, but the fire in her depthless black eyes was beguiling. Her gaze fixed on the heavy black cross that was the only relief on the plain gown. "You are Christian."

Ursula seemed to choose her words with care. "I would rather be the bride of Christ than wed to a Saxon."

From what Autumn knew of the war-making Saxons, she could only agree. Any life was preferable. She thanked the gods for her life on the sea, where alliances and suitors were unnecessary and not forced upon her. "My father has signed to take you to Jutland. He will not do otherwise. He has never failed a contract."

"We will be fine." It wasn't a contradiction, just a simple statement of faith. Ursula had the conviction of innocence. She did not believe evil could befall her. Autumn knew how close she herself had been only two days ago to slavery at the hands of the Angle pirates. For a moment she envied Ursula her belief in fortune. She realized, in that moment, that she would give a great deal to preserve Ursula's innocence, valuing it for reasons she could not yet divine.

Ursula gestured at her companions. "This is Killera, who has been my friend all my life and would not stay at home where she was safe."

Killera, who had been the one to suggest they go inside, greeted her with a cool smile. She was wide shouldered and strong bodied, as substantial as rock next to Ursula's delicate frame.

"Her cousin, Elspeth, who also would not stay behind, though I did ask." The familial resemblance was obvious, but Elspeth was slight where her cousin was broad. She seemed timid by comparison, but Autumn could not believe it was true. A journey like this was not for the timid.

"And this is Hilea, a bard, who is supposed to soothe the savages in Jutland with music."

Hilea scowled. "If they'll even allow a woman to leave the harem."

"There are no harems in Jutland," one of the two older women said tartly. "You'll be lucky to have warm beds."

"Have faith, Aunt." Ursula returned her attention to Autumn. "This is my aunt Justine. Aunt Lillidd you saw on the dock and last, this is my aunt Kaitlynn. They raised me and taught me, and I will miss them terribly." Ursula turned away abruptly, as if she struggled with tears.

Autumn was relieved that the voluble Lillidd was not among their passengers, though it was clear Ursula would miss her aunts.

Killera suddenly leapt to her feet. "What in the mother's name is that?"

Autumn had heard the click of Scylla's claws on the deck. "My dog."

"Wolf, you mean."

Autumn didn't have to bend to tickle Scylla's ears. "There might be some wolf," she admitted without a smile, though she was enjoying Killera's discomfort. She hoped it didn't show.

Ursula was holding out her hand for Scylla to sniff. Autumn's warning died in her throat. Scylla was butting Ursula's fingertips with her nose, inviting a more intimate petting.

Ursula went to one knee to scratch under Scylla's chin. "Part wolf, part puss-cat."

Scylla made an offended noise but closed her eyes while Ursula scratched.

"Scylla will never hurt you," Autumn said. "Tell her what you want her to do and she'll do it."

"Scylla? A six-headed creature devouring sailors to their death?" Ursula's fingers were deep in the fur of Scylla's ruff.

Autumn shrugged. "Better a friendly Scylla at your back then a whirlpool under your prow. She's saved more than one life on this ship." Scylla's light moans of dog ecstasy were getting louder. Autumn took herself to task for being envious. She nudged Scylla with her toe. "Back to the deck with you."

Scylla left with a resentful glare.

"I'll see what's keeping the bunks," Autumn said into the silence that followed. "If there is anything you wanted from the markets, let me know and I'll send someone for it." She had always thought Edrigo's cabin ample in size, but it was overflowing with Ursula's presence. "We probably won't come to shore until Skegness to avoid pirates. Skegness was safe when we left it a few days ago."

Ursula pressed her lips together. "Then we'll go south to Gaul, then east to Germania and north to Jutland? Instead of directly east across the open sea?"

"I believe that is what my father intends. It will take much longer, of course, but it is safer and we can remain well-provisioned and watered." She did not add, *In case we have to run*. Ship's worries were not for passenger's ears.

Ursula's ears were like delicate shells, and Autumn imagined nuzzling them with her teeth. Ursula was staring at her. Autumn flushed to think of her shame if Ursula discerned her thoughts.

Killera spoke abruptly. "We'll settle in, then. Let us know when we're about to cast off, if you will."

She was dismissed. Autumn quit the cabin thoroughly befuddled. Lillidd's grating voice was close enough that she was surely on the main deck now. Autumn took the passageway to the other end of the vessel and tromped up the stairs to the bowman's watch. Padrerus was on duty. She whiled away time until Lillidd went below deck, then she joined Edrigo at the top of the gangplank. A dock crane swung another heavy packing case into the hold. The dock crew would have to be well paid for this lot.

"We're going to be low in the water," Autumn observed dryly.

"Indeed. That's the last one, though, and we'll make the tide. If all is well, we'll pass the pirates in the night."

"All will be well, Father. Enough has gone wrong in the last two days to last us the next ten years." He distractedly patted the hand she put on his shoulder. If Tain were here he would be in the inn, taking money from anyone foolish enough to think they could guess how many coins he held in his hand after he'd shown them three. There had never been three, not when the bets were made.

"Her ladyship is comfortable?"

"I doubt it. But she is determined to make the best of it." She pondered whether she should warn him about Ursula. She felt vaguely disloyal when she said, "She's going to try to get you to take her some place other than Jutland. She says she would rather be a Christian nun."

"The empire may be gone and with it justice for faithless dealing, but to me a contract is a contract."

When the last crate was safely stowed, the ship's mate quickly ordered the loading of market goods and water and wine barrels. Other than an occasional reminder, her father seemed content to just watch and accept Autumn's comfort. He stirred when crew signaled they could raise the anchor.

"We'll make the tide," her father observed needlessly.

"I'll be back in a few minutes. Her aunts need to go ashore."

She hurried around and under members of the crew all hard at work, long practice making it possible to traverse the main deck without getting in anyone's way. She could do it blindfolded in a storm if need be. She clambered down the stairs to the captain's quarters and was met by Ursula coming up.

"We heard the aweigh call."

"I was just coming to tell you. It's time for those going to land to do so." Autumn retreated up the stairs, unaccountably breathless.

The seven women went to the rail, where a great deal of hugging and kissing ensued. As each of the older women left Ursula kissed them quietly on the lips. The gesture had symbolism, obviously. The last of their crew on the dock saw them safely down the gangplank then scrabbled aboard, hauling the gangplank after themselves. Autumn realized then that the dockside crowd had swelled in numbers.

"Hello the deck!" The herald tossed oranges to eager hands, more than enough for passengers and crew. Where had they come from in this remote place? Autumn captured one for herself and smelled it. It reminded her of the southern seas and happier times. She stowed it in her quiver to enjoy later when there was not so much to do. Enjoying the rare delicacy required proper time and attention.

"Hilea," Ursula said calmly. "It is time."

The women held the fragrant fruit in front of them and peeled while Hilea strummed lowly on a lute as she began to sing.

"The garden of life, in a garden of life, we have joined," she sang in upward reaching leaps of breathtaking clarity. Autumn was caught immediately by the spell Hilea's voice cast and the way the music twined in on itself, both sad and joyful. *"We have gathered in a garden of fruits, among the splendor of flowers, to Ursula."*

Autumn saw that the hair that hung below the tie of Ursula's braid was floating, though there was no deck level breeze to explain it. There was light, more than sunlight. She made a reflexive sign of warding and felt foolish for her superstition, but there was no illusion of spellmaking here — Hilea was singing some sort of magic, and her voice carried toward the town and the hills, carried much farther than was natural.

The other three women — Ursula, Killera and Elspeth — were breaking the oranges open and letting the juice within run over their hands. Onshore, the three aunts did the same. Then all six women threw the opened fruit back into the crowd where the slices were caught and shared. There was no mistaking the gesture, Autumn thought. The priestess and her acolytes give one last gift to the well-being of her people before she takes her leave. Autumn felt a chill through her body — she had never been this close to a ritual of this sort before.

Hilea sang, *"When will we see you and be with you, in a garden of fruit, among the splendor of flowers? We feed among the lilies in a garden of fruit. We join with Ursula."*

From the crowd below came a response. *"Ursel!"*

"Ursel!" Hilea answered and her voice rose, and rose again, and rose again, with the power of all the light that streamed around Ursula now. The crowd went to its knees and still Hilea sang ever higher until the hills echoed with the twin cry of sorrow and joy. The hills rang on with the power of it long after Hilea's voice had cracked and fallen silent. Her fingers on the long strings of her lute were still.

The last rope was coiled, the anchor finally raised and the *Verdant Bough* drifted from the dock. Autumn wondered at the calmness of the men who scurried about their work. Hadn't they felt what she had felt, the flashing power that still made her hands shake?

She watched Ursula go below deck, then reached for her orange because now seemed the right time to accept the gift. The first slice exploded in Autumn's mouth with a flavor so bright she had to close her eyes. It made her think of Ursula's red hair. Red hair and red mouth. Her body prickled. She was just a passenger, Autumn reminded herself, and a noble's daughter. A bride of either a Saxon lord or the son of a god.

She told herself, though she was already thinking how to make it a lie, She is not for you.

The sun was growing brighter, and brighter still. Autumn struggled to keep her eyes open, but the tunnel was suffused with white light. She slipped through the spiral gate to welcome darkness and discovered a wall in front of her. It was the moon-and-star painted door of the magician's box. It opened easily when she touched it with her fingers in precise arrangement, but how she knew that special touch was yet another mystery. She stepped through the door and into her sleeping body.

The sun was rising. Scylla nosed her fingers with a quiet woof that meant she needed to go outside. Autumn managed to get to her feet, stiff all over from her long sleep. Her stitches itched fiercely. She felt faint and knew she shouldn't go back to bed without eating something, but her heavy body ignored hunger in favor of sleep. She wanted to look at Ursula again. Ursula, the woman from the tunnel, who had sent her back to life, who had pleaded with Autumn to leave her, had paid a terrible price for Autumn's freedom, had been making love with Killera in a car. Trying to make sense of the faces Ursula wore and the places she seemed to be made Autumn dizzy.

Until now her purpose had been to survive day to day, to wait until something told her who Autumn is, who she had been Before, but that was gone in a blaze of red hair and the brightness of two shining black eyes. She would go back to Ursula. It was what she was here for.

She reached for sleep because that was the only way to find the gate. She needed a magician's box to find the gate for real. Nonsense, she told herself. Part of her knew Ursula was just a hallucination, but that part was getting smaller. She slept and did not see that Scylla's eyes were also closed.

Six

Beyond the gate of her sleep, slipping down the arc of light, Ursula floated the river to Aldtyme and the embrace of its circle. She passed beyond to find her hands gripping the rail of a sailing ship as it drifted from a wooden dock. A silent throng watched its going and she knew them all for her people. At the dock's edge stood three stout figures, lion aunts, and they were weeping.

It was Aldtyme she was leaving again, utterly changed but just as familiar, the fortress, the merchant carts, the cross newly bound to the top of the keep itself. The cross was starkly outlined by the sun as it set behind the moors. The moors were no different. Every copse and rock was as she knew it in both lives.

Both lives, she considered. She remembered walking these moors with Kelly and the flash of memory that had shown the both of them in other garb, in another time.

She looked down. They had worn clothes like these. She looked to her left and Kelly was there, the solid sureness of her, the enduring strength that loved without reservation. Killera, that was her name in this dream. Of course.

You're dreaming, she told herself. Wishful dreams, perhaps.

It was a most incredible dream, then. She smelled orange on her hands and her spirit was lifted by a profound magic woven into the words of the song that had brought her to this place and time.

She did not know the woman who sang, not in her future life. A voice like that could not possibly be forgotten. It soared like light. *"When will we see you and be with you, in a garden of fruit, among the splendor of flowers? We feed among the lilies in a garden of fruit. We join with Ursula."*

It was time to do her part. Ursula lost the sense she had had of watching a film, that nothing that took place could touch her. She was in the scene now, and the power for the spell to bless this place, one last time, came from her. The circle was surrounding this place, as it always had and would in the future she knew. But in this more primal time, the power it raised was like she had never known before — an elemental magic, wild but for her skill at using it.

She faltered in awe of what she felt surging inside her. Then she felt the presence of her beloved aunts coming to her from the shore, their distinct personalities weaving into the mesh of support that had always been there for her, now and in a future that rapidly faded from memory. They were the weavers of this place and could not leave it. Their love and power was hers to have always. She wondered how far she would travel before she could no longer sense them.

Her courage was found. She closed her eyes and cast out with her arms. The circle would endure.

She gave focus to Hilea's final cry of *"Ursel!"* and sent it spilling over the moors. Birds took wing in the distance. She was the strength of the spell, but it took all seven of them, one for each light in the sky of the Great She-Bear's constellation. Tonight the She-Bear's tail would point due east to mark the first day of spring. Winter had ended and the song promised a garden of fruits and a splendor of flowers. Spring would come to her people, even as she left them.

Hilea's voice faded and the spell collapsed in on itself, every nuance completed and every protection given that could be conveyed through the power of the goddess.

Her time as the goddess walking was done. She abruptly felt smaller. When she looked at her hands she expected them to be colorless and insubstantial. It felt strange to be only Ursula. Stars began to dot the sky, and she saw the first of the seven sisters in the Great She-Bear shine forth. East, her tail pointed, due east.

East was where she was heading now, to a Saxon husband as bride price for his alliance with her foster father.

Well, she thought. Time would tell. They were not traveling due east tonight because of the pirates. As long as they did not sail east there was hope. She had no desire to be a Christian nun, but they had their own houses of sisterhood and worship. She understood the message of the White Christ and could live under its rule. Many of the White Christ's sacraments were older than Christ's birth, though in some parts of this world she understood it could mean death to say so. Still, she would choose Christian life over that as a Saxon wife. They had all agreed.

She took one last look at the darkening moors and forests before she followed the others below deck. Hilea stumbled slightly, and Killera steadied her. It was always so with Hilea, who gave all she had whenever she sang. She had sung well, exquisitely well, and the words she had chosen for the spell were her finest work. She would sleep like the dead tonight. They all would. A cup of Aunt Lill's spiced tea would see to that. The scrips of herbs and distillates were, to Ursula, their most valuable possessions, worth far more than the plate and coin sent to her future husband as part of the dowry.

The captain's bed was wide and soft with enough comfort for two, but sufficient cots, thick with wool pallets and linen coverlets, had been provided so they could sleep separately. She knew that Killera wished it otherwise, but tonight Ursula wanted her bed to herself. It was journey's beginning, and she had much to consider. She felt distant from her friends for the first time in a long while, since she had joined them in the circle on the day of her womanhood. The worry she had been ignoring — that she was leading them to a far worse life — began to fester.

There was a gentle tap at the door. Her companions were already nestled, and she waved Elspeth back into her bed as she went to the door. She opened it enough to see who knocked and stood there feeling stupidly confused and out of breath.

How could she have forgotten about the captain's daughter? Autumn's eyes were as deeply green as an old forest, and fathomless for one so young. She gazed at Autumn, and a sensation altogether unsettling and pleasing tickled at the nape of her neck.

"Is everyone comfortable?"

"Yes, and thank you."

Autumn stepped away as if she would go, and Ursula followed her into the tiny hallway. The motion of the vessel was mild this close to shore, and she swayed with her knees bent as she had seen the crew do. "I hope we haven't put you out of your bed."

"No, I have my own cabin — small, but mine." Autumn seemed eager to leave her, but Ursula did not want her to go.

"How long will the voyage take?" No one had given her this information, most likely because they deemed it irrelevant. She was going to Jutland if it took ten years. Men had decided she would go, and so she went.

"My father believes we will be in Jutland before midsummer. Weather could add or take away."

"In time to celebrate a new home," Ursula said wryly. "If't take that long, I am happy. I had not hoped for as much."

The dim light muted the extent of Autumn's shrug. "We can't go directly. It is safer, but slower."

"We'll not complain." The silence between them was prolonged and deep. It no longer seemed as if Autumn was eager to go, but she said nothing. "Do you think — never mind."

"Ask," Autumn said quietly. "If I can answer I will."

"Is there any chance we won't make it?"

"You mean and still be alive?" Autumn's sarcastic tone made Ursula flush.

"Yes."

"Very little. We have never failed a contract." Again she shrugged, but her voice was taut as she went on. "You're the goddess. Don't you know?"

"I am not a goddess, only her servant, and those days are done."

It cost her much to say it so calmly. She would be hard-pressed to raise a circle anything like the one in Aldtyme without her aunts' deep resources that came from the land itself. She didn't know the land she went to, and if anyone there had ever plumbed the depths of its natural power.

"I don't know what you did," Autumn said carefully, "but I've never seen its like before."

"We walk the old ways in Aldtyme, though sometimes the way has new names." It was easy to tell that Autumn was somewhat afraid of her, and Ursula wanted to spare her any discomfort. She did not want Autumn to avoid her for any reason. "The stars rise and fall just the same, no matter the name. Notice must be taken and thanks given. Do not sailors believe in the stars?"

It might have been a flicker of smile on Autumn's lips as she answered. "After the sea, the stars are our way. The only goddess I know is the sea. It's the only truth there is."

"I look forward to learning this truth," Ursula said softly. She tucked her hands in her sleeves because they suddenly wanted to touch Autumn's face.

"Midsummer is a long way away," Autumn said. Ursula could not tell if she meant it as a comfort or a warning. "Breakfast will be placed outside your door after sunrise." Autumn started to add something, then hurried up the stairs. For a moment her lithe body was a dark outline against the starry night, then she was gone.

Ursula returned to the cabin to find only the starlight to light her way to her bed. She disrobed quickly and did not discover she wasn't alone until she was all the way in the comfortable bed's embrace.

"Killera," she said, barely above a whisper, though Hilea and Elspeth would not be surprised to overhear their voices and other, more intimate sounds. They had shared a single chamber whenever they had traveled, most often to York, to her foster father's capital.

Killera's answer was a kiss. Only last night Killera's kiss had brought her body into flower; only last night she had hungered for more. That Killera had slipped into her bed reassured her that Killera's passion was unchanged, but she did not respond to tonight's kiss. Only last night they had wrapped each other in the mystery of the circle and celebrated the first day of spring. They had touched each other as if with sunlight and shared the goddess's kiss of peace before more intimate caresses. A day had passed since, and everything had changed.

She turned her head, and for the first time in her life, she lied to Killera. "I am so weary."

"I know you are," Killera answered, her voice whispering inside Ursula's ear. "I just wanted to hold you."

She let herself be cradled on Killera's soft, wide chest and was still not asleep when Killera's breathing steadied. She lay in Killera's arms and thought about Autumn's eyes. She had lied to Killera, and she thought about Autumn's eyes. She knew herself too well to misunderstand the implications.

She had left the only home she had ever known, and the first night from the shore of that home all she had been was swept away. The tapestry of her life had altered its pattern so abruptly she no longer had the power to know if it meant good or ill.

Killera stirred against her. "Ursula?"

The sound of her name on Killera's lips filled her with a sadness so profound that she could not weep. The ship wavered around her and without seeking it she slipped through the gate.

"Ursula?" The sound of her name on Kelly's lips filled her with sadness, and Ursula opened her eyes to the dim morning light in an unfamiliar house.

"You're crying in your sleep, baby." Kelly smoothed Ursula's forehead with one thumb. "I can't bear it."

"It's not your fault," Ursula managed to say. "It was never your fault." She dashed away the tears on her cheeks.

"I don't care," Kelly said raggedly. "Let me help. Let me *in*."

"I've done nothing but hurt you by keeping you out —"

"I always knew there was something. I didn't care, but I hate to see you like this." She clasped Ursula's hand in hers. "I am strong and I can help. I am not afraid."

You ought to be, Ursula wanted to say. "I've been so selfish."

"Are you going to tell me you don't love me?"

"I do love you — gods, how can you doubt that? I do love you, and that's the problem. It's always been the problem. I love you both."

Color drained slowly out of Kelly's face. "There's someone else."

Ursula couldn't even bring herself to nod. "That and more."

Kelly's fingers spasmed around Ursula's hand, but she did not let go. Her courage should not have surprised Ursula, but it did. "Tell me, then. Tell me everything."

The silence in the car was palpable, a heavy thing that would take more strength than Ursula had to break. How could I have handled it so badly, she asked herself for the hundredth time. *I knew better and still I did it.*

Taylor had been appalled, with good cause. Kelly's cry of anguish had brought Taylor running from the bedroom and, though she had immediately known what Ursula had done, she said later she simply could not believe it.

It had been Taylor who had wrenched their hands apart and used her considerable resources to effectively douse Ursula's attempt to force a rapport with Kelly. She left a badly shaken Ursula to tend to her own pain while she ministered to Kelly's. Liz had frozen in the doorway, one hand over her pale mouth.

Ursula had tried to shudder her way through a relaxing spell, but she couldn't manage it all the way through. She shivered uncontrollably and knew she deserved the blinding pain behind her eyes.

"What were you thinking?"

Taylor's angry question cut into her composure even further. "I thought it would work. I wanted her to believe."

"Stop crying. Remember who you are!"

"I'm not her anymore," Ursula said desperately. She wiped her eyes with her sleeve. "I haven't been Ursula since I left home."

"Kelly? Kelly — wake up. It's okay. You can open your eyes now. Be at peace, you are safe here." Taylor's gentleness faded as she turned to Ursula. "That much is clear. I don't know what you were at home, and I don't know what kind of traditions you had, but this was wrong."

"I'm okay," Kelly said, though her voice was wan. "I asked her to tell me."

"She had no right. She knows better even if you don't. She's supposed to look out for you."

Taylor's condemnation was the final straw. Ursula staggered to the kitchen and jerked open drawers. She needed scissors, or a very sharp knife. She was not the center of the circle and never would be again — not after she'd tried to force contact with an unsuspecting layperson. What had she been thinking?

She found a pair of large shears and slipped finger and thumb into the holes. She lifted her braid with her other hand and closed the sharp blades around it just past her scalp.

"Ursula, no!"

Liz knocked the scissors out of Ursula's hand and they skittered across the hardwood floor. Ursula shoved Liz away and lunged for them, but suddenly Kelly was there, holding her, wrapping her tightly with arms that would always be there to catch her when she fell. She was falling so far and so fast, falling from everything she had been.

Liz returned the scissors to the drawer while Ursula panted into Kelly's shoulder. She tried once to get away, but Kelly went on holding her.

"What have you got us into, Liz?" Kelly's angry demand made Ursula struggle for her freedom again, but still Kelly held her tightly.

"It's not her fault —"

"We were okay!" Kelly was shouting. "We were okay until we came here. It's all" — she choked for breath — "all ruined."

"Don't," Ursula managed. "Baby, don't cry." She was holding Kelly now, trying to keep Kelly whole, but Kelly was breaking into pieces in Ursula's arms, and her sobs sounded like granite crumbling in Ursula's ears.

"Listen to me," Liz said firmly. She put one hand on Kelly's shoulder, and Ursula felt the relaxing spell she had not been able to cast herself. "We have always known we each had a secret and never spoke of it. You knew I was gay like you, and I knew you . . . felt reality the same way I did. We've been silent too long and for nothing."

"The time for secrets is past, long past," Taylor added.

Ursula drew Kelly to a kitchen chair and made her sit. When she would have stepped away, Kelly pulled her down, into her lap, and wrapped her waist with both arms.

With Liz's spell to help her, Kelly seemed to be calming down. Taylor was busy at the counter and returned to the table with tea, milk and a box of tissues.

"I don't think I can talk right now," Kelly said finally. She scrubbed her face with a tissue. "I'll break down again."

"I can help with that," Taylor said. She extended one hand in trust, but Kelly drew back.

"No. I-I can't."

"This is my fault," Ursula said. "I need to make it right."

Kelly's heart was broken, it was written on her tear-streaked face. What she said next was completely without malice, though Ursula would have forgiven her that without a second thought. "It can't be right again."

Ursula had held back her tears then, and she continued to hold them back as the Explorer bumped across the last set of livestock grates before they reached home. Kelly's home, Ursula reminded herself. Whatever Kelly wanted she would do. She owed her that much and more.

Kelly dropped wearily into the closest chair without speaking. Ursula stood in the doorway, wishing with all her might that she didn't do Kelly any more harm. "I'll go if you want me to."

Kelly cleared her throat. Her voice was tight and raspy. "I need to know. About what Taylor and Liz meant. And about . . . her."

"I was trying to force contact, a rapport, to explain it all." She knew it sounded crazy and there was no reason for Kelly to believe a word of it. Kelly's disbelief had been what she was trying to avoid. "I should never have done it. Taylor did it so easily, but she's a master, like my aunts. I don't even compare. I — I don't know what I was thinking."

"Rapport? Some kind of mental touch? You believe in that?" Kelly's face was full of wounded skepticism.

"I believe in it. I practice it. So does Taylor — and Liz. I believe that anyone who wants to can learn how, but it's easier for some than others. Like me. Like you."

"I don't believe in it." Kelly turned her gaze away. Ursula could tell she knew she was lying to herself.

"You've just taught yourself to ignore it. You've always been able to read people's intentions, tell if they're lying, haven't you? Sometimes you know something about them, like if they've recently been in an accident, or lost someone they loved."

Kelly's nervousness was betrayed in the trembling of her lower lip. "I tried to tell my mother, but she got this look in her eye, like I was growing another head, like she didn't know who I was anymore."

"Did your mother have any . . . esoteric pursuits? Something more than going to church?"

Kelly shook her head. "Not that I knew about. I mean, you met her family. They're bread-and-butter people. So was my mom."

"But you're different. So is Liz."

"We have a lot in common, Liz and I. We were both born out of wedlock, and we're both gay."

"Floyd — Floyd isn't her blood father?" Ursula found this information somehow disturbing, though she did not know why.

"No, he adopted her. Aunt Mary and my mom never, ever talked about how they got pregnant. At least not to me. The scandal — both of them and the same year — it's still a family skeleton." She sighed heavily. "I don't know how this can be important to you and me."

"I was trying to explain about rapport."

"Could you come over here?" Kelly opened her arms. "You're too far away, and I just won't be afraid of you."

Some of the ache in Ursula's heart eased. She left the doorway and sat in Kelly's lap as she had at Taylor's. She felt small in Kelly's arms and wanted to curl up, be protected and shushed. But it was time for her to be the strong one. She'd cowered long enough. "I'm trying hard not to frighten you. I don't worship the devil, you know."

"I never thought that. I just don't know what to believe." Kelly rested her head on Ursula's breast. "But you are going to start talking about magic, right? I'm sorry." Impossibly, Kelly was smiling. "I'm having a hard time with this. I sort of see why you didn't bring it up before."

Ursula answered in a more lighthearted vein as well, though she would not allow Kelly to let her off the hook for her lying silence. "No, we're not to magic yet. We're still working on rapport. Everyone can do it, it just takes practice. Everyone has a degree of sensitivity to other people, to anything alive, too. Some people feel it more strongly, like you, and ignore it. Some people, like me, like Taylor and Liz, explore it. In Aldtyme, my aunts are teachers of the way. Anyone who wants to learn to focus, to listen without ears, to see without eyes, to make the most of their own sensitivity, they can learn from my aunts. They taught me. The first thing you learn is how to establish rapport."

Kelly squeezed Ursula's waist. "So you know how to establish rapport with other people like you, and through that you practice . . . what? Magic?"

"I'm getting there, but you're definitely thinking about how this works the right way. Like I said, some people ignore their sensitivity and others explore it. I've had lots of practice focusing my thoughts, tuning out extraneous distractions and, well, some people describe it as turning on antennae, as if their entire body suddenly had sensors. They absorb everything around them, can tell how fast someone else's heart is beating, maybe even their surface thoughts. It takes practice to ignore all the noise and light and hone in on what you're looking for. If another person is actually cooperating, they can share their perceptions, memories, thoughts in rapport."

"So you wanted to show me all of this by being in rapport with me, but you couldn't find a rapport because I didn't know any of this. Catch-22." Kelly had closed her eyes, and Ursula suddenly realized how relaxed Kelly was. She was on the verge of a light trance, as if talking about rapport was helping her unlock the parts of herself she'd kept tightly under control.

"It was wrong of me. The way doesn't have a lot of rules, but that's one of them, and I should never have broken it."

Kelly said softly, "You did it because you thought it would be easier for me. I understand that. But there's more, isn't there? I can tell."

"There's more. Rapport is communication, mind-to-mind. When you've done a lot of it you won't need a conscious circle, or even to be in trance. You don't need to touch someone, either. You can learn to extend your senses great distances. I've been able to talk to my aunts that way since I've been here. It takes energy, but it's very comforting for all of us."

Kelly's eyelids fluttered open. "You mean you could right now just think 'hello, aunts' and they'd be there?"

"Not quite that easy, but, if they were receptive, and they almost always are, yes, I could do it with a little preparation."

Kelly looked up at her, eyes full of a desire to understand. "Can you show me that?"

"I'll try. I don't have a circle, but I think if we keep it simple I can teach you rapport."

"What does a circle do? Why is it so important to you?"

"If anything we do is magic, it's when we work in a circle. We use our rapport to combine our energies. A spell is nothing more than agreed upon words to achieve a certain goal. So instead of ten people hoping the ewes have easy lambing this year, we join together and make one prayer, one hope, and that's one kind of spell. Other kinds a single person can do by themselves, like going to sleep or relaxing when you're frightened."

"That's what Liz did to me."

"Right. She just focused her energy and said the words in her mind."

Ursula saw a flicker of anxiety reflect in Kelly's eyes, but then it was gone. She should have trusted Kelly's strength. "Have you cast spells while you've been here?"

"A few. Mostly trying to sleep. I've — I've lost weight because I've been sleeping poorly."

"You should have told me."

"I know. I didn't want to worry you."

Kelly pressed her lips together for a long moment. "Well, start worrying me. I love you, and I have a right to worry."

"Okay." Ursula swallowed hard. "Okay. I'll try."

"Why is sleep so difficult here?"

Ursula decided to start with part of the truth. "One of the side benefits of working frequently within a circle is the lasting protective energy that clings to the participants and the place they are working. Aldtyme was . . . I didn't know until I left how powerful. Taylor's house is loaded with protection too. I had restful sleep last night for the first time since I left ho— Aldtyme." *And a very vivid dream*, she could have added, but Kelly was absorbing enough for now.

"You know, so did I."

"Your farm has some protections because of your presence, and it was sufficient to keep you from being bombarded by information you didn't want. But if you do this a lot, you're receptive all the time to rapport and you have to spend energy shutting out unwanted contact. The circle in Aldtyme was always there to do that for me, but there's not enough power here. Taylor is right about that. I'm draining myself to keep my mind clear." Ursula was talking to herself more than Kelly. "That was what happened when Taylor and I shook hands. We were both receptive and unguarded."

Kelly shifted in the chair.

"Am I too heavy?"

"No — I wouldn't want you anywhere else for this." Kelly rested her cheek on Ursula's breast. Ursula felt the familiar longing, but she quickly damped it down. Kelly was her student now, and Autumn was in her heart. "I haven't been sleeping very well the last couple of weeks."

"That's my fault. I've generated more . . . because I'm receptive I attract energy to me, not all of it good. I should have realized it would spill over onto you and that your natural protections would start to suffer. You have a quality of strength and stillness that has protected you. I knew it the moment I saw you." *And I've been very bad about protecting you*, she wanted to add, but she would explain her guilt later.

"Back in Aldtyme?"

Ursula nodded.

"We could really talk to your aunts?"

"We'll try." Ursula was almost certain that they would not make it past the gate. The darkness had not stopped lurking. But once Kelly was aware of the gate, she would see how it could work. That would be more than enough for a first lesson.

Kelly still gazed up at her, her mouth soft and eyes filled with longing. "Will you tell me about her, then? That's where she comes in, isn't it?"

Ursula's chin trembled. "I've never even met her." *Not in this life*, she could have added. "I just know she exists. I didn't suspect until I got here."

Kelly pulled her mouth down for a gentle kiss. "Show me then."

Ursula found the words Aunt Kait had used when she was just a child. "Do you see your fingers? Look at each one and look at mine." She hooked her index finger around Kelly's. "They're the same. Feel that they are the same." She squeezed Kelly's finger, hard.

"Okay." Kelly looked as if she wanted to smile at Ursula's small display of strength.

Ursula shifted her grip until they were palm to palm and she invoked the two words that would put herself and Kelly into the lightest of trances. Then she said softly, "Breathe deeply with me, as deeply as you can. In, all the way in. Now out and in again."

Ursula felt the light tingling of the extra oxygen in her fingertips and knew Kelly felt it too. "Most people find it easier if they close their eyes. Do it if you want to. We're very close."

"No," Kelly said. She fixed her gaze on Ursula's eyes. "I think I can see . . . everything's changing. Light . . ." Her mouth parted in surprise. *:Ursula? Is this it?:*

:Yes! Yes, you've found it. I knew it would be easy for you. This is what I was trying to do this morning.:

:It's incredible. I see you, and it's almost as if you were a cartoon before, all flat. But now you're deep — as deep as a universe. You're so beautiful. Oh god, you are so sad, so sad. Why didn't you tell me?:

:I love you. You see that now, don't you?:

:Of course. I see it now.:

Kelly's head had slumped against the back of the chair, and Ursula's own body was cradled safely in Kelly's arms. Using only her mind, Ursula drew an image of herself. *:You can do this, too.:* Ursula wanted Kelly to leave awareness of her physical self behind and visualize, instead, her physical self on this plane. Ursula had enough skill to keep them breathing.

:Like this?: Kelly imagined touching Ursula's face in this heightened state, and Ursula felt the sweetness of it.

:Yes, just like this.:

They drifted for a few minutes while Kelly explored Ursula and herself. Ursula gently urged her to step away from the anchor of their bodies. They perched on a leaf in the dried-flower arrangement over the mantel. Ursula could take that perspective without envisioning her tiny self actually sitting on the leaf, but Kelly needed the physical cues. Some people always did. Aunt Justine said everyone worked in different ways.

:What's that?: Kelly pointed upward.

:The river of energy and chaos generated by every thinking being. Your intuitive flashes — those are leaks from the river. I'll show you how to stop that when you want to. We'll build a gate together.:

:Gate?:

:Come, look at mine.: Ursula gently coaxed Kelly's thoughts to her own mind.

She felt Kelly take a deep breath. *:What do I do?:*

:Any imagery that works for you. Perhaps you see that you are opening a door. That door leads to me.: She created a room with windows for Kelly's ease of understanding, and held out her hand. Kelly took it firmly and stepped over the threshold. *:The more we do this, the less you'll need to see doors and rooms. They're useful images right now.:*

:Is this what it's like to look at the world through your eyes?:

:You're joined with me.:

:Cosmic, baby.: Kelly's laugh, the strongest sign of returning spirits Ursula had seen since they'd left Taylor's, bubbled through both their minds. Ursula let it echo: Kelly's laugh, her perception of it, Kelly's perception of her perception of it, like a thousand reflections in two opposing mirrors. *:What's that?:*

Ursula stopped the echo because it could easily get very noisy. Kelly had seen the barriers Ursula maintained to shut out the river of chaos that flowed endlessly around them. *:This is my gate. It stands between me and the river. I built it to protect me, and you'll need to build one too. The more you work with me like this, the more leaking from the river you're going to feel.:*

:So you open the gate to talk to your aunts?:

:I open the gate and craft a tunnel to take me safely through the river.:

:Is there really a river?:

Ursula felt her body shrug, but that seemed far away. *:It's how we visualize it, yes. An endless stream of energy and chaos. The chaos can overwhelm you, but you can use the river's endless motion to*

117

travel.: She started to think of the darkness on the other side of the gate, but she quickly locked that thought deep in her mind. *:It's how Taylor sees it, how my aunts see it.:*

Kelly was turning to face her in her mind, all loving and wonder-filled eyes. She offered perfect trust, and Ursula could only respond to such a profound gesture. She offered up her awareness of them both in another time, in a distant past she couldn't even set a date to. Kelly's amazement to see herself in that other time was childlike. She asked for more, and Ursula gave her what she could, all of it, every nuance of the dream she'd had, and every soaring note of Hilea's song and the music — so like it and yet not — that called to her from beyond the gate.

Again, Kelly's courage surprised her. *:Let's go find it.:*

:We're too tired. And there's more to tell you, about the music and what's beyond the gate.: A flicker of Autumn's face, shadowed in the hallway of the ship, trembled in Ursula's mind.

:Is that her?: Kelly's sudden distress almost broke their link, but Ursula steadied it again.

:Yes, as I saw her in the dream. I saw her before that, though, for the first time. Earlier in the evening, after we left your aunt's. When we were in the car.:

The memory of the fevered, breathless encounter in the car shuddered between them, made full by their dual awareness of how they had both felt, straining and wanting. Their rapport left the cerebral plane as their bodies awakened. Kelly's mouth was on her throat, and Ursula cursed herself for denying them both this rapture. It could have been so rich.

:Why didn't you show me this?:

: I didn't want to hurt you. Everything I did was because I didn't want to hurt you. You would have known about her. Once you knew it would have changed everything.: It had already changed things. Kelly's desire was marred by the realization that Ursula was not completely hers.

:I'm willing to try.:

:You'll end up hating me. I'm not ashamed of sex or of wanting it. Festival days were always my favorite times.: She showed Kelly a glimpse of Midsummer Night's festival, with the circle in full power.

Priscilla Muldoon and she had found a private glade under the moon. *:Do you see how that is different? Priscilla and I celebrated our bodies for the goddess within us. But you and I are bound more tightly than that. When we touch, it means something more than simple wonder. Something different to you than me, and it will come to matter if we let it.:*

:I can't accept that.: Kelly's mouth was on hers, and Ursula succumbed to the sweetness of it. *:At least let me try to get you out of my system. One last time.:*

:One last time.: Ursula's thought echoed between them, and then Kelly banished the sadness with a throaty moan that pulled down Ursula's crumbling barriers. Her mouth was demanding, almost bruising, with hunger. She lifted Ursula in her arms and took her to bed.

"Did I do that?" Kelly slicked back her cropped hair, wet from her morning shower, and sat down at the kitchen table. Ursula poured her a cup of coffee and resisted the impulse to cover the bruising imprint of Kelly's fingers on her forearm.

She thought to lie and then realized Kelly would know. The time they had spent in rapport had tightened their awareness of each other. To get away with a lie she would have to dampen that awareness, and she wasn't going to do that to Kelly, not when she was taking so much more away. "It's okay. It doesn't hurt."

Kelly looked stricken. "I was too rough."

"It doesn't hurt," Ursula repeated. "Don't worry about it." She had other bruises Kelly could not see, but they weren't unduly painful and last night she had been what Kelly needed for once. She had not known how much Kelly had held back her natural strength, nor how much Kelly had taken cues from her about what course their lovemaking would take. Last night had been for Kelly. Their rapport had let her anticipate Kelly's needs and be ready for them, and to take her own pleasure at meeting them. It was their last time, and she had been strong enough to meet Kelly's demands. Even when she had been exhausted and drained, she had found strength from somewhere to answer Kelly's desire.

"But you didn't — it wasn't what you wanted, was it?"

"If I thought that doing it all again would undo some of the unhappiness I've caused you —"

"That's chicken shit," Kelly snapped. "I don't want that from you."

Ursula didn't know what she had said wrong. "What?"

"A pity fuck. I hurt you and you didn't like it. You think I'd ever take pleasure in that again? I even ruined our last time." She slammed out of the house, leaving Ursula to wipe away a tear with a shaking hand.

The back door flew open again, and all in a rush Kelly enveloped her in her arms. "I'm sorry, I didn't mean to yell. I won't hate you, and I won't be afraid of you."

"I only wanted to make you happy, even for just a few hours."

"I was. You did. It was incredible." Kelly tried to laugh.

"That was being in rapport."

"And you. I'm so sorry —"

"Stop it, will you? It's not a big deal."

"I don't usually get that . . . intense, you know that." Kelly swallowed hard. "Part of me was angry with you."

"Not the part that was loving me." Ursula smoothed Kelly's cheekbone with her thumb. "Don't you think I would have known if you were taking something out on me? Baby, stop this. I was what you needed, and I am happy to have pleased you."

"It won't happen again."

"No," Ursula said gently. "It won't."

Kelly's breath caught. "It really was the last time."

Ursula's answer was a slight nod. She did not trust herself to speak.

Their heightened closeness was abruptly gone, and Ursula realized that Kelly had been the one to withdraw. She was learning. "Please go back to bed, you need to rest. I — I'd rather be alone for a while anyway."

Ursula nodded again and let Kelly walk away.

Seven

Ursula meant to sleep, if only to please Kelly, but her mind was undisciplined by exhaustion. She spoke the three words and sleep came, but just as her muscles relaxed in the moment before sleep, she felt the gate call to her and she entered the dream with a crash of light that left her gasping.

A sudden lurch of the deck made her trip on her robe, and Autumn hauled her back to her feet. Her arm was strong and her hand warm. Every instinct said Autumn was achingly aware of her, but there was antipathy as well.

They'd been in each other's company for fifteen weeks, which could have been an eternity of shared joy. But three of those weeks had been in dock at Yarmouth for repair of torn sails and replacement of burned decking, damage they'd sustained in their only encounter with pirates since leaving Aldtyme. The captain had never doubted the pirates would be repelled. Still, he'd sent them below for their own safety and they'd only heard the thrum of bows and the taunting, victorious cries of their crew as the pirate longboats veered off. Only one of the pirates' flaming arrows had found its mark, but it had done considerable damage.

Autumn had come below to tell them it was safe. Her face had been stained with color and soot, her very essence radiating an almost violent passion for being alive. She'd looked like one face of the goddess as she'd stood in the doorway, her short, nearly white hair wild around her face. Ursula had wanted to crawl to her, to offer her unstinting worship and endless fealty. It was as if she had never really understood love before, though her life had been steeped in perfect love and nurtured by perfect trust. Autumn was outside of that life, and the love Ursula felt was outside of it too.

So, too, was the passion. No proxy in any guise, no matter how well loved or delighted in, would satisfy this new ache. It weighed her down and at the same time lifted her up to the stars.

They'd anchored at Yarmouth the next day, and Edrigo had insisted for their own safety that they board offship at the Abbey of Saint Giles. Ship's crew had stayed aboard, with much maintenance work to do.

Ursula already knew the pain of exile, the wrenching emptiness of leaving behind all her life, her aunts, her power. That suffering was as nothing compared to the ache of not hearing Autumn's voice or catching her eye in some guarded moment. The priests of the White Christ called it a deadly sin, lust, the cause of original sin, the very emotion that barred man from paradise on earth. At mass they were all regularly reminded of the sins of the flesh and threatened with eternal pain for giving in to them. She'd never minded attending service in Aldtyme; at least the priests there had seemed aware that they were raising a circle of their own kind when they stepped through their precise rituals. This abbey seemed empty of that kind of magic, and she missed it.

It seemed that their gentle presence, a company of well-born ladies traveling alone, inspired the priest to tell the story of Eve's wickedness that drove her and Adam from the garden. It had upset Hilea greatly, since they had all been living in such a paradise, free at least among themselves of jealousy and shame. After all, the Great She-Bear viewed sexual love as a sacrament without shame.

The experience had been another blow to Ursula's confidence that she could adapt to a life in a nunnery or a Saxon household. It would have seemed easier to contemplate had it not been for her constant desire for Autumn. She had been so certain in her mind, and she had brought her dearest friends with her on the flood of her faith that they would adapt and survive. Now love threatened all of them, and she had not known that love could bring her to such peril.

They'd sailed south again from Yarmouth, clinging to the populated coast that was far less likely to shelter longboats. In Colchester they'd been warned of a port upheaval in Calais, and they'd waited several days for word that it was safe to trade there. When word came they'd crossed the strait between Britannia and Gaul only to find themselves unseasonably becalmed in Calais as summer drew near.

The captain had apologized for the weather, and looked at Hilea askance. Only the night before, in the warm night air above deck, she had tuned her lute and sung a new work for the enjoyment of the crew, inspired, she explained, by the *Verdant Bough*'s endless movement. Her song had been about an abandoned lover who cursed the wind for carrying her sailor love away.

Ursula had wanted to assure him they had no power over the weather, but she doubted he would have believed her. From the wide berth Autumn gave them for several days after they set sail again, it seemed her superstitions were also aroused.

From Calais they had finally turned east, on the morning after the Great She-Bear's tail had pointed due south. It marked the beginning of summer, when green fruit would begin to take on color, barley stalks would reach for the sky, and husbands of the land would eye their bushels and carts, wondering already if the harvest would be good enough to feed their families and provide for some trade.

The four of them had observed the changing of the season with candles and joined hands, all homesick for the circle they had left behind. Ursula had dreamed of her aunts that night, of them and a ceaseless outpouring of love. She had shared her dream with the others and found that they, too, had been similarly touched.

Their progress along the coast of Gaul was slow. The captain stopped at nearly every port to gather information about the ports ahead. They had taken a long time to make the passage, and it was now quite likely that word of the bride, her dowry, and the vessel that bore her had preceded them. Pirates were no longer the only danger they faced. Every harbor could be a trap, and Ursula made a hostage for ransom by any Saxon, Angle or Southern Jute who didn't fear Cynan of Northern Jutland.

Every encounter with Autumn over the many weeks had been fraught with semantic games about truth and faith that always had a simmer of anger on Autumn's side. Ursula had not been able to find a way to break through Autumn's reserve, and as she stood on deck, steadied by Autumn's hand, she wondered if she ever would. They drew daily closer to Cynan of Jutland's lands and farther away from opportunities for some kind of dignified exit to a Christian abbey that had a house for nuns. If she was to be a Saxon bride, she was unwilling to go to that life without at least having told Autumn what was in her heart. If she remained silent she would regret it for the rest of her days.

She realized she had been staring at Autumn's face and that Autumn had not let go of her arm. She swallowed hard and Autumn startled out of her daze. She dropped Ursula's arm and turned away.

"Aren't you ever going to try this?" Killera's voice floated down from the crow's nest. Of all of them, only Ursula had not adopted shipboard attire. She hesitated because it would mean asking something of Autumn. Hilea hadn't hesitated, and Killera could hardly allow Hilea to appear braver. What Killera did, Elspeth would try to do.

"You're much taller than I, but I think I have one pair of leather leggings that might fit. If you wanted to climb up there." Autumn was carefully noncommittal.

Ursula did not know how far down this path of irresolute weakness she would go. The farther they went from Aldtyme, the weaker she became about matters of personal honor. She had lied to Killera not once, but several times, trying to spare Killera hurt while she had feelings for Autumn. She knew Killera wondered about the loss of intimate moments. She was no doubt suspicious of the cause, which meant she was hurt anyway. Her vacillation was hurting all of them.

She followed Autumn below deck, to the door Ursula had long known was Autumn's. The room beyond was hardly big enough for the small cot and the tall bureau bolted to the windowless wall.

Autumn struck a flint to light the oil lamp held snug on the bureau top. Ursula had to sit on the bed to allow Autumn to close and latch the door behind them.

Autumn opened and closed several drawers and then turned with a pile of clothing. "I think these will work best. Other than height we are of a size." Autumn handed her the clothes looking only at her face, as if to say she was not evaluating the shape and depth of the other woman's body.

The same could not be said of Ursula. She let her gaze rest selfishly on Autumn's shoulders, her hips, her breasts. The longing in her was painful, deep in her stomach, and she had never experienced its like before. She wanted something she could not have. So focused was her desire that she had a brief flash of rapport with Autumn's turmoil and clearly heard her thinking, "She is not for me."

Aunt Justine had a saying about getting what you deserved when you played with things that could hurt you. Ursula knew she deserved to get hurt, mostly because at that moment she did not care if what she did next would wound anyone. She knew she was being unspeakably selfish even as she did it, but, great mother and all the gods, she could not stop.

She unknotted the cord at the throat of her robe and slipped the heavy fabric off her shoulders.

Autumn was like a statue. Ursula did not even think she was breathing. She fumbled with the cording to unwrap her waist and Autumn suddenly moved. "I'll leave you alone."

Ursula tried and failed to find Autumn's studied nonchalance. "You don't have to go." It was a plea.

Autumn put one hand on the back of the door and the other across her stomach. "Yes, I do."

It was unexpected, that Autumn was strong enough to fight the same yearning Ursula found irresistible. "It need not mean anything." From the way Autumn's back stiffened, Ursula knew immediately she had said the wrong thing. "I didn't mean that," she said hastily. "I didn't mean it."

"Yes, you did."

"No. I was trying to make you turn around."

"I can't."

"Why?" She felt cheap to press her barely covered breasts into

Autumn's back, but she could not stop herself. "Have you given pledge to someone else?"

"You have. A Saxon dog or the White Christ."

"I've given nothing of myself or my honor to either. I intend to keep myself free as long as I can."

"Am I a means to that end?"

"I don't understand." Autumn's back was warm against her breasts. The scent of her skin was intoxicating.

"Is it more pleasant to seduce me than my father?"

Ursula reeled back. "How can you think that?"

"What else can I think?" Autumn turned finally from the door, and her eyes were heavy with desire and yet a tenacious dignity burned there as well. "You and Killera — Hilea told me. You have no need of me."

"We were much to each other, and will always be. But you — what I feel when I look at you, hear your voice, it's profoundly different. I've not been with her since I felt it, since your eyes slipped inside my mind." In desperation Ursula cast out with her mind, wondering if she could show Autumn her intentions were born of honest desire, but she was met with rigid natural shielding that made her instantly withdraw. Autumn would have to let her in if they wanted to truly know one another.

"That could all be one of Hilea's pretty songs. Or one of your witching spells."

Ursula drew herself up with what was left of her shattered composure. The brief contact with Autumn's shields had made her realize she was preoccupied with Autumn's body and had not thought about her mind. She had done Autumn an injustice, and Autumn was fully aware of it. "You don't know me or trust me, then, so you're right. This will not work." She wrapped her robe around herself and gathered the clothes Autumn had chosen in her arms. "Thank you for these."

"You are welcome," Autumn said through stiff lips.

She stepped up on the cot so Autumn could open the door, then clambered past her as if she was used to exiting rooms by stepping down off a bed with her robes half undone and tears in her eyes.

She put the clothes on in her cabin and went back on deck feeling like a fool. What had possessed her to tell Autumn that to lay with her could mean nothing? No wonder Autumn seemed not to like her at all. She had behaved like a . . . like an ill-bred, tavern-trawling man. Gods.

"It's about time," Killera called down.

"Are you sure you want to do this?" Elspeth shaded her eyes as she studied Ursula's face.

"I'm fine," Ursula said, knowing she had not answered Elspeth's question.

Hilea started one of her bawdier songs, and Ursula realized her interpretation of Killera's insistence. They would be very alone for the first time in many weeks.

"You don't have to," Elspeth said softly.

Ursula no longer knew if Elspeth was referring to the climb. "I think I do." She had behaved badly toward Autumn and Killera both, and this would be a chance to at least set one score right. She did not want to hurt Killera, but pretending nothing between them had changed was a lie. It was wrong.

The climb was exhilarating. She'd not had as much exercise in far too long. The captain gave them three weeks to Jutland, landing not quite a week before Midsummer. She could not hope to convince Autumn that they could share something, if only briefly, while she tried to keep Killera in the dark about it, as if Autumn was a dirty secret.

She rested halfway up, enjoying the rush of wind past her ears and the sense of weightlessness that came at the peak of every swell. When she'd gone beyond the gate in their circle it was like flying, but not like this. That was all mind; this was all body. Her stomach lurched and nerves tickled her throat and she liked the sensation. It was unlike anything she had felt before. It was part of Autumn's world, part of her truth of the sea. She wondered if being in Autumn's arms, being loved by her, would feel like this.

Killera's head popped over the edge of the crow's nest. "What's taking so long? I was up in half that time." Had she not dreaded being alone with Killera she would have enjoyed sharing this experience with her, enjoyed even a casual coupling, as sweet and earnest as they had ever shared. But that time was past. Because of the way she felt about Autumn, there would never be anything casual between her and Killera again. She needed to remember who she was, or at least, who she had been. It was time to show Killera perfect trust and tell the truth.

Hilea and several of the crew cheered when she reached the top. Killera helped her over the lip, and she plopped down to catch her breath. They swayed through the sky, arcing forward and back with a motion far more intense than that of the deck.

"Is this how birds feel?" Her stomach was taking its time adjusting, but the dizziness passed after she could breathe normally again. The wind roared past her ears and she felt as if she could touch the sky.

"I don't know, but I like it," Killera said. "I feel as if we could all leap from here to freedom."

Ursula pulled herself upright and looked down at the deck. Elspeth looked upward with concern, so Ursula waved. "Death is not the freedom I am looking for."

"Nor I." Killera put one gentle hand on Ursula's back. "My freedom is with you."

Ursula turned to Killera to speak only to find Killera's lips close to her own. She couldn't help her impulse to lean away.

Killera's eyes widened, those golden, honeyed eyes. They were bright with Killera's inner light, a light that had warmed Ursula to her soul so many times. "What is wrong?"

The lie wanted to be said, a denial that anything was wrong, but Ursula forced herself to speak truth. "I am wrong."

Killera ruffled the loose curls at Ursula's ears. "Tell me why."

"When we came aboard — no, just before that. On the dock, I changed. One moment you were the center of my heart..." Her courage faltered as Killera's eyes darkened.

Killera was the braver of them. She always had been, and yet Ursula had never learned to trust that. "And the next moment?"

"She was there. I didn't know it then. I thought it was just my body wanting something new, wishing it were festival."

"I've seen the way you look at her," Killera said slowly. "I had hoped — I thought you would be with her and come back to me, like at festival. You know I like festival as much as you. It's a celebration, for joy."

"What I feel — it's not like that."

"How do you know?" Killera's eyes said she didn't want anything Ursula had said to be true.

"I tried to...just now. She said no." Ursula could no longer bear to look at Killera. "I insulted her by pretending it wouldn't mean anything. As if she was mine for the taking just because I wanted her. Of course it would have meant something to me."

Killera's hand tightened on her arm. "What would it have meant?"

"I don't know. Just thinking about it frightens me. Since we left the circle I've felt lost, as if I no longer feel the earth under my feet." She tipped her head as she considered that. "And of course there is no earth under my feet, only the sea. And she is the sea to me. I want to understand and feel the wonder of her. I feel incomplete now, and I never did before."

"I think . . . I cannot truly understand how you feel. I wasn't the goddess, and I can't know what you lost. I know that delving into mysteries, trying to understand everything — that's who you are. Maybe she is just a new mystery and once you understand her you will come back . . ." Killera's voice faded because Ursula was slowly shaking her head.

"She is that and more," Ursula said slowly. This was the most difficult truth of all. "I, I resigned myself to going to a husband's bed if we weren't delivered before we got to Jutland, though you know I believed that day would not come to pass. I could do that — it means nothing to me. And I would always come back to you because you are my rock and I love you. No stranger husband could change that, ever."

"But she changed it." Killera's voice was tight.

"If I thought she would stay with me I would do almost anything — no, *anything* — to never get to Jutland. I would run, though I know we would be caught. I would lie, I would steal, I would ruin her father's honor. I would be less than I am for the chance to spend my life with her, and I know that doesn't make sense. I know it's wrong being willing to sacrifice so much, not just of myself, but all of you. It scares me, terrifies me, that I could even consider doing such things. I even have thought — forgive me," she pleaded.

"Dearest, anything, please don't be upset."

"You don't know what I've thought. It's terrible. I thought that if I could somehow trade the rest of you for my freedom to be with her I would do it, I would do it!" Her voice choked with unshed tears.

"You are only thinking it, but I know you would never do it." Killera was trying to be gentle, but Ursula knew her words had upset her.

"You know it, but I don't. And not knowing, not trusting myself — I lie awake nights and wonder why this is happening. Why do I feel this way? And I know it's pointless to worry, because she will never come with me. And I know . . . even when she is gone, I could not bear to be with anyone else. Not a husband, not . . . you . . ." She faltered, surprised by her own vehemence. "I love you and I can't let you touch me — oh, don't cry!"

She had never seen Killera cry before, and the tears felt like acid on her hands when she wiped them away. Why had she done this? What had Killera done to be treated so cruelly? Was this the reward of perfect love? "I am so sorry."

"Why her?" Killera dashed away more tears and her anger, almost as rare as tears, made Ursula draw back. "She's not one of us. I might almost understand if it was Hilea. But Autumn has never traversed the gate with you. She knows nothing of the way."

"I would teach her all of it, if she would learn. I would bring her into the circle — she could do it, I feel it whenever she lets me be close enough. But she'll never agree. She thinks I'm trying to use her against her father. She thinks I'm — I'm some sort of witch seductress."

Killera's hands were shaking. "I can't believe this, any of it. You love me."

"I love you, but I can't —"

"Don't say that!"

"Killera, I —"

Killera's mouth was on hers, and it was nothing of the arousing gentleness or even the needful, demanding passion that she knew so well. Killera's teeth bruised her lips and yet she kissed Killera back because of what they had meant and would always mean to each other.

Killera's hands were on her clothes, under them. She pushed Ursula down to the narrow bottom of the nest, onto her back and lay over her, an immovable force that suddenly frightened Ursula.

But she did not say no. Killera's anger was building and Ursula knew she had caused it, her faithlessness had caused this. She should have remained silent. She had no chance of a future with Autumn. The obsession might have passed, given time. Instead she'd ruined a future with Killera that could have given them both joy.

She need only have stayed silent and kept the hurt to herself. But that wasn't perfect trust. How could perfect trust ruin perfect love?

She did not realize, until it was almost too late, that Killera would not stop herself. She pinned Ursula to the small decking of the crow's nest and ruthlessly stripped away the clothes Autumn had given her. The next kiss was as bruising as the first and there was something more, the press of Killera's desperate and angry mind, unbidden, without the calming joy of the circle.

:*I can make you love me again. I can make you forget her.*:

:*Please . . .*:

:*You are the center of my world, you always have been. I worshiped you as the goddess incarnate and loved you as a woman and I can make you love me again.*:

Killera's hand was gripping too tightly; what should have been a caress was a pinch. Teeth that should have grazed soft skin bit down instead.

There was a moment, just before Killera took her, when Ursula could have stopped her. Her own mind was strong enough to take control. She need only say no, with her mouth or in her mind, and it would be over.

She did not say no.

She sobbed into Killera's shoulder and let Killera hurt her because she believed in perfect love and perfect trust, and those beliefs did not allow for this to happen.

She held tightly to Killera's neck, just held on and prayed for it to end and prayed that nothing of lasting evil would visit either of them for this moment, for the pain she had caused and the pain Killera gave. Prayer for once seemed useless, useless against all of Killera's strength and the anger that spurred that strength to take revenge so brutally, so intimately. Killera's body was pressing the air out of her and she could not breathe.

Ursula only knew it was over when Killera got to her knees with a ragged sob. :*Mother's grace, gods, what have I done?*:

Ursula could not answer then. Her stomach wanted to empty itself, and she struggled to control it.

"There's blood, Ursula." She sounded so childlike, utterly confused by the aftermath of her strong arms and hands on a body far more frail.

Ursula made herself look, then said weakly, "My moon blood."

Killera wanted to believe her, for just a moment. Ursula could see it in her eyes. She wanted to pretend it hadn't happened. Ursula nodded, yes, she would let Killera believe that she wasn't hurt. Nothing had to change.

But already Killera was shaking her head as she stared at the blood on her fingers. "What have I done?"

"I'm all right." More lies, but she would say anything to take away the terrible grief in Killera's face.

"Ursula?" Killera was not looking at the woman she had violated, but for the goddess who had always given comfort, had explained the unfathomable, the unthinkable.

Ursula tried, but she had left that path. "It is all right. We have turned to an unexpected door and are strong enough —"

"I've hurt you, it's not all right!"

"You didn't mean to —"

"Yes, yes I did!"

There was the truth, and Ursula wished it away, for Killera's sake, more than her own. She had not known that truth could be evil. She had not known that love could lead to this door.

She clasped Killera's bloody hands between her own, palms together in a potent gesture that could not be lost on Killera. With this gesture she had once accepted Killera's oath of worship and love as the goddess incarnate. "I love you," she said lowly. "That cannot change."

Killera tried to jerk her hands away. Angry, bitter tears poured down her cheeks. "I don't deserve your love."

Ursula held fast, though her aching flesh made her momentarily feel faint. "Please don't take your love away, not this love, not your friendship, not the past. This is my fault-"

"No, don't say that. You didn't deserve what I did."

"It is done and we are here. We are strong enough to walk away from this."

"Are you — do you mean that nothing I do to you, *nothing*, not even that, matters to you any more?" Killera's eyes were dim where once they had been golden.

"That's not what I meant. I wish it were undone, that we could go back. But we can't. I can only say that I love you, that nothing you do to me can change that."

Killera succeeded in pulling her hands away. She spread the bloody fingers in front of Ursula's eyes, and it was all Ursula could do to stay conscious. "Even this?" She looked down at Ursula's body and then touched thighs and arms where her fingers had left dark, mottled bruises. She moaned high in her throat when she brushed the teeth marks she'd left in Ursula breast. "Gods, even this?"

"I can forgive it all, and I do so freely —"

"You forgive me, but how do I forgive myself?"

The honey and gold were gone from Killera's eyes, and Ursula knew she would never see them again. Tears came, finally, and Ursula swooned, reaching for the arms that had hurt her, finding her perfect trust. Those arms wrapped around her, and Killera's voice crooned her name. It was heavy with guilt and would always be. Guilt was too hard to let go of when you'd devoted yourself to nurturing it, when you clung to it because you'd become used to it being a part of you. It was too hard . . . she knew it would always be true of her own guilt.

The line between past and present wavered and Ursula rode the edge of it, not sure where she would wake up when she opened her eyes. She was in Kelly's bed, in a farmhouse in Paradise, and she knew that her Kelly had never had honeyed eyes. They were as murky as Killera's had become, as if the guilt still lingered, even to this lifetime. She remembered what had happened last night, and it did not begin to compare to the violation she had suffered at Killera's hands, but the brutal echo of Killera's one moment of rage, one lapse in a lifetime of gentle strength and perfect love, sounded between the two lives. An evil had touched them, then and now. Kelly felt it, and suffered it.

She heard, for just an instant, from beyond the gate, evil's laughter. A woman triumphant, and ever hungry.

Exhausted sleep was rolling over her as she discerned a new truth. *I could have stopped the evil*, she told herself. *I trusted that evil could not come when I should have faced it and fought for both our sakes.*

Eight

The two men at the lumberyard handled the one by eight planks of cured yew as if they were pure gold. Considering the price, Autumn thought, the unfinished pieces were almost that valuable. She'd eased herself on shaky legs through three nights of carefully scripted roulette to pay for the shipment. Ed had driven her to the lumberyard to order them and again to pick them up. The same wad of cash had settled up her rent with him and paid next month as well.

She'd only been out of the hospital for a week, but the compulsion to build a box like she had seen in her dream was too strong to ignore. She'd only told Ed that she was planning a new trick for her act, and sometimes she briefly convinced herself that was all it was. His concern was that she was pushing herself to do too much too soon.

He was right, of course, but she had to be ready in time. She'd told the club owner to expect her back on the first of August, a day she now knew was Midsummer on an ancient calendar, and called Lammas on some calendars slightly less old. She would use the magician's box for the first time that night. She had only two weeks to build it.

This was all a delusion born of both the shock from nearly dying and from some excellent painkillers during recovery. The part of her that had learned so carefully the rhythm of Las Vegas and the skills she had needed to survive completely on her own reminded her that what she was thinking about — somehow finding Ursula, her Ursula — was a fantasy.

Fantasy it might be, but having died and been revived, she was willing to suspend dry realities for fantasy, especially one so detailed, so rich in feeling and so full of the promise of meaning to her life. Every night she dreamed of that life, picking up where she had left off, or knowing what had passed since her last dream.

She tried, one last time, to be practical. She had lived ten years believing in nothing but herself and what she could touch and manipulate with her fingers. I don't believe in Ursula, she told herself.

You believe.

The voice never lacked for conviction. It had told her she was not a thief, not a cheat, not crazy, and now it told her she believed in something utterly unbelievable. It was fickle, the voice, but she no longer resented it. She was finally learning to accept its limitations.

She also accepted the limitations of her memory. After ten years of darkness, she was remembering information — not about herself, but about her craft, like how to build the magician's box. In the moments between waking and sleep, between sleep and waking, knowledge was trickling into her mind like flashes of light through a dark curtain. The box had to be made of yew wood, and the way it was built, the order in which everything was done, was important. The colors and arrangements of stars on the outside were also vital if the box was to function when it was completed.

What the box's function was — well, that was yet a mystery. She had faith, for little else had come to matter, that it would lead her to Ursula. Yet her natural caution was wary of Rueda, who also was sometimes in that moment between sleep and waking. This knowledge could come from her.

But not Ursula — the dreams of Ursula did not come from Rueda. They were yet untainted by anything but yearning and love for a beautiful woman who had never been meant to love her. Because she had dreamed of Ursula she no longer dwelled on the searing pleasure of Rueda's touch on her body. Being caught between aversion and desire had made her weak, but now it was resolved as all her focus turned to Ursula.

She could not fathom a purpose for her dreams and had learned nothing useful from her growing stockpile of books about Saint Ursula. There was little to know. Ursula may or may not have existed, but if she did she might have been a Christian woman sent to marry a pagan. Instead she undertook a pilgrimage to Rome in a quest to become a nun. She was supposedly surrounded by an impractical hoard of eleven thousand virgins. When Ursula refused to marry a barbarian lord, Ursula and all eleven thousand companions were slaughtered. Most of Ursula's legend had been written several hundred years later, justifying the sanctity of some relics found during the restoration of the abbey where the massacre supposedly took place.

If the Ursula in her dream was the same woman, then it would account for Autumn's growing sense of urgency. Some sort of darkness was going to overtake Ursula on her journey. Somehow, Autumn knew she could change that fate. They had to have made mistakes, and there could be a chance now to fix them. If the box took her back to that time or brought Ursula to hers — it was madness to even consider it, she knew. But this madness had brought her more joy in her sleep than she'd had in her waking life. I'll take the madness, she thought.

You are not mad.

Thanks, voice, Autumn answered. I needed that.

She had likewise learned nothing from her collection of different recordings of the music that had seemed to begin this phase of her life. She had heard Hilea sing some of the same phrases of the chant, centuries before they had been written down in a German abbey. The music was a key her mind lacked the skill to turn. But the magician's box and its use — that she could and would master.

It was, perhaps, why she was here. She had no past to hinder her from applying all her skill, strength and will to the mystery.

Ed helped her unload the wood and offered her the use of his tools and workspace, as well as his expertise. They stacked the planks against the wall as Ed admired their clarity.

"Even unfinished they're beautiful," he said. "And the grain is fine, no knots or warp."

She had no idea why yew was required. "It's pliable but resilient," she said, which was what the lumber guy had told her. The bow Autumn had carried in that other life was made of yew and she had watched that bow made. She reached for a plank, but Ed stayed her with a hand on her arm.

"You're beat. Start tomorrow with a clear head."

She wanted to tell him that time was running out, but a yawn took the words out of her mouth before she could say them. It was only late afternoon, but every day before this she had had at least one nap by now.

Scylla whined when Autumn said it was time to go home, so Autumn left her to Ed's TLC. She knew Scylla would not go far.

She made herself eat a slice of turkey and drink a large glass of orange juice before she crawled into bed. Every time she closed her eyes it was easier to dream: a few deep, steady breaths, visualizing the door of the box opening, feeling the spiral pulling her in, then reveling in the swooping sensation of stepping into that other Autumn's body. That world was always moving, the deck beneath her feet rising and falling as the wind blew them ever toward the day and place when Ursula would leave them. That day was coming upon them quickly.

For the last week Ursula hadn't been well. She'd become sick her first time up in the crow's nest and had only managed to get back to the deck with Killera helping her move her hands and feet, every painful inch. Killera's arms had trembled with what it had cost her at times to hold all of Ursula's weight against the riggings. Crewmen had helped them at the last, her father carrying Ursula to bed while Killera insisted she could stand. The ropes had bloodied her hands, but she had insisted she was fine. To this day, however, she was still pale and uninterested in food while Ursula was returning to more robust health.

Autumn heard someone on the riggings below her as she stood watch on the busy port of Wester Brugge below. She combed the faces of passersby for any sign that the *Verdant Bough* was of undue interest to anyone on the dock. Stopping at every port since they had left Calais was wearing on the energy and temper of the crew, but her father's caution was well placed. She welcomed their creeping pace toward Jutland, grateful for each day that passed. Too soon they would turn north again toward Friesland, then arc to the northeast to their final destination at Rijsbrucke.

From the whispered curses and out-and-out swearing below her, she knew it was Hilea climbing up to the crow's nest to join her. She liked Hilea. Hilea would have made a fine sailor.

"Why is it always so hot when we're in port?" Hilea swept her brow with her sleeve.

"You've gotten used to always having the wind to cool you," Autumn said. Sweat was dripping down her back, a sensation she disliked. She glanced at Hilea and went back to watching the dock for any signs of trouble. Edrigo had gone to the portmaster's office to pay their tithe and pick up any useful news. One of these days they would find themselves expected by agents of Ursula's future husband, if not actually met by a ship. It had been a risk, taking the slowest route. Cynan of Jutland would get advance word of his bride's whereabouts and perhaps take measures for her safe passage when she approached the domain he controlled, but others with less pure motives could easily learn their whereabouts as well.

"Will I distract you if I stay up here?"

"Not at all," Autumn assured her as her eyes continued to scan the activity on the dock.

"Pity," Hilea said dryly.

Autumn had to laugh. Hilea made no secret of her carnal interest and her honesty was refreshing. "I will wager that no one has ever called you coy."

"Only men."

"Do you find it curious that all of us prefer our own sex?"

"Curious, yes, but that is something that binds us together. It might not be the reason why we found ourselves together, but it is one reason why we hold fast to each other. It's not all of us, though," Hilea said. "Elspeth hasn't tried it either way."

"Truly?" Elspeth was almost twenty-two, the oldest of the five of them, though most of the time she seemed the youngest.

"Even festival failed to move her. She says that she will know when the time is right."

They sighed together at the mystery of it. "Perhaps she's been listening too much to the priests of the White Christ."

"They talk about the prize of virginity, but what I've seen of them they value it little when it comes to their own needs. I don't begrudge them their desire for women — how could I? But to preach one thing and do another does not build faith."

Autumn could only agree. "I don't understand much about your faith, about the she-bear goddess, but what I do understand seems straightforward. Love is good. To receive love you must give love. Trust in each other is good. Give thanks. These things are easy to do and don't require a priest who talks to a bishop who talks to a pope who talks to a god."

Hilea leaned her head against Autumn's arm. She was tiny compared to the others, and the top of her head barely reached Autumn's armpit. "You understand it all perfectly. There is no more than that."

"There must be." Autumn saw her father exit the portmaster's office. He casually set his cap on his head and turned toward the market stalls. Autumn relaxed. All was well or he would have kept the cap off.

"You know enough to experience the joy of the way every day — and, in fact, I believe you do just that, you just don't know it. You wake gladly and do everything with an aware joyfulness. That is the goddess within you, within all of us, especially Ursula."

Aware joyfulness — yes, Autumn thought, that described Ursula.

"Now, if you're talking about becoming an initiate," Hilea went on, "perhaps joining a circle and being more active in the way you give thanks, then yes, there is a lot to learn. It has astonishing rewards, fulfilling experiences. But with knowledge comes responsibility. If you would know the goddess in all her faces then you must help others know her too through your example. In this, Ursula is the best of us and I am the worst."

"Why is she the best?" Autumn glanced at Hilea again and flushed at the expression on Hilea's face.

"I don't know why the two of you just don't get it over with."

Autumn let that remark go unanswered. It was not comforting that everyone seemed to know how she felt about Ursula. Even Edrigo had made an offhand comment about Autumn's preoccupation. "I don't understand how she was the goddess and isn't now."

"I didn't at first. I'm not from Northumbria, but from father north, Caledones. The she-bear of course is over that sky, too, but she is not regarded as the . . . doorway to love and faith as she is in Northumbria. Caledonians do not believe such a doorway is necessary. Gods and goddesses are within every rock and spider and mote of dust. Ursula would say it is all the same thing. How you find the wonder of our daily gifts is unimportant. Finding, celebrating, loving — that is what matters."

Autumn shrugged. "I find no reason to believe in this goddess of yours, but she neither demands my belief nor attempts to bar me from her gifts if I believe differently. Is it strange that this makes me more willing to believe?"

"It was why I first opened myself to her. She asked nothing of me so I was not afraid to let her into my heart. A single act of trust changed me forever. It could be the same with you."

"I trust in the sea and the stars."

"The goddess is the sea and the stars," Hilea said firmly. "As I said, you already believe in her, already embrace the joy of your life. You just don't know it." She sidled one arm around Autumn's waist. "You could be one of us so easily."

She clasped Hilea's shoulder companionably. Hilea sighed. "You're as bad as Elspeth."

"Not hardly," Autumn said. "I'm no virgin, nor do I aspire to be."

"Well, that's something, I suppose." Hilea leaned over the rim of the crow's nest. "Are those wine barrels for us? Ursula's father had wine from this region at one time. It was very good."

"My father knows his wine. I'm sure it'll be drinkable." She signaled all's well to the mate, who nodded and went in search of crew to hurry them along. All's well meant they would catch the tide this afternoon instead of waiting until early morning. "Hilea?"

"Yes, fairest fruit of my eyes?"

Autumn had meant to be serious, but snickered instead. "If I wanted to be one of you, what would it mean?"

"You would have to be initiated into the circle. But we haven't raised a circle since we left home. I don't think Ursula believes she can do it without her aunts and the power of the goddess within her."

"Wouldn't I upset the numbers? Make it one too many?"

"It doesn't work that way. I know the White Christ's priests are terribly concerned with numbers and balances, four of that and twelve of those and three priests on special days and — I don't understand why it's so important. How can another loving presence intent on faith and goodwill upset the balance? If we are actually working, casting a spell if you like that term, then balance is important. It takes the skill of the center — that's Ursula's role — to balance it, but it doesn't matter if it's four plus one or five plus one or ten thousand plus one. She balances it and the spell takes power. There's usually at least one woman who is an anchor as well, in case the center is overwhelmed."

Autumn knew who that had to be. "Killera."

"Absolutely. She cannot be swayed from her task, not for anything."

"If I may," Autumn said slowly, feeling an unaccountable nervousness, "what kind of spells do you cast?"

Hilea's laughter tinkled like bells. "You were thinking we call up demons or wish a plague on our enemies."

Autumn frowned. "I've heard of such, so I don't know what is so amusing."

"I'm laughing because I thought the very same. I thought the world was like Caledones, where witches sometimes consorted with less pleasant deities than the she-bear. In Caledones, you can find a pixie under a rock and lose your soul. Or not. Depends on the pixie's mood. The she-bear is nothing so capricious as that, nor will she send a thousand plagues on you to see if you'll still love her on the morrow. Our spells are for healing, for growth, for well-being."

"It seems too pure for an imperfect soul like me to stand."

Hilea laughed so heartily that faces turned up to look at them. "You and I are much alike. All that goodness, gods I found it cloying at first. But the she-bear allows for a wicked thought or two, just no wicked magic with her power. Last winter we did do something more unusual. The Saxons had sacked all the other regions and were ready to take Cressius's lands."

"I wondered why they had not."

"The circle worked in full power for six weeks. We cast the same spell every day. It was simple and truthful. We sent an awareness toward the Saxons — Ursula directed it. We said that this place had treasures that could never be taken, only received in the fullness of time. The Saxons hesitated, and reinforcements arrived in sufficient force that they negotiated. They had had a long campaign, and sitting in the icy muck for six weeks had taken some of the edge from their desire for conquest. Of course, Ursula didn't know that her selfless desire to spare her foster father and her peoples bloodshed would result in exile for herself."

"That's what I don't understand. Why did the she-bear allow this?"

"She does not serve us," Hilea said softly. "We do not serve her. All that we do is from perfect love and perfect trust. What comes from that is sometimes a mystery. The she-bear does not carve a path and tell us to walk it. The path makes itself, and as we walk we thank her for her succor and her love."

"You must do what is laid before you, but are aware of her love all the while." Autumn did not really understand. "They say the White Christ had a similar faith. He knew that death would come from his actions but accepted the path, feeling only love."

Hilea was nodding. "Yes, that is what their sacraments celebrate. I think that is one reason why so many of our people go happily to the White Christ's church. I just wish they did not begin to feel guilty about celebrating the goddess as well."

"The priests of the White Christ are a jealous lot." Autumn thought of the towns now under the shadow of the cross and places farther south where the she-bear's followers would not be welcome.

Hilea was scrabbling in her pocket. "Want some?" She bit into the apple, then offered it to Autumn.

"Thanks. It's dry up here, and I forgot my waterskin." She

crunched the tart fruit and thought, just to see what it would be like, Good apple. Thanks she-bear. She felt silly.

"Who were your mother's people? Every time I look at your skin I wonder. You didn't get that skin from the captain."

"My mother was from Gotaland, from far north. She died bearing me, so Edrigo took me to sea with him."

"Some of those in northern Caledones are as fair as you, but I've got my grandmother's brown Pict skin. She claimed her grandmother had scars from her cheeks to her knees, all stained with blue. She said the wild Picts all went underland long ago, when the Romans first came."

"How did you end up in Northumbria?"

"It was a combination of my voice and my father's tendency to lose at wagers. He lost me to a lord, who thankfully was only interested in my singing. That lord in turn traded me to Ursula's foster father for arms. The day I met Ursula was the first day of my life I wasn't angry. It was the first time I sang for the joy of it, and I sang to give thanks. After that, the way of Ursula's goddess was easy for me."

"You never did answer my question about Ursula being the goddess."

"Oh, you noticed." Hilea had a wicked laugh, and Autumn knew she was being teased. "Ursula was a foundling, some even said a changeling, though she's too tall to be faerie."

"She's too beautiful not to be," Autumn murmured.

Hilea sighed. "I'm not going to get anywhere with you, am I?"

"Ursula was a foundling," Autumn prompted. She spotted her father on his way back to the ship.

"A foundling. Her three aunts told her foster father she was a child of great nobility and that if he raised her as his own child he would be rewarded for all eternity. The crones have a lot of influence and always have had. There are people in Aldtyme who swear that they never age and have lived in Aldtyme since time began. So he took the child in and raised her as his own and called her Ursula because the crones told him to. From the day she was found it seemed she was meant to follow the goddess."

"And then he sold her for an alliance."

"He was an impatient man and a practical one. He did not see how the people's fanatical devotion to his daughter would keep the Saxons from burning his fields. He was unwilling to acknowledge that Ursula and the circle were why he still had fields."

Autumn waved to her father as he reached the gangplank. "How does this relate to Ursula's relationship with the goddess?"

Hilea laughed. "You are familiar with the concept of obsession, aren't you?"

"Hilea, please."

"Oh, all right." She shook her brown hair out of her face, and her blue eyes were bright with humor. "I came into my womanhood before Ursula did and was initiated first. The circle is made up of women because they give life, as the goddess does. There is an outer circle, which is very casual. Any woman who has acknowledged the bonds of the circle and participates in recognizing the goddess's goodwill among us can participate. The outer circle meets just about anywhere and for any reason and not always to do ritual."

"So there's an inner circle," Autumn prompted. She waved an all's-well signal to three crewmen who were carrying another load of cheeses and bread between them. Her time for idle talk was just about over.

"There's an inner circle. If you believe that the goddess has power and if you believe that that power can be directed to help the land, then the inner circle is how that happens. Ursula was the center of the inner circle, and when she was initiated it was . . . made known. I'm sorry, I can't say how. The crones said it happened sometimes that the goddess wished to feel the earth and sun the way her people do, and Ursula was the way she chose to do it. She was both herself and the goddess for nearly three years. When we set sail she had to leave the goddess behind. I don't know why I would tell you all of this, because you don't really believe any of it."

"You were hoping if you answered all my questions that I would be kindly disposed toward you." Autumn flashed Hilea a grin.

"I'd almost forgotten since you so thoroughly rebuffed me, not once, but twice." Hilea pouted prettily, her blue eyes veiled behind dark lashes. "I'm only asking for a quick tumble. It would not mean anything."

Autumn stiffened. Ursula had said almost the same thing. Hilea, however, meant it. "It wouldn't work."

"Would so, I assure you it would."

"If you would please me, sing me something."

Hilea wrinkled her nose. "And what would I receive in return?"

"Only my everlasting goodwill."

"Well, that has some value, I suppose." She cleared her throat and sang lowly, so her voice would not carry, *"Like the grassland touched by dew and immersed in its caress, your flesh has known delight. O most fair and delectable one —"*

"That's enough," Autumn said.

Hilea's laughter again turned faces on the dock up toward them. Autumn heard her father's whistle and saw that Padrerus was waiting for the two of them to descend so he could replace her on watch.

Hilea went first, and she quickly followed the men with the fresh food toward the galley. For a little thing she ate with as much abandon as a man twice her size. Autumn saw that more crew were being dispatched to acquire additional foodstuffs. Her father told her why as soon as she joined him on the foredeck.

"There was a message waiting for our passenger with the portmaster. I can only guess that it waits at every port between here and Jutland. We'll sail directly for Jutland now. I don't want to further announce our whereabouts now that we know for certain that our coming is anticipated by the right people."

Autumn's heart ached with the news. The days with Ursula were dwindling, and she had so stupidly turned down Ursula's offer to bed simply because it would mean far more to her than it could to Ursula. A few stolen minutes were better than none. "What was in the message?"

"I gave it to Lady Ursula. It was sealed and I didn't know the signal."

"So you don't know what it said?"

"You shall know." Ursula's voice brought heat to Autumn's face. "I would appreciate your help, Captain."

Autumn lingered because Ursula seemed to expect it and because she could not make herself leave. Recovered from her sickness, Ursula shone like a star in Autumn's eyes. What Hilea had told her was fresh in her mind as she memorized, again, the curve of Ursula's lips and the color of her hair. *The goddess has lived through Ursula. If I were a goddess,* Autumn thought, *I would want to do the same.*

Autumn read the short missive over her father's shoulder, which was also over Ursula's shoulder. It was for the best light, she told herself.

Edrigo was working through the message word by word. It had been penned in cramped Angle-Saxon dialect. "Uda Cynandottir — that's the proper name of your husband-to-be, isn't it? Cynan?"

"Yes," Ursula said. "So this message is from his daughter. I was told she is his eldest child, and older than me by some ten years. But that is all I know."

Cynan of Jutland was old, then. Autumn had to swallow down a sourness in her stomach.

"Uda Cynandottir to Ursula, daughter of Cressius, lord of lower Northumbria, who is to become sister to my uncles and mother to my brothers and sisters, greetings."

"Is it greetings, or glad tidings?"

"Greetings, though the scribe was sloppy. Interesting that she does not say you are to become her mother as well."

"Yes, I noticed that." Ursula sounded detached, and yet Autumn could sense that she was badly shaken by the message, not so much for what it said, but for its very existence.

"Lady Uda of Jutland bids welcome — that's welcome, not greetings — to Lady Ursula of Britannia. Uda of Hjerring pledges the kiss of peace to Ursula of Aldtyme. All is in preparation for midsummer nuptials if the *Verdant Bough* proves fast and secure. That's all," Edrigo finished.

"That's about what I had fathomed," Ursula said. "She greets me first as the daughter of a lord, like herself, then as a noblewoman of my homeland, like herself."

"And the last?" Autumn suspected what Uda's invoking of the place where Ursula was from meant, as well as the esoteric meaning of "kiss of peace."

"She greets me by my association with the old ways and places herself in that realm."

Edrigo moved uncomfortably. "It's a fair guess that she is warning you that she is your equal and expects to be treated as such."

"It's a lot of effort for a message that simple. She could have imparted that in person." Autumn reached between Edrigo and Ursula to touch the lady's signature. The moment she did she felt dizzy. The next thing she knew, Edrigo was shaking her arm.

"You need some rest, daughter."

The strange sensation of lassitude was gone. "Make the sun rise later tomorrow and I'll catch up on my sleep."

Ursula was wrapping the message in the oiled paper that had protected it. "Thank you, Captain. May I ask what your plans are now?"

Edrigo paid Ursula the compliment of showing her the map and his calculations. "We'll leave Wester Brugge and sail northwest until we've left sight of land. Then I intend to turn due north so we can give Friesland a wide berth when we shift east again. Once we pass the islands we'll of course turn north, but we'll not go into port at Tonningo, which I would think anyone interested in our whereabouts would assume we would do. Instead, we'll sail light to Rijsbrucke and Jutland to finish our journey."

Autumn raised her eyebrows. Sailing light meant to trim close on the wind for greatest speed. Their stores of fresh foods would get low. Hard sailing on cheese and journey-bread was never any fun.

"Thank you," Ursula said quietly. "How many more days, then?"

"The wind is with us now for our entire eastward journey. We'll not stop at port — I believe eight days at most. We'll have you in Jutland in time for a midsummer wedding."

Edrigo's voice faltered at that last, as if he felt Autumn's wince. More likely he was responding to the mute plea in Ursula's liquid black eyes. "I signed a contract, my lady," he added gruffly.

"I know, Captain."

The mate's announcement that the new supplies had been stowed interrupted them. When the last of the crew returned the *Verdant Bough* would be ready to catch the tide. Autumn turned from the discussion of the best route in the crowded harbor to find that Ursula had left them. She was still gazing after her when her father finished with the mate and turned to her.

"Were it not for the contract . . ." he began.

"I know, father." Autumn was not given to tears, but they trembled in her eyes now. "She was never for me." Scylla butted her hand, and Autumn absently scratched her ears.

"Aye," was his only answer, but he gently pulled Autumn's head against his shoulder. "I hate to see you unhappy."

"Do you remember last winter, when we were dry-docked at Cherbourg?"

"Of course. You were desperately in love with the innkeeper's daughter."

"Desperately," Autumn echoed. "I thought she made the sun rise and fall. Now I yearn for a woman who really does make the sun rise and fall, or something close to it. What I feel — it's nothing like last winter. It's far more fatal and reaches into me to places I didn't know could hurt. I didn't know."

He stroked her hair for a moment. "I forget that you are seventeen. Most women your age are married with a brace of children hanging to their skirts by now. I didn't tell you that last winter I was considering leaving you ashore for the rest of the season."

"Father! Whatever for?"

"To make a family of your own. You would never have the chance living aboard ship. I lost my confidence that I'd chosen the right life for you. I thought you needed to choose."

"I'd always choose this life. Why didn't you ever discuss it with me?"

He sighed. "Tain forbade it. He said it was too soon to turn you into a land creature, that you needed at least one more season."

"Dear Tain," Autumn said softly. "I miss him." Tain would have joked her out of her doldrums and helped her through the long evenings by teaching her new tricks with his coins and dice. "He'd have suffered for bunking with the crew instead of you, all this time."

Her father merely grunted and shouted a reminder at the mate, who was chivvying crew to their stations.

They were preparing to sail light and in eight days Ursula would be in the hands of her husband.

Nine

Over the next few days, Kelly's troubled mind was obvious to
Ursula. They did not speak of the gate or try to initiate rapport
again. Ursula did not know if Kelly preferred to act as if it had never
happened, or if she was dealing with perfectly understandable fear
about what the future was going to bring them. She wished she had
told Kelly about the darkness that waited beyond the gate, but that
time would come, and too soon.

They worked out of doors harmoniously enough, and slept in the
same bed, even woke cuddled comfortably. Ursula sensed no rancor
on Kelly's part that they no longer stole a morning here and there
for more pleasurable pursuits, at least not yet. What she did sense,
with growing distress, was Kelly's guilt over hurting her that night,
and that the guilt was out of proportion to what she had done. It

was as if Kelly linked to Killera's grief and did not know it. She hoped when the last bruise faded Kelly would let it go.

She saw the car turn in at their gate and flipped back the brim of her large straw hat to study it. None of the local farmers drove a compact car. She wiped her brow of humidity-caused sweat and focused on the car. She sensed nothing at all, not even how many people were in it. The car was close enough now that she ought to have been able to tell. She stripped off her gardening gloves and called out to Kelly. "We have company." She only knew one person in this country who could shield so well. "Taylor and Liz, I think."

Kelly was pale when she emerged from the barn. Ursula wanted to assure her that everything was going to be all right, but she lacked conviction. She did not know what this meeting would bring, but she knew something continued to change. She was not done with Taylor, or rather, Taylor was not done with her.

Taylor looked ordinary in her jeans and sleeveless T-shirt, but even when she stepped out of the car Ursula could palpably sense Taylor's protections. She came this time with her guards fully engaged. What happened next would not be an accident.

They did not waste time on pleasantries about the weather or how lovely it was to see one another again. Kelly led them inside and poured out tall glasses of iced tea. The slow-moving ceiling fan cooled Ursula's skin.

"I've been talking to various authorities — people of my acquaintance who have personal knowledge or access to knowledge about what may be happening beyond the gate," Taylor said without preamble. "I have a lot of questions and some answers and an idea of what we can do."

"Why does anything need to be done?" Kelly was still pale, and she fiddled nervously with her glass.

"You still don't know?" Taylor gave Ursula a hard look.

"I've told her some, but I'm not forcing anything. She hasn't wanted to talk about it."

"Don't defend me," Kelly snapped. "I've been a coward. I admit it. I'd prefer to pretend this is all going to go away."

"It won't," Taylor said shortly.

"There's something out there, isn't there?" Kelly turned to Ursula, her eyes dark with fearful impotence. "It wants you."

Ursula slowly nodded. "I should have told you about it, but . . ."

Kelly's eyes darkened as she remembered what they had done instead. "Why didn't you ask me about it?"

"I didn't know it had to do with you. I just know it's there." And it frightens me, her eyes said.

"It's an old lesson, and I have been such a poor teacher." Ursula wondered how many ways there were to say she was sorry. "We're stronger when we talk about what frightens us. I should have brought it up. With something like this I shouldn't have waited for you to come to me."

"Don't blame yourself. I know why you didn't." Kelly's gaze flicked over Ursula's arm where only the faintest hint of bruising remained.

"No!" Ursula's sharp tone startled Taylor and Liz. "That was never the reason, and it never will be."

Kelly did not believe her, but she only said, "From everything you told me, about how I would start to feel more and more pressure from the river, well, I should have asked. I just wasn't ready."

"I know. Listen," Ursula said, knowing that Taylor understood only a fraction of what was happening. Liz perhaps understood more. "We're working too hard trying not to hurt each other. That's not trust. I am stronger than I look, and no matter what you say or do, I will not leave you because of that. I will not be afraid of you," she added, knowing Kelly would remember saying that to her.

"You're going to leave me, though."

"But never because you have hurt me. I know that doesn't seem like an important distinction, but it is. Stop being gentle with me." She let her irritation show.

Kelly's eyes swam with tears, and it made Ursula ache to see them. She cried so rarely and always, it seemed, because of her. "I'll try, I promise, but you must stop trying to protect me. I might get freaked out, and I might be scared out of my wits, but I won't walk away."

Ursula took a deep breath and told Kelly the truth. She did not care that Taylor and Liz heard it too. "I know that you are stronger than I am, and that you have more courage than I have and that I have never learned to trust it. That's my failing, and I will do better. I, I thought that always expecting you to be strong was unfair to you. Because sometimes we all need to be weak, and I" — she choked in air as her voice cracked — "I've been the weak one all along. I've been counting on you being the strong one, and I thought it wasn't fair. But it's who you are. I'll try to trust you. To let you be what you are."

A lone tear escaped the shimmering pools in Kelly's eyes. "And what is that?" Kelly knew the answer, but Ursula knew she needed to hear it from Ursula's own lips.

"My rock, my anchor, forever."

The darkness in Kelly's eyes lifted and for a moment, one shining moment, they were honeyed brown. "I will always love you."

"I know." Ursula accepted the burden, the imbalance of being loved more than she loved in return. Denying it meant denying Kelly. She could not do that again.

There was a prolonged silence as Ursula looked her fill at the change in Kelly's eyes. They were darkening again, but not like they had been. They looked more like Killera's had, in those happy, early days.

"Can I assume our visit has so far been a good thing?" Taylor's tone was cool and dry.

Ursula wiped her eyes with a shaky laugh. "So far, so good. We needed to talk." Kelly took her hand under the table, and Ursula felt the tingle of rapport. Kelly had such trust of her, and Ursula swore she would repay that trust tenfold. :Thank you for this.:

:I think they're ready now.: It was Taylor's thought that intruded, and Ursula realized that she and Liz had been in rapport since before they had arrived.

Her sharp glance alerted Taylor that she had been overheard. :We are always in rapport.:

Ursula could feel that now, as well. The two were bound by deep oaths, more than initiate and adept. Their bond was deeply intimate, sexual as well as platonic. The Elspeth she knew from her dreams had none of this depth. :Blessed be.:

Taylor and Liz shared a similar smile. Liz finally spoke. "Since the night you were at our house, I've been having dreams, as if I've lived an earlier life —"

Kelly knocked over her glass, spilling tea and ice cubes across the table. After the flurry of paper towels and assurances that nothing was harmed, Kelly took her seat again, but her pallor was extreme.

152

"What is it?" Ursula pressed her hand to Kelly's shoulder. Their rapport had shattered when Liz had said the words "earlier life."

"Since that night I've been dreaming too." Kelly looked at Ursula as if to say she was sorry for having kept silent.

Ursula stroked Kelly's shoulder, then let her hand fall away. "It's all right. Leave be. I've been having dreams as well."

"I suspected as much, which is why we came." Taylor leaned her elbows on the table. "I'm not having any dreams, so I think that this doesn't involve me. Which makes me the perfect person to monitor you all if you want to share your dreams in rapport. I think this is *very* important."

There was more that Taylor knew and suspected, but Ursula let it go for now. Her suggestion was logical, and she was prepared to show the others her dreams. If she could, she would hold back what happened in the crow's nest, but given the heavy weight on Kelly's spirit, she had a feeling that Kelly had dreamed of it too. "I'm ready." She put her hand on the table, palm up.

Taylor took Liz's hand and reached for Ursula. "Let's begin this way, you and me because we've done it before. Then I'll bring in Liz and when we're balanced, you bring in Kelly."

Ursula nodded reassuringly at Kelly. "This will work best. The strangeness of it won't be as intense. This is one of those times you don't have to prove you're strong. It's easier for all of us, not just you."

"Okay." Kelly tried to mask her trepidation with a smile.

Taylor's hand was warm and comfortable. All at once Ursula was aware of Taylor's incredible shields and how much background irritation had been leaking through her own thinning gate. Her gate was abruptly shored up, and she reeled a moment at the blessed silence. It had been wearing her down, day after day. :*Thank you, oh thank you.*:

When she looked over at Kelly, she could tell that Kelly was somehow deeply moved. "What is it?"

"You're glowing. You know, you did that once before. The day you got here, in the grocery store. You seemed like a light, and your hair at the very ends, it was floating, like it is now."

Ursula looked down and saw that it was true. "I didn't know it did that."

"I've missed that light. I didn't know it had gone out." Kelly had only wonder in her eyes. Without another word she took Ursula's free hand in hers. *:I'm not afraid.:*

:I'm ready, Taylor, and so is Kelly.:

Taylor relaxed the wall she had been keeping between them, and Ursula let Taylor come to her. It was easy since they were both so practiced and had done it before, that night at Taylor's house. They sorted each other out with a light spirit. It had been a while since Taylor had worked with her circle, and she was hungry for a useful purpose for her powers and skill.

Ursula became aware of Liz then and let Taylor draw them gently together. Liz was still undoing her guards, lowering her shields, and then Ursula saw why. Liz wasn't naturally withdrawn, it was self-preservation. She felt everything that happened around her, felt it as deeply as if it was happening to her. What must it have been like as a child, buffeted endlessly by the emotions of others? A schoolyard of playing children surely had been misery for her.

:All my life everyone said I was timid.: Liz shared just a touch of what it had been like, enough to make Ursula swell with pity. *:I was a basket case until I met Taylor.:*

Taylor had taken the noise away, had helped Liz build her shields until she could be in a crowded room and not suffer anger, love, desire, humor, hate — suffer them all at once with no control.

:How did you meet her?:

:At a friend's wedding where she officiated.: Liz shared the memory. The ceremony had been overflowing with love and commitment. Even the families had been in harmony, and the intensity — positive though it was — had left Liz shaking with anguish.

:She was like a lightning strike in a calm sky.: Taylor's nurturing instinct was powerful, and yet it was balanced by need of Liz's love.

:She asked me if I could help her with something, and we stepped into the little room behind the reception hall.: Liz's joy spilled over to Ursula, and Ursula found herself smiling as nostalgically as Liz, as if she had been there. *:I love that little room.:*

It came to Ursula all in a flash, Liz's memory of that moment and Taylor's, overlapping with their slightly different perceptions, but clearly conveying what Ursula could see had been the single most profound moment of their lives. Taylor had taken away the noise for Liz and found herself instantly, fatally, in love. Liz had felt alone for the first time in her life, and into the silence she had had a single thought. *:I knew I would find you again.:*

Past lives, Ursula thought, as she carefully gathered Kelly into the rapport. *:Meet your cousin for the first time,:* she invited.

Kelly's curiosity was infectious. *:What on earth were you doing? You all have the goofiest smiles on your face.:*

Liz showed her, and Ursula did not have to look to know Kelly's smile now matched hers. Then Kelly was showing Liz and Taylor the day she had walked into a tiny, crowded herb shop in Aldtyme, a world away, and had seen Ursula for the first time.

Ursula did not recognize herself in Kelly's memory. She was not that beautiful, and her hair did not shine like that. She didn't walk that gracefully, and her voice was not that lovely to the ear.

:If you say so.: Kelly was laughing at her because Liz was agreeing to Kelly's perceptions. Taylor stayed carefully neutral.

:Are you ready to share your dreams? This is going to be easy, I think. I'll monitor for intensity. Kelly, don't fight me if I try to relax you with a spell. You too, Ursula. I know what Liz can handle, which is far more than any of us, but I don't know you yet.:

:I won't resent it.: Kelly's ability to trust was so evident to Ursula. She had wasted so much time being afraid of Kelly's reaction to the idea of rapport, to the idea of the kind of magic she worked.

:Ursula, stop that.: Taylor's emotional presence faded, and the adept was more evident. She seemed like Aunt Lillidd for a moment. *:We're not here for you to wallow in guilt.:*

Suitably chastened, Ursula refocused on the rapport.

Liz went first, and nothing she showed them surprised Ursula. She was on the ship, journeying with Ursula and her cousin because she had no other purpose. She worked the circle and yet could never be touched by it, so tightly wrapped were her own guards against the intrusion of other people's emotions. She'd seemed so colorless and shallow to Ursula because she dared not show her real depths. There was no Taylor for her in that life.

At the end of Liz's dream she had been looking up at the crow's nest where Killera's anger and Ursula's pain spilled down on her. She had felt faint and woken up with a migraine. Kelly jerked her hand, but Ursula held tight. *:That's in the past. It wasn't you.:*

155

:Peace.: Taylor invoked a relaxing spell and Kelly settled, even felt chagrined for Taylor having to intercede.

:I'll do better,: she told Taylor. *:But thank you. I need that to share my dream. It's . . . hard.:*

It was hard, hardest of all for Liz, who had not really known what had happened in the crow's nest, but now saw the blood on Killera's hands. Kelly hadn't meant to start there, but she was little practiced. She abruptly took them back to where it had begun, as the ship had left dock. Killera was not frightened to leave because she left with Ursula. Ursula had faith they would be together and so she had no fear of the future.

That had changed over the weeks that followed. Ursula had withdrawn, and Ursula saw herself as Killera had seen her, the naked longing on her face whenever Autumn was near. She felt the burning desire Killera had coped with, watching her lover's body voluptuously ripe for another woman's touch. Killera had suspected what Ursula was going to say to her when she climbed up to the crow's nest wearing the other woman's clothes and thinking about another love.

She had known fear for the first time, then, when she realized Ursula no longer had faith they would be together. Fear bred anger, and she had known anger even less than fear in her life. Overwhelmed, distraught, abandoned, she had forgotten how strong she was.

Kelly tried to stop the flow of vivid images, but the memory of the dream was too intense for her to handle. They all shared, with a shudder of horror, the feeling of Ursula's tender flesh tearing as Killera pushed too hard and did not stop, and then the horrified shock that had numbed Killera to incomprehension.

Liz had pulled back, deftly using her shields to spare herself. Kelly tried to break contact, but Taylor held them together. *:It was a dream.:*

:It happened.: Kelly was shaking with aftershock. *:It almost happened again.:*

:But it didn't.: Ursula shoved her own shock into a tiny ball as far down in her mind as it would go. She was an adept, and if she dwelled on something that had never happened to this body Kelly would be lost again. *:That's not what happened between us. You know that. I know that. Let it go.:*

Kelly tried. She tried, but Ursula knew they would have to deal with it, again and again. She had let the evil touch Killera when she could have stopped it, and it was her error that haunted Kelly now. Kelly had to understand or they would never get past this. It was time to take them through her dream.

Liz and Kelly had showed their dreams as just that — dreams. They had lacked clarity and form. Many parts were blurred nuances of events or words. *:My dream was different.:*

She showed them the harbor, the people gathered round them. She gave them every word Hilea had sung, and every sensation she'd had of the ship's motion and the smell of the sea. *:I felt it all as much as I feel what we're doing right now.:*

Conversations with Autumn, her all-too-physical desire, the clumsy attempt at seduction — she showed them all of it and spared herself nothing. When she reached the crow's nest she felt Liz begin to withdraw. *:Please, stay.:*

:I don't think I can bear it again.:

:It's important. Please.: She didn't linger on what Killera was doing, but rather on her own thoughts and on the moment when she had consciously decided not to stop Killera. *:I could have stopped her, but I didn't. I trusted that she could not hurt me.:*

Kelly's anguish erupted again. *:And I hurt you anyway —:*

:It wasn't you. It wasn't her, either. It was my own innocence, my unwillingness to believe that evil could happen. I should have fought it, for her sake, if not my own. It was as much my fault — more my fault, because I was the one who could have stopped it.: Ursula put her heart into what she was trying to convey to Kelly.

:You should have never needed to stop me.: Kelly was near tears. Their rapport trembled and nearly severed.

Taylor did not use a spell to relax Kelly again, but she washed their link with a calm influence. *:You have more work to do and Liz and I should not be part of it.:*

:I understand.: Ursula was worried by Kelly's inability to separate herself from Killera, but dealing with it was for another time.

Taylor turned all their thoughts to more productive channels. *:We need to think instead on why you all had the same dream about the same events, from your different perceptions.:*

:Because it happened to all of us.: Kelly's answer was the only

one that made sense to Ursula. *:We've known each other before. It seems like we're making some of the same mistakes again.:*

:When did we know each other? Why are we dealing with it now?: Liz had lowered her shields again now that the most intense moments appeared to be behind them.

:I wish I could discuss this with my aunts.: Ursula wondered, with Taylor's immense protection, if she could go beyond the gate and pass by the darkness she knew was there.

:How do you know they would be there?: Taylor was willing to try, but only if there was some chance of success.

:They're always there.:

For the first time since they had joined, Taylor wavered. *:Are you saying your circle is always open?:*

The question puzzled Ursula. *:Wasn't yours?:*

The obvious answer was no, but Taylor didn't immediately reply.

:Isn't this what you mean by a circle?: Kelly's curiosity was piqued again.

:This isn't a circle, only the first step in creating one.: Ursula knew her answer confused Kelly. *:Can we show her?:* Ursula's appeal was to Taylor, who was in control of their rapport.

:Show us all.: With hesitation, Taylor gave control to Ursula. Her shields were carefully blank. *:Show us your circle and what you do with it.:*

She had done it hundreds of times in Aldtyme, and it was just as simple now with Taylor's calming presence. She balanced their energies and raised the protective circle, then corrected when Kelly seemed to understand her own part better. The circle protected them from unwanted intrusion. The ease it had taken to raise, Ursula felt, was mostly thanks to Taylor's seemingly limitless resources.

The circle was also a focus for their power. Ursula wove their four very different energies into one usable force and turned her thoughts to what was nearest. The garden, she thought, of course.

She took them out to the garden where they'd planted tomato seeds that morning. Visualization had always been her best method, and she imagined running her hands through the soil, dark and rich with nutrients. Then she visualized dropping in seeds, breathing life into each one as it fell. The spell was easy. *:As a seed finds water, let leaves find sunlight.:*

From the garden to the well, then down the well, into its cool presence. She whisked them through the water itself, a lovely sensation, cool and still after the humidity of the day. *:From sky to land to sky to rain to life.:* It was not really a spell, for she knew of nothing that could compel an element like water to do anyone's bidding, but rather a hope for rain. *:This is what a circle does,:* she told Kelly. *:Our combined energy makes this possible. I could not do it without you.:*

She was so thrilled to be feeling the land again that she quickly forgot she had companions as she combed her essence through rows of plants. She found a fungus beginning on the summer savory and sped toward a gathering of ladybugs, dancing with them until they were inclined to follow her. She showed them the fungus and left them to their meal. Then she saw tomato worms, and she pushed herself into the sky, calling the drowsy robins in a nearby alder tree to their rightful feast. She did nothing but help nature along, encourage all creatures to do their part, to thrive in the dance of life, the gift of the goddess, to feel the fecundity of her body and know the joy of ripening desire — it was so wonderful to dance again — midsummer was near — she would dance —

:Ursula, come back.:

She wanted to ignore the voice, but it was ruthlessly pulling her back to her body. For a moment she didn't know which way that was, but then she sensed Kelly, her rock, her anchor, and with a happy sigh, she settled beside her again. For a sublime moment, there was no past and no future, just the touch of skin and the essence of life.

The minds of the others were quiet, and Ursula turned her thoughts to Taylor. *:I'm sorry I got carried away.:*

Taylor was trembling, but with what emotion, Ursula did not know. The light surrounding her was searingly golden, and Ursula fought an unnecessary impulse to shade her eyes. *:Ursula.:*

:What? What is it?:

Perfect trust. Taylor's response was to open herself, every memory and thought, to Ursula's examination. *:I am your servant. I walk in awe of you.:*

:I don't understand.: Taylor's own power far exceeded Ursula's. She balanced their rapport as if it cost her nothing and had personal shields and protections that defied Ursula's comprehension. *:I am in awe of you.:*

:I have never experienced anything like what you just did.:

:But that's why — that's the purpose of our circle in Aldtyme. To encourage nature and of course to nurture love and trust in one another. What else is there?:

Taylor's incredulity was directed at Liz. *:Gods. She asks what else there is. How can she not know?:*

Ten

Edrigo quelled the pushing and shoving match between the boatswain and the mate. Autumn knew their hearts weren't in it, but everyone was tense. Sailing light was wearing on the nerves. Every shift of the wind had to be responded to or their trim would slacken and then their speed. The *Verdant Bough* was not the typical corbita, and could travel half again faster than most of its class. The mainsail was heavy, though, and only balanced at this speed by Padrerus's expert control of the bowsprit fabric.

They'd left sight of the Friesland coast two days ago and relied on the stars to steer them north-northeast. They'd made numerous course changes throughout the day to keep the wind. Now that the stars were coming out it was clear they'd been more east than north. Edrigo was afraid they'd find themselves back in sight of land come morning.

He barked an order to rein in the sail and turned the tiller toward the north again, even though they would slow down. There was no other cautious choice.

The sun was fully below the green ocean horizon, and as the last light faded the lookout shouted, "Ship to starboard!"

Autumn took the tiller to let her father look, but in a few moments night had fully come.

"Douse all lights!" Her father's shout had crewmen scurrying to the watch lanterns. "Silence now, you wine-soaked bastards, and bring down the main."

"I'll tell our passengers," Autumn volunteered as he took back the wheel.

"We'll let them pass us in the night."

Autumn flew down the stairs and didn't knock. She surprised the four women in the midst of changing their clothes for the night. Before she doused the lamp she had the clear view of Ursula's smooth back and the way her long braid coiled around her waist as she bent to take off her boots.

That image was burned in her brain as the light went out.

"I'm sorry," she said breathlessly. "Haste was important."

"What is it?" Ursula's voice seemed to come out of the darkness, but Autumn's eyes were slowly adjusting.

"Another ship. We saw them just as the sun set and have no idea if they saw us, or who they are. We're going to drift and be silent. The moon is waxing, but there are clouds to help us. With luck, they will pass us in the night."

Ursula said quietly, but firmly. "They shall do so."

"You can guarantee that?"

"Yes, I can."

Killera was already pushing bunks into the corners to make space on the floor.

Ursula turned to her companions. "Will you try this with me?"

Hilea said simply, "Of course."

"I believe we can do it," Killera said. "We could do it before the goddess walked with you, and I don't know why we can't now."

Autumn sensed a desperateness in Killera, as if she needed to prove something to Ursula. Ursula's manner toward Killera was unchanged that she could discern, but something had definitely altered between the two. She remembered Ursula saying she'd not been with Killera since seeing Autumn for the first time and wondered, finally, if it might be true. Why would a noble woman care about such scruples and the feelings of a woman of no rank, who sailed the sea like a man?

It was Hilea who turned to her and said quietly, "Join us. Your place is here."

Elspeth's face glowed white in the dim light. "You can be of help."

She wanted to say no, but Ursula was holding out her hand from where she sat cross-legged on the floor. Autumn did not want Ursula to feel how hard she was trembling, but the moment their fingers clasped the trembling stopped. Hilea took her other hand and helped her sit.

"Be not afraid," Hilea whispered. "Nothing ill can happen to you here."

They were all still for several minutes, then softly, lovingly, Hilea began to sing. Her chant had no words, only deep, melodic tones that Autumn could feel relaxing her. Each note brought Autumn closer to a place of stillness, where she heard not the ever-present sound of creaking timbers and the slap of the sea against their hull, but the whisper of her own breathing, then the beat of her heart.

When the voice came, between her ears, she was not frightened. It was Ursula and she welcomed her presence.

:We are joined.:

Hilea continued to sing, her low, even tones modulating only slightly.

Ursula's voice sounded again, behind Autumn's eyes, and she let the words roll over her, wanting to be a part of this magic, whatever it was, because she felt ever closer to Ursula. In time, she might finally understand her.

:We find our balance now, Autumn. Don't worry.:

Similar assurance came from Hilea on her other side, then she was aware of Elspeth's distant energy, an orb that paled next to the vital, dark gold of Killera.

:It is time. Autumn, do not be afraid to try.:

In the next instant Autumn felt cold air on her neck and through her closed eyes she saw the curtain of blue light springing up around them. She opened her eyes in panic, afraid the other ship would see it, but there was nothing there. She closed her eyes again, and the blue light surrounded them all. She even found, if she thought about it, that she could make the light nearest her brighter, until it was the same intensity as the rest.

:Well done, Autumn!: Hilea's approval was clear, though she never stopped singing. From Ursula was only a continual pulse of calm that regarded them all equally.

Just as Autumn was relaxing again, everything changed. She felt an enormous pressure on the top of her head. With her eyes firmly closed she looked up to see a thick but unlocked gate, reinforced with heavy bars, and Ursula's hands raising the latch.

The gate flew open and Ursula said something Autumn could not understand. Beyond the gate was a spiraling chaos of light and sound, roiling like floodwater. Ursula spoke again and it was as if a tunnel opened to allow her to pass safely through the river of chaos. Autumn watched her rise in stunned incomprehension, then realized that all of them were going with her.

She felt the hard pressure of Hilea's grip. The weight of her body on the cabin floor never changed. Just as surely she felt herself rise, a spirit of thought, and she followed the others through the gate and into the tunnel Ursula had made for them.

They were above the ship, far higher than the crow's nest, and they soared ever higher. On the remote edge of the horizon, leagues away from the landmass that was dotted with lights, Autumn saw a longboat. Ursula was taking them to it.

It had no markings on its sails, and the name was obscured by tar — a pirate who wished any affiliation to be secret. The men who sailed it could have been any of the tribes who sailed these waters. The heavy beards made it only certain they were not Romans.

Autumn looked at what interested her most — how many in the crew and what kinds of weapons. She saw fire arrows in plenty, but only four bows. There were two racks of throwing spears, and the captain wore a sword. There were twelve, perhaps fourteen crew, equal in size to their own, and each man had his own dagger, just as Autumn wore in her boot.

Ursula had her own intentions. Autumn heard the merest whisper of it, like a flash of intuition.

:The ship has turned south.:

That was all.

:The ship has turned south.:
It was elegant in its simplicity.
:The ship has turned south.:
Ursula continued the persuasive message for several minutes. Autumn looked up at the stars and wondered if they could go there.

She felt a faint flicker of amusement from Ursula, who had stopped sending her thoughts toward the pirate vessel. *:Some other time, perhaps.:*

At that moment, all things seemed possible to Autumn and nothing Ursula could suggest would frighten her. She watched in amazement as the longboat turned to starboard and tacked back to the south, away from the *Verdant Bough*, which still drifted north.

Killera's thoughts whispered through Autumn, though they were not directed at her. *:Come back, Ursula.:*

They floated back to their ship, to Killera's golden, unwavering presence. Autumn wanted to ask what the river was that Ursula had helped them enter with the safety of the tunnel, but it did not seem the proper time. The blue light was fading, and she no longer perceived anyone else's thoughts.

The sensation of waking from the trance left Autumn as sluggish as if she had fallen asleep in the sun. The others did not seem to feel it, but then they had done it before.

Hilea clapped her hands like a child. "That was wonderful!"

Killera likewise seemed pleased, though she regarded Ursula with anxiety. "You didn't overtax yourself, did you?"

"I'm fine." Ursula flashed a brilliant smile in the dark.

Autumn became aware that the cabin door was open and her father stood there, thoroughly bemused. She jumped up, feeling as if she'd been caught doing something forbidden. "Father, it's a most amazing thing," she said nervously.

"I came only to see what kept you. I did not mean to see what was not meant for my eyes." He spoke directly to Ursula. Autumn had never seen her father flustered in this way.

Ursula rose from the floor, her robe still loose and her long braid uncovered. "I understand, Captain. You did nothing wrong."

The silence was awkward, so Autumn said quickly, "The other ship has turned south. I saw it turn."

Edrigo nodded tightly, and Autumn realized he did not want to know more than that. He looked at her as if she had stepped over some mysterious line that kept him from understanding her actions. "Thank you, then," he said to all of them, and he bowed and left.

Autumn was trembling again, with fatigue and giddiness. The wonder of what she had just experienced was at war with the part of her that still did not believe such things were possible. She did not believe in Ursula's goddess, and yet that journey had happened. She believed, then . . . in Ursula.

She wanted to say something to her and could not find words. Her body was waking up and aching to be near her. The feeling was impossibly more intense than it had been when she'd burst in to blow out the lamp. Her body's craving was compounded by a new desire, more powerful, that wanted the caress of Ursula's mind again, to hear her thoughts. She wanted Ursula's laughter inside her heart again.

"Would it be all right if I went up to the top of the stairs?" Killera was already at the door. "I need some air."

"Don't go all the way onto the deck," Autumn warned. "The crew won't be expecting you, and all the lanterns are out."

Killera just nodded, then she was gone.

Autumn ran her shaking fingers through her hair, still searching for something to say to Ursula.

"Have a cup of wine," Hilea urged her. "It can be draining the first time." Her lips quirked and she said dryly, "As with other things."

"Oh, Hilea," Elspeth murmured, then she went to her own bed and was quiet.

"No wine, but thank you," Autumn said. "I think I should rest as well." She stepped toward the door, only to stumble as her feet refused to obey her mind.

Ursula and Hilea both moved to help her, then Hilea stepped back. "I think you should help Autumn get safely to bed," she murmured, her tone just as dry.

"Perhaps you should do it," Ursula said.

Autumn felt the heat of Ursula's body all through her own and could not have born it if Ursula let go of her. "No." Her voice quavered. "I want you."

She meant it on so many levels, and she heard Ursula catch her breath.

166

She needed Ursula's arm around her as they negotiated the dark hallway. She stepped carefully and still stumbled twice. Her body was not obeying her, not her feet, not her hands, certainly not her eyes, which wanted to close in sleep.

Ursula was the one who managed to get the door open, and Autumn levered herself past the threshold and fell onto her bed. The darkness was absolute when Ursula shut the door. Autumn closed her eyes to stop them from straining to adjust for light that didn't exist. She wanted desperately to sleep, but her hands had other plans as they pulled her rough wool shirt over her head. She sensed Ursula bending over her and reached upward, wanting to pull Ursula down to her.

"Will you be all right?"

Autumn encountered Ursula's robe, then found one hand. She pulled sharply on it, dizzy with exhaustion and swollen with desire. "Stay with me."

She kissed the fingers she clasped, the palm, the wrist. Ursula knelt beside the bed to press one hand to Autumn's forehead.

:Sleep.:

When Autumn woke, her first awareness was that the *Verdant Bough* was moving again, but at a moderate rate. Then she felt the strange combination of being half dressed; part of her was too cold, and the rest a little too hot.

She swung her feet over to the floor and her toes touched something soft and warm, and it wasn't Scylla.

The events of the previous evening flooded into her mind, and she knew it was Ursula sleeping on her floor. "Ursula?"

Ursula stirred, and in a rush gathered herself out of Autumn's way. "Oh, I'm sorry. I didn't mean to fall asleep. I was monitoring you for a few minutes, just to make sure you were resting comfortably, and I must have . . . oh . . ."

The rest of Ursula's explanation was lost as Autumn slid to the floor next to her and followed the sound of her voice to find her face. The touch of her hand silenced Ursula, and then Autumn felt Ursula's cheek burrowing into her palm, inviting exploration of her face and neck.

Autumn's heartbeat was in her fingertips; all her awareness focused on the heat and softness of Ursula's skin. She pushed curls back from delicate ears and brushed thick lashes with her thumbs. Ursula brought one of Autumn's hands to her mouth, her lips first pressing gently against Autumn's wrist, then trailing lightly toward Autumn's curling fingers.

Autumn opened her eyes because she sensed light beyond her closed lids. A faint shimmer of silver, like a lamp under a blanket of fog, outlined Ursula's face, her hair, her shoulders, everywhere that Autumn looked.

The soft light seemed to startle Ursula too, for she looked as amazed as Autumn felt. Her amazement faded as she gazed at Autumn's face, then moved closer, raising her lips as she closed her eyes.

Autumn closed the distance between them, grazing Ursula's chin and cheeks with her mouth. Ursula gasped once and shuddered as Autumn pressed her lips to Ursula's eyes. "Kiss me."

With her heart pounding like gull's wings in the wind, Autumn turned Ursula's face to hers and drank from the petaled cup of her mouth. Her eyes felt seared with the brilliance of spring. Her nose tickled with the scent of flowers and tilled soil. She thought she heard the bubble of water as it danced in a fountain or what could have been rainfall on newly opened leaves that sheltered them from a warm, loving sun.

The kiss deepened and left Autumn longing to fill her hands with Ursula's skin and hair. But she did not lift her arms or make any other gesture, just continued the astonishing kiss, breathing in a love that she had never imagined, not even in a dream.

Ursula finally lifted her mouth with a gasp for breath that was also a moan and turned her gaze upward to Autumn's face. Autumn lost herself in the glistening depths of those amazing black eyes.

She was remotely aware that Ursula was unfastening her robe further, and yet she could not look down at what she knew must be profound beauty. Her hands hungered, her fingers thirsted, and she could not look at the legs that uncurled when the last of Ursula's clothing was shed.

"Autumn . . ."

Her name on Ursula's breath was like Hilea's song, and it took her to a still place where she was aware of her body's every sensation. Blood pounded in her ears and throat and her stomach tightened with desire.

"Touch me, please."

Autumn could not make herself move. She closed her eyes and knew want mingled with fear. "I can't."

"Please."

She was trembling with aching need. "I want to."

:Please.:

Autumn cried out, the touch of Ursula's mind was so tender and yet needful. She tried to form an answer, but did not know how to convey what she felt.

:Let me.: Ursula leaned closer again, her lips nuzzling Autumn's throat. *:Let me touch you, then.:*

:I can't!: Her fearful response was so loud in her own mind that she felt Ursula wince and sit upright again. Finally, she let her eyes take in the soft shoulders, the full and supple swell of breasts, the curve of thighs. A goddess's body, too beautiful to profane, too perfect to mar with mortal desire.

"I am a woman," Ursula whispered. "Not a goddess."

Autumn shook her head mutely.

"I am a woman," Ursula said again. "Desire is in her design, and your touch her gift. You are the goddess because I was made for your love."

The next kiss left Autumn disoriented and her mouth did not want it to end. Ursula drew Autumn's arms around her waist and moved into their grasp, offering everything.

The shock of their cool, bare skin meeting made Autumn moan again. She did not know which way was up, only which way led again to Ursula's mouth.

:I am a woman, like you.:

Autumn slid slowly onto her back, pulling Ursula with her. Ursula's mouth went again to Autumn's throat and Autumn grasped Ursula's hips, drawing them ever closer. The cold of the floor helped her to focus and she let her hands glide over Ursula's ribs, over flesh that seemed as fragile as a rose petal. But her fingers felt the strength of bone and muscle as Ursula moved, and she held her more tightly.

Ursula groaned and twined in her arms, her teeth rasping over Autumn's shoulder. Emboldened as Ursula grew less and less ethereal to her senses, Autumn let go of her last fear. She formed the words and prayed she would not regret the risk. *:Does this mean something to you?:*

:Yes, yes, yes. Everything.: The answer rang in Autumn's mind like a bell, bringing clarity and purpose to the fevered movements of her hands. She stroked Ursula's ribs again and then the soft sides of her breasts. Ursula's arousal resonated in her mind and Autumn answered it with her own, sending sparks into their already burning passion.

Autumn still wore her trousers and she needed them off. She pushed Ursula up to her knees and sat up to fumble with the cording. When it wouldn't give, she shimmied out of them, glad she had not tied them too tight. She tugged them off and turned back to Ursula and was shocked into stillness as Ursula's mouth closed around her breast.

Each movement of Ursula's mouth as it explored her breasts, her stomach, was painfully welcome. Autumn trembled in places she had never known could feel pleasure — the crook of her arm, the inside of her knee. Her legs were slick with her want and she was momentarily afraid Ursula would be repulsed.

:This is the blessing of a woman, shimmering like daybreak.: Ursula tasted, then again and again until Autumn thought she would faint from the tenderness of it.

:There . . .: What Ursula's seeking tongue did not find, Autumn exposed with her mind, with her fingers, with shudders of her body. *:I am yours.:*

The gate was above them and Autumn's pulsing emotions were pushing it open. Ursula glowed crimson and the tunnel opened, carrying them as lights in the night sky until they were stars irrevocably attracted, blazing with heat, shimmering like daybreak.

Even when Autumn's body cooled, even when Ursula wrapped Autumn in her arms and they shared tears, even then they remained in the tunnel and Autumn felt the cool light of stars on her face. Dreamily, she asked, *:Are we a constellation?:*

:The lovers, of course.: Ursula's mind was trilling with delight and satisfaction.

Autumn had a passing thought about tomorrow, about the day after, but she found it easy to push from her mind. Right now, for these selfish moments, there was no tomorrow.

:Know me.: Autumn did not at first understand Ursula's invitation. Then her spirit was gently pulled inside the ordered, vaulted rooms of Ursula's mind and shown their doors and windows, the people who occupied them as memories, the experiences that had painted the walls.

She saw a Killera no more than six, sitting bravely while Ursula pulled a bee stinger out of her foot. She was a giggling Ursula, rolling down a damp hillside crusted with wildflowers. She lived Ursula's past, in a few heartbeats, not absorbing it all, but taking its measure. The innocence and joy were in spite of the world's cruelties, cruelties she saw as goddess and confessor in troubled times. Autumn came to the only door Ursula would not open and knew that behind it lay mysteries she was not yet able to comprehend and confidences that had come to Ursula while she walked as the goddess.

What Ursula did show her was the feeling of the goddess within her. *:I breathed in everything, the smallest creature, the largest tree. I breathed them in and gave back love.:*

:I don't think you've ever stopped doing that. The goddess is still there.:

Ursula rocked Autumn in arms streaming with light. *:Beloved,:* she breathed, and the tunnel pulsed with each syllable.

Autumn danced through the rooms of Ursula's mind, twirling to music she had never heard but would always remember. *:Beloved.:*

They slipped down the arc of the tunnel, back toward their entangled bodies. If Autumn had been more experienced she might have known that the darkness that slowly swirled behind them was not just an absence of light. Then the gate was closed and her fingers found Ursula's quivering welcome, honeyed and salty, a soft pliant welcome that quickly became the fierce gasp of flesh craving more. She crushed Ursula's breast to her mouth and found her way to the goddess in both of them, like the shimmer of daybreak.

Ursula panted against her pillow, shocked awake by an echoing ecstasy that had penetrated every nerve with hunger for the touch of a woman she had never met. When her heartbeat finally quieted she heard Kelly pacing on the porch and, from the guest room, low, gasping moans as Liz, more fortunate than her cousin, found release in Taylor's willing arms.

Autumn hugged her knees to her chest and tried not to give way to tears. The music in her head was louder than the CD player, painfully so. *When can I see you and be with you?* She had almost understood, almost been able to touch the dream memories. She could nearly inhale the scent of Ursula's hair. Her naked body could . . . almost . . . feel Ursula's mouth on it. She had felt incomplete all her life, never knowing her past, but she had no way of coping with this new misery.

If she could divine the mysteries of the magician's box, and she was able to somehow intervene in the past she dreamed about, there was no guarantee that this endless longing would be sated. You're not doing this for yourself, she told herself firmly. You're doing it for her. For Ursula.

In a crowded amphitheater, a lone guitarist finished a scathing solo, every note assailing the heavens to the pulsing approval of an angry, unfocused crowd. As the echoes died, the musician brought the neck of the guitar close to her magenta-streaked hair and her fingers caressed the strings as if it were a violin. She crooned an ancient melody into the microphone. "When can I see you, in a garden of flowers . . ."

Part Three:

Spiralig Tor

I alone remember.
I will never see you again.
Fuck this world.
— Lea Battle, "Battle Hymn"

Eleven

Her fingers worked their fastest now. When she took the time to practice for her return to the House of Cards, coins, cards and dice appeared with a suddenness that transcended human ability. Where once Autumn had only cursed the ability because she didn't understand why she had it or where it came from, she now felt a sense of wonder. It was a gift she was learning to celebrate.

She planed the last plank of yew and used a grooving tool to create the channel that would knit it to the planks on either side. Her ability to work with her hands no longer stopped at sleight of hand. They worked as if she was long practiced at woodworking, almost without her conscious direction. She had had no idea she knew how to do this, but it was also something to celebrate.

The box was almost done and needed only paint. Every day she grew stronger as her stitches slowly disappeared and the weight she'd lost came back. She found herself dining almost nightly with Ed, either appreciating his bachelor cooking skills or repaying his hospitality by treating him to dinner at Marge's Diner. She was eating better than she had in the last ten years, and in a short time she'd become one of Marge's regulars. She found she liked the feeling of belonging. Short but well-timed and choreographed visits to roulette tables all over town continued to leave her with no financial worries. She no longer feared harassment from the casinos, no longer felt like a shadow afraid of what the light might show her. She didn't even need to go back to her show at the House of Cards, but she would. She had met Rueda there.

She did not know what role Rueda played in the life she might have had with Ursula, but she knew there must be one. Maybe the box would help her find it.

Or maybe the box was just a box.

She set the last plank in place and tacked it to its neighbors with small finishing nails. It was not just a glorified closet. Every step of the way she felt some sort of power building, and she was not afraid. She did not yet know how to use the power, but she would when she needed to. Her memory had almost become reliable that way.

"You've been at that day and night." Ed's disapproving tone was not new, and Autumn tried to mollify him with a smile.

"I want to get it done before I go back to work," she told him unnecessarily. He knew her reasons, he just didn't agree with them.

"I was going to toss a couple of burgers on the grill." Ed never argued with her, he just made his worry plain.

"No, no," Autumn said. "It's my turn." She tapped in the last nail. "And I'm done. I could use a brief celebration. Tonight I'll do a layer of primer, and tomorrow I'll start painting."

"It's amazing the way it went together." Ed raised a hand to stroke the side nearest him, but snatched it back at the last moment.

"What is it?"

"I, I just had the idea that I shouldn't touch it. It's meant for you."

She tried to reassure him, to take the apprehension out of his eyes. "Magician's trade secret."

He looked at her as if he finally believed she was a magician, that she didn't just play one on stage. They gazed at each other for a long minute. Autumn wanted to tell him that she didn't believe she was a real magician — yet — and that he should not worry, but any protestation on her part could be taken for confirmation.

Finally, he gulped. "I don't want to know." He tried to lighten the air. "But if you could tell me how you get so lucky at the tables, now that would be worth feeding you supper for the next year."

They walked companionably to Marge's Diner, with Scylla loping by Autumn's side. The heat and Ed's leg made their pace slow, but it suited Autumn's recovery as well. Scylla agreed with a soulful sigh to wait outside on the promise of leftovers. Autumn ordered a large steak and milkshake. Ed approved heartily when Marge included a heaping helping of steamed broccoli. To please him further, Autumn ate the broccoli first.

She was deep in the dregs of the tall steel shake container when she felt a shadow on one shoulder. Her senses chilled and the fog of pleasant company and good food fled. She felt like she had in the hospital, when Staghorn had tried to touch her, coiled to protect herself and ready to strike. In her mind she could almost hear Scylla growling.

It was indeed Staghorn who stood slightly behind her, watching her lick the teaspoon free of chocolate ice cream.

Autumn would have gone on ignoring him, but Ed abruptly said, "What do you want, fella?"

"Cool it, pops." Staghorn's smug, insulting tone brought an angry flush to Ed's usually serene face. Autumn was tempted to let Ed beat the crap out of Staghorn. He might have twenty years on Staghorn, but he was a big man and his upper body had compensated for the weakness in his legs. Staghorn was a coward, however, and would no doubt pull his gun.

Autumn stayed Ed with a gentle hand on his. "Leave be," she said and realized she had quoted Ursula. What would Ursula do to the Staghorns of the world, she wondered.

"How are you recovering, Autumn, honey?"

"My health is no concern of yours." She met the feral gleam in his eyes with her own cold stare, feeling suddenly like Scylla facing down a pirate.

"You know I worry." His eyes deliberately traveled the length of Autumn's body.

Ed started to get up again, but Autumn waved him down and shook her head sharply. She said loudly enough for her voice to carry,

"I had no idea Las Vegas P.D. was so concerned about follow-up, Detective Staghorn."

Several conversations at nearby tables quieted. The neighborhood wasn't one that welcomed strange cops. Autumn had seen the off-duty sheriff, who sometimes borrowed equipment from Ed for his own sculpting hobby, sitting at the counter. She was counting on the lack of love between the two branches of law enforcement to get Staghorn out of her hair — for now.

Marge's voice cut across the clatter of plates and silenced what conversation still continued. "Is there a problem here?"

Staghorn glanced over his shoulder. "Only if you don't butt out." He quelled the angry murmur that swept through the diner with a glance around. When he looked back at Autumn, she sat with her hands in plain view. He did not notice that Ed's fury had mutated into satisfaction.

He reached for one of Autumn's French fries, but she swatted his hand with the flat of a table knife that was suddenly in her grasp. "That's rude."

He shook his hand, then grasped her shoulder with it. "You need to step outside with me, babe, so we can get a few things cleared up."

Autumn smiled reassuringly at Ed as she stood. She touched his shoulder as she walked by, then stumbled into the busboy, and patted a friendly shoulder here and there on the way to the door. Just before they reached it she said quite loudly, "Wait — I think I should see your badge first."

Staghorn wasn't an idiot. Beyond searching his pocket once, he didn't waste any time looking for his missing badge. He smiled as if he'd won. "I think I will run you in for stealing this time." He spun her around to face the cash register and kicked her feet apart, holding her in place with most of his weight on his hand in the small of her back.

"Hey, cop, you dropped this." Marge's mouthy busboy tossed the wallet at Staghorn's head. Staghorn didn't let go of Autumn to pick it up.

"Now what exactly did I steal?"

It was then that Staghorn reached for his cuffs and discovered they, too, were gone. One of the men Autumn had so briefly touched on her way to the door held them up. "Can't you keep track of anything?" He slid them across the floor at Staghorn's feet.

Staghorn's response to the resulting laughter was to shove her face down onto the glass display case. It hurt, a lot. She'd pushed the right buttons and hoped she didn't regret it. "You're going to pop my stitches," she gasped.

"What is going on here?" The new voice was the one Autumn had hoped to hear.

"Stay out of it."

"Don't think so." The sheriff's deputy flipped his ID open. "I'm not one to usually interfere with a brother cop —"

"Then shut the fuck up." Staghorn ground her face harder into the glass and Autumn yelped.

"I'm gonna have to ask you to let go of her. I don't want to mess up my boss's day off, and you don't want him in a bad mood when he calls your boss. Don't put me in the position of having to testify when she sues you."

Autumn closed her eyes and found the quiet place that had always helped her avoid the night creatures in the train yard. Ursula had shown her how to use the skill in the most subtle way. :*She's not worth the trouble.*:

"This has got nothing to do with you." Staghorn's grip on the back of her head slackened ever so slightly.

:*She's not worth the trouble.*:

"I know that," the deputy said. "But I live here and have to face these people. You gotta let me keep my own nest clean."

:*She's not worth the trouble.*:

Staghorn let go of her head and hauled her to her feet. He held her for a moment, with her back against him, then pushed her away hard enough that the deputy put out a hand to steady her. "You aren't worth the trouble."

Autumn gazed at him with equanimity. Just three weeks ago she'd have been livid at his touch, but it didn't matter now. He'd had nothing of her though he'd meant to take everything. There were many different ways to win.

"But you better hope, bitch, that you never cross my path again." He snatched up his badge and cuffs and slammed out the door.

"What an asshole!" Marge's vehemence brought a round of agreement.

"Thank you, Officer," Autumn said breathlessly.

"Aren't you the little girl who got attacked on the Fourth of July?"

Autumn nodded, not sure what to make of being called a little girl. She did her best to appear vulnerable and guileless, but it was a stretch. The deputy was trying to put the information he had together and figure out exactly why a brother cop had taken such an interest in Autumn. He was too much of a cop not to wonder if there was fire he just didn't see.

"Oh my god!" One of the waitresses was staring down into a tub of dirty dishes with horror.

The deputy turned away as Autumn sidled back to her seat, stopping briefly to squeeze Ed's shoulder. Ed was seething with indignation on her behalf. "I'm fine."

"That creep could have seriously hurt you. You should file a complaint."

"It wasn't going to get that far, and he's not worth it."

Several people began to laugh, and Ed turned to look. Autumn tried to keep her expression innocent as the deputy used a pencil to fish Staghorn's service revolver out of the dirty water. He turned to look at her suspiciously. She could not hide the gleam in her eye.

Then his mouth crumpled into a grin, and everyone began to laugh with released tension. "I'll guess I'll have to drop this off with his desk sergeant. Staghorn, wasn't it?"

Autumn nodded and bit her lower lip to keep from grinning. The rush of self-confidence tingled in her fingers and toes. It was an addictive feeling.

She did not know who she had been, and she did not know how she knew what she knew. What she knew was that she was not a thief, not a liar, not a cheat, not a pickpocket.

She was a woman and she was strong. She had been a warrior and was one again. She had been a magician and would be one again.

You are a woman. You are strong. She didn't need the confirmation, but Autumn thanked the voice.

You are a warrior. You are a magician.

There was more and, for the first time, Autumn thought the

voice might actually volunteer something other than denial or confirmation of her thoughts. The voice was almost a palpable presence, something — someone — she might recognize.

The moment passed. That it had even existed was, however, enough for the day.

Ursula found it hard to make eye contact with anyone as she poured herself a glass of milk. Kelly was scrambling eggs, and Ursula was glad that kept her on the other side of the kitchen. They had all shared an erotically charged dream in which Ursula had figured prominently. She felt naked this morning, and not in a good way.

"Having had time to think about it, I think we need to plan a major working," Taylor said. She dumped a great deal of sugar into her coffee. A quick glance told Ursula that Taylor wished morning did not come so early on a farm.

"To accomplish what?" Ursula watched Kelly's rigid back. She knew Kelly had felt everything in the dream.

"To tie you into the power you ought to know about. Something is keeping you from it, something in you."

Ursula considered that and shook her head. "What I know my aunts taught me. They never . . . held anything back. I mean, could someone in your circle keep a secret like that from you?"

"Perhaps they don't remember it anymore."

Ursula blinked. "Remember what?"

Taylor flushed and she hurriedly set her coffee mug down. "I meant perhaps they don't know about it."

Kelly dumped eggs on Ursula's plate, then moved on to Liz's. She said firmly, "No you didn't. You said they didn't remember it. From when?"

Ursula said nothing, but Taylor glanced at her and saw the same question in her eyes.

"I'm sorry. I'm still a little sleepy. I didn't mean to put it that way."

"Why did you?" Kelly ran water into the frying pan, then joined the rest of them at the table.

Taylor cleared her throat uncomfortably. Liz was carefully neutral, though Ursula was certain Liz knew what Taylor was going to say.

"Saint Ursula has always been a favorite saint of mine. A woman who repudiates marriage with mortal men and is killed for it while surrounded by women, well — she's always intrigued me. The fragments of legend in the broadly available histories paint her as a Christian acolyte in a pagan world, but that never rang true for me. Most of those accounts were written hundreds of years after the fact. I've always imagined her as a strong-willed noblewoman who just didn't want to let male society rule her. The feminist in me, you know." She paused to eat a bite of eggs.

"I didn't know there was a Saint Ursula until you showed me the music." Ursula made herself eat, though every word Taylor said made her increasingly tense.

"After you left the other day I brushed up on my research. I have access to people who have access . . . to a lot of history. I will explain more when we — I'll explain that part later." She sipped her coffee with more nervousness than Ursula had ever thought she would see from Taylor. "They gave me a variety of histories, some legends, some fabrications long after the fact, and some bits and pieces that sounded eerily familiar to what Liz and you both described to me."

It was Ursula's turn to sip nervously. Liz's expression gave away nothing. "Like what?"

"That Ursula was a priestess of the old ways, ways that were pre-Christian and still thriving into the fifth century. A nobleman raised her and gave her his house name, but she was not really his daughter. She was a foundling who was brought into her power by three witches."

Ursula gulped. "Three w-w-witches?"

"There's more," Taylor breathed. At least two . . . sources . . . named the witches."

Ursula shook her head. Kelly had gone deathly still.

"I had heard the names before, and when you told me your aunts' names it resonated. I confirmed them again, to be sure.

"No," whispered Ursula.

"Kaitlynn, Justine, Lillith with the double-D spelling."

"What does it mean?" Kelly's frustrated question was a half cry. "What's happening?"

"I don't know," Taylor said through gritted teeth. "I wish, you have no idea how much I wish that I did."

"You're saying I'm her — that Ursula. Who becomes a saint."

"Maybe. I think we should use a full working, amass some serious energy, and go looking for answers. The river has answers for us, if we're brave enough to look. That's one of the powers you should have."

"But — she died, you called her a virgin martyr. What happened to them all?" What happened to Killera and Autumn, to Elspeth, to Hilea? What dark future did the distant past hold for all of them now?

"We can't be sure. We only know that the popular version says eleven thousand virgins were killed when they took refuge in a German abbey, sometime in the late fourth century. Maybe even the middle fifth century."

"I can't handle this." Ursula pushed away her plate. "I don't believe it."

"And I think," Taylor went on, her tone more ruthless, "I think the reason you don't really know what your power is capable of is because you've been deliberately short-circuited, bound in some way. You never perceived the darkness that's hunting you, not until you left the protection of your circle. But maybe it was there all along, it just didn't know where to find you because you were so securely sheltered — and you never really displayed your power."

"But now it does know where I am," Ursula said numbly.

"Maybe you were bound for your protection, to help hide you. But you have to be able to defend yourself now."

Ursula had a horrible, nauseated sensation in the pit of her stomach. She knew what Taylor was going to suggest.

"If we do it right," Taylor said more gently, "it ought to free your power and maybe even your memory of your past."

"Do what?" Kelly moved protectively toward Ursula.

Ursula pulled her braid over her shoulder and let the long coil rest in her lap. "I know . . . at your house I was going to cut it off, but that was because I felt I was no longer worthy of it."

"I'm not suggesting we cut it. Only unbraid it, then braid it again, giving you the same initiation that I had."

"Unbraiding it is the same as cutting it."

"I don't think so."

183

"But how can you know? I can't do it!" Ursula abandoned her breakfast and the conversation, a wild panic in her throat. She bolted to the porch and then to the vegetable garden where they'd most recently been planting.

Her braid was her link to the circle. It was a storehouse of energy, the only lasting symbol she had of what her aunts had spent a lifetime teaching her. Unbraiding it — it was unthinkable. Braiding it again with some other intention was petrifying to consider.

She sat down on the only bench, her legs no longer reliable. Raw panic threatened to overwhelm her, and she felt enormous pressure on her gate. Clutching her braid in her hands, she sent all her strength to reinforcing her ever-thinning protections. The darkness receded, just as she thought she could fight it no longer, and she slumped on the bench. She tried to close her mind to the present and escape to the far simpler past.

She woke when Hilea's morning song was done. Her limbs were heavy with satisfaction. Further desire was stirring, and her mind was preoccupied with thoughts of Autumn.

If she thought long enough about being in Autumn's arms she felt suffused with light, almost choked with the power of it. She did not know if a mortal woman should experience such soul-inspiring pleasure. Given what her future held, when the *Verdant Bough* finally turned east to Jutland, she could almost wish that she would die in Autumn's arms, her last sensations and thoughts completely of her.

Life was not like that, and she knew it. She had a road to follow, to rejoice and suffer in, to survive to the very end. She could do no less. Loving Autumn so much only made her more aware of that.

She heard someone on deck shouting and did not understand at first, then more loudly, and closer, she heard the cry again.

"Ship to starboard! Longboat to starboard!"

She lurched to her feet and found Killera there at her side, Killera, whose misery was so obvious. Hilea had knowingly thanked Ursula for the pleasant dreams, but the dream had not been a pleasant one for Killera. Elspeth was likewise pale this morning, as if she had also felt more nightmare than dream.

"Help me," she said to Killera. She didn't wait for an answer because she did not have to. Killera was her anchor. She cast out with her senses, opened her gate.

A different ship, but equally as menacing. She plunged toward it, looking for any information that would help, and felt Killera's familiar strength buoying her. Fourteen crew above deck, perhaps two more below. Their intentions — they knew what the *Verdant Bough* carried and wanted both the bride and her dowry. She tried to probe harder and something dark, like a dense, black curtain, fluttered between her and the ship. She closed her gate sharply, feeling pursued, and Killera's arm was around her waist, holding her steady.

"I must tell Autumn."

Killera winced, but nodded. "I'll go with you. Ursula —"

Ursula found the courage to look into Killera's darkened eyes.

"Don't ever hesitate to draw on me. Nothing has changed."

:I know.:

:Thank you for trusting me this way. If this is what we will have, it is enough.:

She clasped Killera's hand. *:I do love you.:*

:I know how much.:

If there was a hint of bitterness in Killera's wording Ursula did not sense it, though she would have understood.

They met Autumn on the stairs as she was coming down. "I'm to see you into the secret hold."

"We can be of help."

Autumn bit her lip. "I know. But Edrigo's given me an order."

"I've been given no such order," Ursula said, and she nodded to Autumn to go back up the stairs.

The activity on deck was frenetic. Arrows were being stacked at the base of the sail riggings. Two lanterns were quickly lit, and arrows with tips wrapped in oil-soaked wads of cloth were placed close by.

"She's coming fast!" The crewman in the crow's nest waved in a series of signals Ursula didn't comprehend.

"My lady, you'll serve us both best by getting below." The

185

captain was in no mood to argue, Ursula could see that, but she would not be dissuaded.

"My ladies and I can help. This is not the same ship as last night, and it won't be turned back by a trick. I can get you more information, but you have to let us remain here. We can help in the battle as well."

"No woman fights on my ship —"

"Father!"

The captain looked even angrier. "You know what I mean, Autumn."

"We'll not fight," Ursula said.

"Yes, we will." Killera's flat tone brooked no discussion. "If it comes to going with them or fighting, I'll fight."

"Before it comes to that we can help you," Ursula added urgently. "We helped when the Saxons began their first assault. We helped discourage them until weather was a bigger enemy than we were."

"She can do what she says, father."

"It's our lives, too." Hilea had her lute with her, held in one hand like a sword.

"The gods forgive me," the captain breathed. "All right."

Ursula was already triggering her trance as they settled with their backs against each other more for warmth than anything else. She had seen Autumn take the dagger and sheath from her boot and hand it to Killera. She could sense the weapon as it rested in Killera's lap. She looked up to find Autumn watching them. "You should do what you do best."

Autumn fingered the bow slung over her shoulder. "It's my turn."

Ursula did not know what that meant, but she accepted that Autumn had a duty. They all did. "I need a moment," she told the others. "I'll be right back."

Autumn followed her to the stairs, out of sight of the others, if not completely out of their minds. They lost themselves for a moment in the depth of their kiss.

"No matter what happens," Autumn murmured when their lips parted, "last night was enough. Of course I want more, but it was enough."

Ursula blinked tears out of her eyes. "There will be more nights," she said with conviction. There was no other option.

Autumn ran up on deck and Ursula heard her calling to the other archers. She went to her own place, knowing she looked both kissed and stricken.

She set it aside. There was no other option.

She closed out the sounds of the three crewmen plus the captain who strained to trim the sail for greatest speed. More than half the crew were at the railings, bows in hand. Ursula glanced up and saw that three of the archers had taken posts tied into the rigging themselves, and would fire handicapped by the ropes over their chests but from great strategic advantage. They were all too vulnerable, far more so than the crewman in the crow's nest or those on the deck, and sure to draw the most enemy fire.

She blinked again and realized the topmost archer was Autumn. Her turn . . . her turn to be the most likely to take an arrow, perhaps fatally.

She set the fear for Autumn's life aside. She had no other option. The others were waiting, as aware as she of the stakes. The circle almost raised itself, they were so in tune about their task.

The gate opened and Ursula crafted the tunnel with care this time, using the strength of the others. She turned their search toward the other ship's energy and the intentions of those who pursued them so doggedly.

The other vessel moved lithely in the water, built for speed, not cargo. The sailors themselves were buoyed with confidence of catching their quarry, and the distance between the two ships was slowly closed.

She saw arrows in plenty and archers to match the *Bough*, though none had taken position in the riggings. She honed in on the man at the tiller and watched his hands. He was shifting to port, for some reason preferring to close on them from behind and to port instead of starboard. His vessel had all the speed he needed. Of course. The *Bough*'s riggings were off center to starboard, and the archers would have to shoot farther. They would be that much less accurate.

:I will stay with Ursula.: Killera's steadiness was a gift beyond measure.

Ursula gave distracted approval as she continued to gather information. Hilea and Elspeth went to the captain to tell him what they knew, and once he was listening to Elspeth's quiet voice, Hilea went forward to keep the mate informed as well.

The *Verdant Bough* wheeled to starboard and the pursuing vessel had to correct its course as the gap between them widened.

:They still intend to come to our port side.:

The *Bough* continued a wide turn to starboard until they had almost gone about-face. They lost speed in the opposing wind, and the boom swung hard over, missing the heads of the experienced crew by inches. The deck jolted as the sail luffed.

The other vessel overshot them, turned almost as sharply and was forced to either engage their starboard side or withdraw and try again.

:They come.: She knew without sensing it that Elspeth and Hilea repeated the words to the crew.

Ursula saw the archers ready and the first arrows flew on both sides. Each vessel was nearly dead in the water, sails falling quickly as they made their stand. Edrigo trusted his archers and had chosen the direction of the confrontation. The sun was to Autumn's back.

Ursula focused her attention on the enemy archers. Her plan was to discourage them, for she knew that believing you cannot do something is a guarantee that you will fail. She sent energy to make the sun seem ever brighter, to blot the *Verdant Bough* from their sight. *:They cannot be hit with the sun in our eyes.:*

Arrows volleyed again, sounding like wasps as they parted the air. Ursula felt the keen edge of Autumn's exultation. Her last arrow had found an exposed thigh, and one of their archers was down, nearly useless for further combat.

:We cannot win. They are too strong.:

The enemy archers were shouting about the sun, shielding their eyes and shooting wildly when they fired at all. Arrows flew from the *Verdant Bough* with frightening precision and men screamed with surprise and pain.

She felt Elspeth's horror and sent a spell to quell it. The other captain was giving distance as his archers dug into the fire arrows, hoping for one lucky shot. Burning arrows were already lancing from the *Verdant Bough*'s deck, and three found a home in the other vessel's decking, causing more panic than damage.

:We cannot win. They are too strong.:

Ursula listened for a moment to their cries and learned their fears. For many who clung to the old ways, nothing terrified more than the White Christ, whose angry father had drowned a world and destroyed a city. *:The White Christ protects them. :We cannot win. They are too strong.:*

She was deep in trance now, and aware of Killera's steady presence, keeping her anchored to her body when her stretched perceptions cast further into the opposing vessel.

A jolt of fear from Autumn jerked Ursula away from the other crew, and she turned in the tunnel to look back at the *Verdant Bough*. A lone archer had taken bead on Autumn and was shooting with care and precision. One arrow was so close Autumn had to duck it, and she could not fire back while hard pressed for her own safety.

Another arrow, fletched in white with a flaming tip, soared across the space between the two ships, and Ursula saw its destination was Autumn's heart.

If she had had any doubt of Killera she would not have attempted it, but she had no doubt and so she tried. She abandoned the tunnel and her gate and threw all her energy into the circle, visualizing it as impregnable and ever larger, until it encompassed Autumn as well as most of the *Verdant Bough*.

The only thing that seemed to move was the ships themselves. All eyes turned to the fire arrow, which hung suspended a mere inch from Autumn's chest. The shaft quivered as if it had sunk into wood.

Autumn slowly raised her hand to pluck the arrow from the air. She looked down at her body, as if to confirm that it had indeed not reached her, then she nocked it to her bow. She was within the circle now, and Ursula heard her thoughts.

:Find your owner.: She let fly.

The fire arrow would have sunk into the man who had launched it had he still been in that position, but he'd thrown himself to the deck. The arrow instead found coils of rope and old sailcloth — plenty of fuel to quickly spread its blaze.

A ragged cheer went up from the *Bough*'s crew, and Ursula

realized she was cradled in Killera's arms. Nothing had seemed important except saving Autumn. She was breathing only because Killera's mind made her.

She did not perceive her own gate was left open by her carelessness, until a presence had passed through it.

Killera saw it first and struck out with all her psychic strength. In a heartbeat, Ursula joined her, and she felt Hilea and Elspeth surging to their aid. Even Autumn was abruptly there, fighting this new assault.

Ursula did not know what it was and had never experienced the violation of her own gate before. A darkness swept over her, heavy and choking. She felt the claws of another mind raking over her, trying to pull her back through the gate and into the river, into the chaos.

She would not go there, and so she fought. She no longer knew what was happening with the ships. Her life was suddenly unimportant. The darkness wanted her in the river, and the river was forever, chaos beyond life and death.

She would not go there and she fought with all her strength, all the strength Killera had and everything she could take from the others, from every man, even the enemy. She found strength in the deep life of the ocean below them, in the sunlight on her body, in the sharp edge of the wind. She fought because there was no other option.

The darkness still came. She was losing.

Autumn felt as if the ropes across her chest were choking her. Through her blurred vision she saw fire swelling on the other deck, and that a few pirate archers were taking up positions again. She knew that Ursula's protection was gone and that she was fatally vulnerable.

She heard her father screaming at her to climb down, but she could not move. Everything she had in her was for Ursula now, to repel an attack from beyond the gate that seemed to have no ending. All she could do was watch the fire blaze on the other vessel. It was all that saved her as it finally burned through the deck, taking the supply of arrows with it. Some of the other crew began to jump into the sea.

A flash of bright blue caught her gaze, and she saw that a woman wrapped in a blue cloak had joined the other vessel's captain. She was very tall, and from the distance, seemed overpoweringly beautiful. Autumn felt a stirring of pity for the other woman's plight, but then she saw that the woman appeared singularly unmoved by the drama around her. If she felt the heat of the fire she showed no sign of it, nor did the wildly pitching deck seem to rock her. Her hair, thick and chestnut-hued, was coiled on her brow like a crown.

Autumn saw the woman gather herself and spread her arms, and then she sparkled with the same kind of light that had glowed around Ursula last night. The same kind, but nearly indigo where Ursula's was silver or sometimes tinged with the red of her hair. The light was behind Autumn's eyes, too, and she realized that she was looking at Ursula's attacker.

The other captain was using what little control he had over his tiller to bring his vessel closer to the *Verdant Bough*, most likely hoping to either jump to relative safety or burn the *Bough* along with his own vessel. Edrigo heeled them over to avoid any contact.

Autumn struggled to sever her link to the circle. She knew Ursula needed her strength, but right now Autumn needed her arms, her eyes. She felt Ursula's disbelieving pain, then the swell of Killera pushing her hard out of the link.

:Leave us, then. You don't understand.:

There was no time to explain. Autumn nocked one of her green-fletched arrows to string and took aim. They heeled over again, and she lost sight of her target. Her heart pounded three times in her ears, then they rocked back into view. Their two decks were nearly touching.

The air was split by a twin cry of anger and purpose. Scylla launched herself across the two rails, howling with battle fever while Hilea's voice soared to a tone that Autumn thought would surely split the sky.

Hilea's unearthly cry broke the woman's concentration. The dark light behind Autumn's eyes faded as she took aim. Scylla howled again, and then Autumn's arrow slammed into the woman's shoulder, spinning her around. A scream, a gruesome snarl, then there was only a sharp, empty quiet.

Autumn remembered to breathe, and her ears heard the sound of the fire and falling timbers again, with the thumping of the ocean against their badly trimming hull. The other ship was sinking as water poured over its port rail. A bundle of gray fur, stained red and singed in places, leapt to their deck, then a muffled explosion settled the pirate vessel further into the deep.

The mate did not need to be told to raise their sails again, and the *Verdant Bough* heeled over one last time, leaving Autumn clinging breathlessly to the riggings, her mind finally clear. Too clear, for she could no longer sense Ursula or any of the others.

Shaking hard with exhaustion and shock, she used her dagger to cut herself free, nicking herself in the process. When she managed to gain the deck again she just breathed for a minute, trying to remember why she had wanted to be on her feet.

They were finally free of the smoke from the dying ship, running ahead of the wind.

Autumn found herself with her arms tight around Scylla, holding fast to a dog not nearly as large as the one who had leapt so daringly to the defense of those she loved.

"Even then," Autumn sobbed into Scylla's thick, comforting fur. "Even then, you knew." Her stitches ached horribly, almost as much as they had the first day after the dagger had cut her open.

Scylla wuffled in Autumn's ear and was soon pleased to have a dog biscuit, which she crunched contentedly before going back to sleep.

There was no sleep for Autumn. Her mind churned in too many directions with the feeling that the crisis had not passed, but only paused. She could not sleep because she now knew, not what, but who threatened Ursula. The cold beauty of the woman on the ship was all too familiar. Autumn had let Rueda into her bed, her arms not yet knowing that Ursula waited in her past and future. She did not sleep and she wondered what price there would be to pay for her mistake, for having gone willingly into Rueda's arms. She did not sleep, and she prayed that no one paid the price but her.

Twelve

The droning voices of women working together in ritual had always triggered stillness in body and mind, but tonight of all nights — Midsummer, her favorite festival — it terrified Ursula. She wanted badly to hide, but she could not let Taylor down. Taylor had made her choice between church and circle. Circle had won. Ursula could only guess at what cost Taylor had hung up her vestments for the last time.

Even now, Taylor's friends, including Liz, were walking a ritual circle, sanctifying the ground they had chosen inside the smaller of Kelly's barns and readying it for what was to come.

She heard the quiet step on the path where she waited to be summoned, but did not turn.

"You don't have to do this." Kelly had played devil's advocate since Ursula had made her decision, arguing relentlessly with Taylor about the necessity of what they were going to do.

"Yes, yes I do." Even a week ago Ursula had not felt the steady drain of her energy that went to shore up her protections. Now keeping her gate strong was a conscious effort. It mystified Taylor that Ursula could not seem to access the power necessary to repel the darkness. They both believed tonight's ritual unbinding of her braid would unbind the power as well, though she did not know what that ultimately would mean.

Kelly examined her face in the light of the full moon. "You look like you're going to faint."

"I probably will." She was impossibly cold in the humid night air. The gray ritual robe Taylor had provided her was thin, and she knew that the temperature would probably get higher inside the circle. The cold came from inside her.

Ursula stepped into Kelly's open arms, and the warmth of Kelly's body through her matching robe did much to quiet Ursula's trembling. "You know I don't understand why you're doing this, but I will watch over you."

"I know and I thank you." Perfect love and perfect trust — Kelly offered both, and Ursula knew she would have need of them. She heard a steady tread on the path and knew what words would be next said.

"The circle waits."

She was glad it was Liz sent to bring her to the circle. Her day's fast and ritual meditation had left her feeling weaker, not stronger, and she had need of a friendly face. She was going to open herself to complete strangers. No matter how kindred they might be in spirit, the prospect was humbling and frightening.

Kelly walked behind her and stopped at the barn door. "Ursula, are you absolutely sure?"

She lifted her chin for Kelly's sake. "Yes."

Three pairs of bare feet crunched on the path of freshly strewn dried flowers and hay, sending up a perfume of all seasons. The circle, demarcated by a line in the dirt floor, was free of all debris and plainly visible in the soft light of four lanterns, one for each quarter of the circle. One portion of the line, a scant shoulder's width, was yet unclosed. Something other than Ursula's eyes saw this was the threshold into the already raised circle, left open for her to enter.

Liz stepped through without pausing and Ursula followed. Kelly stopped at Liz's gesture and had to be content with waiting just outside. She was untrained and unknown to these women. They had enough to handle with Ursula's untested skills.

Ursula did not turn to see by what means Liz closed the circle, but the palpable easing of the pressure on her gate told her it was done. She felt some of her anxiety bleed away and realized it had been coming from the darkness that pressed ever closer to her weakening protections. Taylor's circle was as inviolate as Ursula had hoped it would be. She knew that Kelly believed she could step over the now completed line on the floor any time she wanted. Kelly still did not understand and yet she trusted. Ursula hoped she had not lied to Kelly when she had told her everything would be fine.

She and Liz were two of the ten who had gathered. She stood where she had entered, and Taylor had to be the figure in the center. Now that the circle was closed, Taylor walked from the center to stand in front of Ursula. She carried a long, dried bundle of white broom like a scepter. She reversed the bundle so the stiff florets brushed the dirt floor. At Taylor's nod, Ursula began to walk, between the two women to her right, then between the next two, back to front to back, until she had completed the circuit twice. She could hear the bristles of the natural broom on the floor behind Taylor, tracing the path that Ursula walked.

The pattern completed so that the path in the dirt interlaced the other eight women, including Liz, Ursula went to the center and turned to face Taylor, who had left the bundle of broom parallel to the circle's now-closed threshold.

Taylor's face was lost in her hood. She was all priestess now and Ursula needed no reminder to kneel. "Who comes to this place?"

"I am Ursula, a daughter of the old ways."

"Why do you seek this circle?"

"To find a new path." She unknotted her plain robe and let it fall to the ground around her knees. Taylor had not told her she needed to do that, but she had gone naked to her initiation and naked again when they had made her the center. She should be naked now. "I am bound by a commitment I can no longer keep and ask your help to release me."

They had argued for a long time, she and Taylor, about why her aunts had not undone the braid once she had formally given her place to Priscilla Muldoon. In the end she had agreed with Taylor — it could not have been an oversight. Her aunts overlooked nothing. They had sent Ursula out into the world with the only protection they understood.

She wished she had asked their help early on, but had gone too far from them since. She could not guess why they hadn't told her what might happen if she left the protection of the circle — perhaps they did not know and only hoped to protect her from all harm. She knew they must be concerned that she had not come to them through the gate, but it was also entirely possible they expected her to make a visit later this evening, when Aldtyme's public Lammas festival and more private Midsummer rituals would both be in full swing. It would be all over by then, she told herself firmly. She would tell them all about it and learn what they had known or suspected. Answers, at last, she thought, with only one detail to be taken care of.

Taylor asked sternly, "Why do you shirk those responsibilities?"

"I left them freely for love and another took my place. Yet I am still bound and cannot seem to find my way."

She raised her face at Taylor's faint gesture. The fingertips Taylor placed on her forehead were scented from the white broom and Ursula inhaled the comforting, familiar smell. Taylor then raised her up for the kiss of peace and Ursula sought to find her perfect trust.

She knelt again and bowed her head, aware that Taylor was blessing the short dagger they would use to cut the ties around her braid. She concentrated on her pulse and her breathing, finding stillness. Then Taylor knelt facing her and bent her will to balancing the circle, to protect them from anything that might happen next.

She did not flinch when the hands of strangers lifted her braid from the dust. She heard the snick of the dagger leaving its sheath. The cool presence of the blade as it approached the first tie was like a cold breeze at the small of her back.

All was quiet until the blade had done its work.

~ ~ ~ ~ ~

"Well, that has to feel good," Ed said. He chuckled as Autumn stared at the marquee that blazed, "Tonight! Autumn Bradley Returns!"

"Wow — I didn't know they cared." She was also surprised to see a line already queuing up for her midnight show. In the mingling light from the marquee and the full moon, she recognized a few faces from the diner and even spied Marge and her boyfriend near the front of the line. Ed had insisted on driving her since he, too, wanted to see her in action. He left her at the stage door and went to pick out any seat in the house as Autumn had promised him.

After sunset the temperature had dropped to below one hundred, but just barely. It seemed much harder to wear her three-quarter-length leather jacket in the heat, and she knew the recent events of her life had softened her in some ways. They had also made her harder in others, harder than she had known she could be.

Tonight she would unveil a new illusion, polished for an audience that would not know she was still practicing. They also would not know it was not an illusion. She must use the box in front of an audience, with another person to play guinea pig. Doing so was not the box's final use, but a necessary step in its preparation. The final use was still a mystery, but it was Midsummer's Night. If her dreams were real, then she knew that Midsummer festival had always been a glad time for Ursula of Aldtyme, a time of reverence and thanks and celebration. If there was a time when Autumn would learn its purpose, she felt it would most likely be tonight.

She hadn't dreamed of Ursula for the last two days, nothing since that other Autumn had collapsed on the deck of the *Verdant Bough*, exhausted from the battle with Rueda's pirate ship. It was almost as if the past waited for the present to catch up. She had spent the day focused on her memories of Ursula and the feelings of the other Autumn, who had spent one incredible night in Ursula's arms and mind. Her sense of inner calm was not disturbed by backstage chatter with the club owner, nor by the surprising visit and quick interview with a local entertainment reviewer.

The only nerves she felt were just before the curtain went up. She was in her regular uniform, tight all-black bodywear with the leather jacket over it and her hair freshly trimmed to white stubble. A last glance in the mirror helped her find the cool distance she had always taken on stage with her, but the facade was paper thin. She was not this person anymore.

The decidedly partisan ovation broke the facade immediately. Her austere stage face gave way to a brilliant smile she didn't even try to hold back. As she went to front center stage and perched on the tall stool that waited there, she felt suddenly among at least a few friends. She rubbed her empty hands together, faster and faster, then opened them to reveal two white dice with black spots.

"Who wants to play?" She closed her hand around the dice and rolled her hand upside down and back, opening it again to show two red dice with white spots. Another turn over and all four dice were on her palm. Her hand began to tingle and a decidedly odd but very pleasant sensation tickled the pit of her stomach. She could almost feel the raising and spreading of what she had always thought of as the intimate magic of the small nightclub. The cool sensation on the back of her neck was like what the other Autumn had felt when Ursula had raised the circle.

Yellow Shirt was just about to burst when she gestured for him to join her on stage. He said his name was Craig after he had bounded onto the stage.

"You can add, right Craig?"

"I'll try."

Craig leaned over the small table as Autumn threw two dice and snapped her fingers like a craps player on a hot streak. "Eight," she announced, before the dice stopped moving and with her gaze distinctly turned toward the audience not the table. Cards, roulette, dice — they had no secrets from her.

Craig blinked, then nodded excitedly. "Yeah, eight."

She scooped up the dice, added one from her sleeve and tossed three. "Thirteen." She winked at Ed, who sat at the closest table with Marge.

She hardly waited for Craig's confirmation before scooping them up again, adding another, and throwing all four. "Twenty-one!"

Craig contradicted her. "Twenty." Without looking at the dice, Autumn gave him a exaggeratedly patient look. He counted again. "Oh. Twenty-one. Sorry."

The audience's laughter made Craig blush, but Autumn didn't

tease him overmuch. She abruptly realized she wasn't thinking of him as a sucker. She was inviting him to be amazed, to wonder, to be touched, ever so gently, by the magic she could feel coursing through her hands.

It pulsed so strongly at times that the tricks were actually harder to do. She felt as if she was holding herself in. Instead of knowing in advance what the dice would reveal, she thought perhaps she could make the dice roll the number she chose. She fanned playing cards, changing them from all red to all black and in the middle of the trick had the crazy idea she could not just switch them in her palm, but actually *change* them.

She felt a little dizzy as she continued the performance. She was willing to give control to what was almost a memory, and she knew the crowd was loving her panache and wit. She was loving it.

"Time for something new. You probably know I had a heck of a summer vacation, but I think you're going to like what I developed."

She did not wish for an assistant to muscle the tall box onstage. She did it herself with a handcart, letting its very solidity speak for itself when she thumped it into place. Low tech, low glitz was her trademark. The yew was black now, and a precise pattern of runes and mystic symbols — none of which she understood — was painted in white and edged with yellow and blue. The wood was unnaturally warm to the touch, or at least it seemed so to her.

"This is a magic box," she said simply. "Who wants to give it a try?"

Tight Jeans, Julie, was happy to try and she would add an element of eye candy if Autumn found herself off-center for any reason.

"Okay, you stand right here."

"Sure." Julie had an infectious giggle.

"I'll just get the not-magic box." She zipped off stage for the moment it took to lever an ordinary cardboard wardrobe, as tall as the magician's box, onto the handcart. It was the kind that people sometimes used in their garages or that turned up as stage props in cheap theater productions. She wheeled it into place next to the magician's box so that when she raised her arms, she would be able to place the flat of each hand to the side of each box. Standing between them, she gave the wardrobe a little shove to demonstrate its flimsy quality.

"This box is not magic. Think of it as a low-budget launching pad." She then rapped her knuckles on the solid yew wood. "This is the landing pad." She smiled provocatively at Julie, who giggled nervously.

"Ready?"

"Okay! What do I do?"

"Nothing," Autumn said. "Absolutely nothing." She opened the door to the cardboard wardrobe and Julie stepped inside. "The door doesn't even lock."

Autumn walked all the way around the wardrobe, thumping on the flimsy sides and back and jiggling the door. Julie giggled every time she bumped it. The audience started to chuckle with her. Once Autumn paused in her rhythm of thumps and Julie giggled anyway. Autumn let herself laugh with everyone else. She should not be this relaxed, considering what she was about to do, but she couldn't help herself.

She opened the sagging cardboard door to smile at Julie, who squeaked in alarm. "Everything okay in here?"

"Um, sure." More giggles.

"Okay." Autumn closed the door, then took her position facing the audience between the two boxes. The smile she gave Ed was meant to reassure him, but a flicker of concern crossed his dark face as she crossed her arms over her chest and slowly closed her eyes. Other illusionists would have pulsing music and laser lights ramped to maximum right now, but she worked in quiet. The more still she became, the louder the silent expectation of the audience seemed.

She had no rational basis for thinking this would work. She wondered if she was breaking some sort of cosmic rule by using unsuspecting people for far more than an illusion. Probably. But this was what her flashes of memory said she must do if she was going to be ready. She needed an unaware, possibly uncooperative subject for practice.

Ursula had raised a circle and then opened her gate to the river of chaos. She could travel the river safe in the tunnel she crafted by focusing either her own energy or that of the circle. Autumn knew she was not capable of that. She had no circle, and her own energy was not like Ursula's. Not at all like it.

Her mind steady, she touched her left hand first to the papery surface of the wardrobe, then raised her right to the warm, solid yew. The magician's box had a power of its own to give Autumn. Not a circle, but a source she could tap and master. She could feel her fingers going nearly numb as the power surged through her and she harnessed it, holding it ready to use when she needed it. Julie's giggling had stopped as she waited for something to happen.

Fueled by the latent power in the box that she had built with her own hands, Autumn opened her own gate for the first time.

She was in the tunnel of light again, the one that had carried her the night she had died. Autumn went with it, knowing her body remained poised between the two boxes. Her spirit arced toward a silver lake to skip like a stone across its surface.

She stood like this, exactly like this, on another smoky stage, wearing a skin-tight and low-cut spangled costume. The audience that watched her was exclusively male while women wrapped in feather boas regarded her from the wings. She twisted the energies rippling under her hands while Ed gestured and made it appear the magic came from him. A pianist banged out an energetic ragtime tune that further frayed her nerves. She wasn't doing it right, didn't really understand the gate or the tunnel she was trying to access, but Autumn could tell she was close, very close.

She stood like this, exactly like this, in a bright drawing room, wearing clothing so tight and heavy she could hardly breathe. Well-dressed gentlemen and ladies had watched indulgently as she entertained them with her "gypsy" parlor tricks, but now they seemed almost frightened by her straining body. It wasn't going to work, Autumn thought. Wanting it to work, being willing to die for it to work — it wasn't enough.

She stood like this, exactly like this, in a man's worn breeches and dirty cotton shirt. The barn was deserted and she tried again, tried for what seemed like the hundredth time. Each attempt drained her further as she sobbed in desperation, not knowing why she tried. And Ed, clad in buckskin, did not intervene until her eyes had rolled back in her head and what came from her mouth was no longer English. Autumn wanted to tell him she wasn't crazy, it was Latin — a poem about a garden of flowers and interminable longing.

The next skip felt colder, as if she had traveled deeper. It came more quickly, leaving no time to process what she saw. *She stood like*

this, exactly like this, when the black-robed figures came for her,
pitchforks gleaming in the night. Fear made her heart beat even
faster. She could smell the fire that waited.

She stood over the shattered remains of a crudely made box. Her
tattered gown covered a body gaunt with hunger. She wept in the
ruins of hope and knew she could not build another. Her gown
became a shapeless shift as she raved in a pit of muck and filth,
surrounded by the insane, who had never known the touch that drove
her mad and could not understand why she cried out endlessly:
Ursula . . . Ursula . . .

The muck and filth were gone, and she crouched in a rain-soaked
field to count her winnings. She needed a plane and stains and both
were far beyond her purse. It had been a good idea to cut her hair,
to pad her shirt. They'd thought they would separate the country boy
from his money and instead the boy had walked out with theirs. The
field grew to a forest, and she stayed safe in a dense thicket with a
wolf at her back, while servants of darkness combed the world for
her. She held two coins in her hand, then three, then four, then none.
Practice made perfect and she had nothing but time.

The skipping ended and she knew she had gone back, far back.
She needed to leave the gate and traverse the river of chaos — there
was something to be done. Tonight was the right night, but she was
losing track of the years. Time was so fluid. It seemed to exist only
to keep everything from happening at once.

Heat was pulsing under one hand. Autumn felt the tunnel coil
on itself, then, like a rock in a sling she was flung back, across the
silver lake, back to her gate, her body, to the expectant hush of a
not-yet-restless audience.

She fell to her knees, her hands still pressed against the two
boxes. The gate opened again, but this time she was the gate, from
fingertip to fingertip, and the river of chaos was all around her,
roiling with the terror of voices and music and emotions she couldn't
hope to sort out.

Chaos pressed in on her, on every inch of skin, but she did not
drop her hands. Her eardrums were strained by music too beautiful
and too ugly to bear, her eyes blinded by a thousand suns, but she
was still the gate and would not fail. A blazing heat seemed to shoot

through the stitches that ran down her chest. She saw the dagger again. It arched toward her helpless body, but she did not let go.

She screamed and did not let go.

Ursula's scream would have shattered her own gate were it not for the strength of Taylor's circle. When her breath was gone she still screamed, then Taylor was in her mind, rigidly controlling her breathing.

The circle's power, all that stood between Ursula and the darkness that wanted her, was in jeopardy as Kelly rebounded again and again from the threshold.

:Tell her you're all right.:

:She knows I'm not.:

Another twist of her braid was gently uncoiled and her next scream overcame Taylor's controls. The pain was all over her skin, in her head. *:I can't go on, I can't.:*

:I didn't know — gods, I didn't know it would be like this.:

Kelly's rage-fueled thoughts were very faint, and Ursula almost didn't track them. *:You bitch, you fucking bitch! Let me in!:*

Was Kelly talking to her? Ursula couldn't tell. She remembered Kelly asking her to let her in before, when she had been keeping a secret — what had it been? A secret that no longer mattered. The hands tried to be gentle, but she screamed again and had no voice left for it. They didn't mean to hurt her. Gods, it was only the beginning, only the outer braid. When it was done, a lifetime from now, there were the three inner braids. *:I can't go on . . . I can't . . .:*

They let her rest and she didn't know if that was mercy. She felt Taylor's helplessness as she conferred with the rest of her group. The circle had lost Liz, who had suffered nearly as badly as Ursula. She was likewise on the ground, but in Taylor-induced sleep.

She wanted to suggest the same sleep for her while they did their work, but never had she heard of any ritual happening while the primary participant slept.

:If I thought it would work I would try it, Ursula. I can't — you can't go on, and I can't either. We're going to stop.:

Of all that Taylor could have said, this was unexpected and, Ursula knew in an instant, wrong. Something had been woven into her along with the braid, and even if it had been done in perfect love, it now hindered her. The pain could be a warning not to go on, or a test of her resolve to become something more than what she had been.

She pulled herself up out of the dust, streaked with it where it clung to the sweat that slicked her body. "I can go on," she said weakly as she rested on her hands and knees. "We have to go on."

"No —"

"Let Kelly in." Ursula closed her eyes for a moment because everything tilted to the left.

"We're going to stop."

Ursula wasn't confident that she could stand, and every muscle in her body shouted outrage that she tried. She swayed on her feet and managed a step, then a second.

Taylor realized where she was going and stood between Ursula and the threshold. Ursula raised her head and though she was panting for breath, she said steadily, "Get out of my way." From somewhere deep, somewhere that had been awakened by the pain, she put the force of her will behind her words.

Taylor went pale and stepped aside as if she did not want to.

Ursula faced Kelly through the circle's rim. "I need you."

"I'm getting you out of there before they kill you!"

"No, I need you to help me get through this."

"No! Are you crazy —"

"Yes. And you are my anchor. I need you."

Kelly eyes glittered with angry tears. "How can you ask me to do this? I can't let them hurt you."

"I need you, but I can't let you in if you're going to interfere. I can't get through this without you, and I must do this. I don't know why —" Ursula stopped herself. Hysteria wouldn't convince Kelly of anything. She took a deep breath. "You must trust me."

Kelly looked as if Ursula had punched her in the stomach. "I can't —"

"Then I will do it alone. Please — please stop trying to get in." She gestured at her body and was certain of every word she said. "I'm more naked than you see. If the circle fails I'm lost to the darkness."

She turned back to Taylor and said hoarsely, "I'm ready."

From behind her, more welcome than any sound she had ever heard in her life, came Kelly's quavering voice. "I'll help you. Please let me in."

The silence in the club was absolute, even the clatter of the bar. Autumn had felt the enormous surge of power in her body but had no idea what had transpired. She tried to gather her wits and knew that in only a moment Ed would storm the stage, not at all convinced her scream was part of the act.

She was saved by a frantic pounding and nearly hysterical laughter.

Julie, in her tight jeans, with her eyes wild and hair almost standing on end, succeeded in kicking open the door. It was not the cardboard wardrobe she stepped out of, but the magician's box made of yew by Autumn's own hands.

The audience went crazy as Julie whooped and jumped like a cheerleader whose team had just won the big game. Ed pounded the table with his big hands and looked proud enough to bust a gut.

Autumn hid her face in her hands as the voice, that nearly useless voice, rang in her head so loudly she thought everyone would hear.

You are a magician. You are the daughter of yourself, always a magician, suffering to grow and learn. You are a magician, you are a warrior, you are a woman, and you are ready.

It was her voice, all her voices, in all the languages she had learned over the many years that she had labored on this one trick, her one hope.

She was ready.

Ursula did not know how Kelly's arms could still be around her. She no longer had any voice to scream, but her body writhed in agony while Kelly held her and cried with her.

The hands were unmaking her, thought by thought, breaking her into shards of herself so small, so pitiful, that Ursula had to battle not the pain, but the despair that it was for nothing. There was already so little of her left.

She was surrounded by strangers, but for Kelly. Strangers were unraveling everything she had ever been, all her trust, her love, her innocence, her wisdom. She would never be that again. The pain was bringing clarity, a level of perception that equaled any she had ever worked with. Kelly's heartbeat was loud in her ear, along with her choked gasps when Ursula couldn't stop herself from digging in her toes and pushing against her with all the strength she had left. She could feel every speck of dust on her skin and each weighed on her like a mountain. Nothing was her friend, nothing danced for her or filled her with light. The darkness was coming just as it had on the ship. But this was her darkness. It was enormous. She had never known it was in her and never made it part of her.

The hands began on the last of the three inner braids, and she shuddered with an agony so intense that Liz, deep in induced sleep, cried out. Taylor's exhaustion was also plain. She was all that held the circle together, drawing on her companions and herself beyond what they had known they were capable of. They were all finding their abyss and falling toward the bottom. It would be sunrise soon, and with it a small boost of energy from the new day. Ursula knew in her heart that none of them could make it that long.

The club was deserted but for her. Even Ed had finally agreed to leave about an hour earlier, after extracting a promise from her that she would take a cab home. It was nearly three A.M. Autumn was sleepy and tired, but it was still Midsummer's Night.

She made sure one last time that she was alone. The doors were locked and she only sensed herself. There were no ripples against her gate.

Her gate — it was a part of her now. She had always had it and not known it for what it was. It was made up of her intuition and self-reliance, her fierceness and instinct for survival. She could not open it as Ursula had, because she did not know how to make the tunnel. Instead she had the power of the *Spiralig Tor*.

The *Spiralig Tor*, the Spiral Gate, what she had only known as the magician's box, was a tool she had labored lifetime after lifetime to create. Failure in its use had always cost her memories until only instinct drove her forward. She had been forced to start over, again and again, a new person in a new life who knew less and less.

She had built its energy by making it with her hands. She had tested it and herself tonight, by bringing a living thing, a giggling, unsuspecting woman, into its confines. It had been a journey of only a few feet, only the span of Autumn's arms, but it was more than she had ever achieved. If her visions in the tunnel were true, she had made hundreds of attempts, and had died or gone mad with each failure.

She was ready, but she still did not know for what. Learning the secrets of the *Spiralig Tor* had been her one hope for a very long time, and she knew she had only begun. She would not leave until Midsummer's Night was ended. Perhaps she had learned all she was to learn for the night, but she had only a few hours to wait.

She sat with her back to the door of the box, feeling its power almost like a heartbeat. It was some time before she realized she had slipped into a light doze. She woke with a start and realized her hands were tingling. Her back was covered with sweat as if there was a fire inside the box.

She checked her personal gate, the one that stood between her and the river of chaos. She envisioned a heavy padlock on its latch and heavy steel bars securely sealing it. She would not travel that way. Then she carefully touched the door of the *Spiralig Tor*. The yew wood was almost hot enough to burn.

The door opened onto a spiraling mass of dust and light. The river of chaos was a whirlpool here, with a solid center that could be a tunnel. To find out she had to put her hand in it. A single act of courage was all that was necessary.

From the center of the spiral came a low, throaty laugh, hungry, insatiable and familiar.

Ursula had nothing left. None of them did, except Kelly. Her last braid was loosened to the final coil of strands. No one, not even Taylor, had the strength to undo it. The circle wavered in its intensity and would soon fall.

She was stripped of power, almost of consciousness, and all she knew was failure.

She felt loving hands at the nape of her neck. No longer strangers who unraveled her essence, but Kelly, whose tears were the source of some of the salt on Ursula's face.

She was beyond words and tried to express her gratitude with a smile, but when their gazes met Kelly faltered.

"Don't look at me," she whispered. "You look like — like when I was Killera. Oh god." Her voice rose. "I can't hurt you any more. I can never make up for it."

:It wasn't you and this pain . . . not you.: She wasn't getting through, she could tell.

"All I wanted to do was love you, all I ever longed for was your love, and I ruined it. I ruined it on the ship, and it's ruined for all time because I did it again."

:No, no, don't.: Kelly felt more than she had let on, far more, and Killera's ghost was heavy in her. The centuries-old guilt stayed Kelly's hands as Ursula hung suspended between her past and future, with the pain so intense that all at once she wanted to die. Anything was better than this.

The darkness surged against what was left of the circle. Its cruel emptiness hungered for her mind. Something flickered so far inside her that its dull, exhausted light was almost not enough to remind her she still had something to lose, more than her life. *:I will not go there again. Never again.:*

Kelly was a broken mountain. Ursula felt as if all the crumbling stone had fallen on her. Her throat was choked with dust and she coughed to clear it. "Kelly." It was no more than a croaked whisper.

Kelly's eyes opened at the sound of Ursula's voice. "Save your strength —"

"What she did . . . Killera . . ." She swallowed hard, nauseated by what she was going to do, and afraid of the price her desperation would demand of her if she survived this. "What Killera did. It hurt and I forgave her. What you did . . . it didn't hurt much at all and I of course forgave you. But if you don't help me now . . ." She coughed once and could not catch her breath until she nearly fainted. "If you don't help me now, I will not forgive you."

Kelly moaned. "Ursula, don't."

"If you don't help me now, it will mean you never loved me."

208

"Don't!"

"Please," Ursula pleaded. "I can't do it myself. They're all exhausted. What they have left is for Taylor to protect us." Ursula knew that none of them could break their concentration to move, and Taylor had already dangerously depleted them and herself. Daybreak was too far away. "Please. Prove that you love me."

Kelly's fingers were at the nape of her neck again and Ursula knew that perfect trust was not why. Not even perfect love, not any more, but manipulated guilt. She felt surrounded by debts to be paid with her own potent coin and this would be one of the largest. Kelly would never forgive her. Two guilty souls could not heal each other.

The last strands parted. She did not have anything left in her to even wince although every nerve burned. Every thought and memory was a throbbing blur.

She had nothing left. Taylor and the circle had nothing left. Kelly, finally, had nothing left.

The circle was coming down.

Fear paralyzed Autumn as she heard Rueda's laughter coming from deep within the spiral. It seemed unrooted in time or place, ever present and ever seeking. Had she labored for this moment only to die again? Was that her destiny? What had she done to deserve that kind of fate?

And then she heard, shimmering like daybreak, a single voice, raised in longing. She listened as the voice rose, and rose, and rose again. Autumn had traveled so far on its strength.

So many journeys . . . seabirds taking wing over the moors of Aldtyme . . . echoes of a stone abbey in the German countryside. She pressed her face to a locked grill separating the guest quarters from the abbey cloister. She violated the abbey's hospitality by her very desire to enter where she was forbidden. But the music drew her in, and few locks had any power to stop her. She touched it gently and the grill noiselessly swung open.

She walked the newly cut stairs toward the quarters of the abbess herself, who had built this place of honor to Saint Ursula. The abbess had also written a liturgy for Saint Ursula's feast day. Ever since Autumn had heard a single strain, a snippet of verse, she had known she must speak personally with this woman. But the abbess was seeing no one this week. The prioress said the abbess was consumed with the Living Light, the force that worked through her to pen the verses and responsories of masses for all the sacred hours, commissioned by bishops, lauded by popes, and singularly familiar to Autumn. She had not yet forgotten why this music called her.

"The burden of fire is upon you," the voice sang in Latin, melancholy even as it rose in clear brightness. "The blood of Ursula is upon us, now let us all rejoice."

The door was slightly ajar, and through it Autumn heard the scratching of a quill. She further opened the door and saw that the abbess's back was to her. The abbess repeated what she had just sung, then wrote vigorously on the parchment before her.

Having come this far, Autumn paused, and sought for the best way to interrupt the abbess's work.

The abbess put the pen down. "I've been expecting you. I did not know I would have to wait so long."

Autumn held to the threshold as Hilea turned to face her. The spiral washed over Hilea's face and Autumn was not in an abbey, but on the dimly lit stage, clinging to the edge of the Spiral Gate, about to fall in.

Rueda's laughter still echoed, and Hilea's voice surged again. After her voice came her face, the wimple of a twelfth-century abbess replaced by a shock of magenta-streaked hair. "What the fuck took you so long?"

"I don't know what you mean."

"Of course you don't. How did I get so lucky?" A spasm of pain washed over Hilea's face. "No! Not again!" Her mouth opened and no sound came out, then the light of her visage and the power of her voice was gone.

The spiral glowed as a cry of unsurpassed victory almost shattered it. Rueda had what she craved.

Autumn knew what that was.

She was ready.

They had all fallen, even Hilea's voice. It was up to her now. It had always been up to her.

She plunged her hands into the spiral. A burning heat seared them, but Autumn did not pause. Her spirit fell into the spiral's embrace.

Someone was singing and Ursula felt the burden of fire upon her. The circle was down and the darkness from the ship, the darkness that had lurked outside her gate, that had kept her from all the answers she had needed to avoid this moment, that darkness was all around her. Its claws raked over her mind and would never be sated.

:I won't go there again. I won't.: But she had no strength left to fight. What she had been was gone. Her unbound hair felt like bonds, holding her immobile as the darkness claimed her body and her soul.

:You came willingly to this place.: The terrible caress of the darkness was all over her. *:At last.:*

Fight, Ursula told herself. She had nothing left to fight with, not even Kelly, whose breathing was frighteningly shallow. The darkness would win again and she would lose all she loved again. She had not even found Autumn, her Autumn, and the darkness would win.

:You don't have to find her. I already did. She was delicious.:

The last flicker of light in her went out. She had no reason to fight now. The singing abruptly stopped and the darkness laughed with a woman's voice, triumphant.

For the time it took for Ursula's heart to beat once and once again, nothing happened. It was as if the world held its breath. Then Ursula's head began to pound with the wings of a thousand birds as the unbearable scream of a single note from an electrified guitar pierced the darkness with the shimmer of daybreak.

Hands reached for her from the shimmer of light. They were not the darkness, so Ursula strained to clasp them. She had done this before, in the backseat of Kelly's car, and she reached up, reached up —

This time hands joined. Hands coursing with magic, hands nearly drained of life. They stretched across a continent, and this time were met.

211

Thirteen

There was no torch light to help find the shore, only the impression of what was water and what was land. Ursula just saved herself a stumble that would have drenched her traveling cloak with salt water. She found more sure footing once she was on the matted roots where forest met ocean. They came to shore just south of the greatest of the rivers that broke the coast of Germania.

:I am safe.:

Hilea was next over the side of the small boat that tendered three of them to the shore. Though the crewman handled her gently, she also nearly fell, but kept a tight rein on her mouth. *:Damnation, the water's cold. Not the way I would have spent Midsummer's Night.:*

Killera had no trouble finding her feet even after so long at sea. She was a solid, comforting presence at the dark forest's edge.

The boat pushed off for the second of its two journeys. Elspeth and their bundles would come on the second trip, and the four of them, armed with wits, coin, and Aunt Lillidd's herbs and teas, were free. How long they would be free was another matter.

When they'd left Aldtyme, Ursula had wondered if she was leading her dearest friends into a worse life. She wondered still, but that fear was nothing compared to the wretched ache in her bones and the misery that pounded at her temples from a prolonged bout of crying. She had not cried until the pain of holding back the tears was more bitter than the tears themselves.

Autumn . . . Autumn . . . She longed to reach out with her mind, but Autumn was not for her. They were to part and had always known it would be so. Fate had made the place of their departure not Jutland, but Germania, a gift from Edrigo, who placed high value on his daughter's life and his ship. Ursula knew he would suffer for this decision, but the *Verdant Bough*'s scars from battle with the pirate ship had been enhanced to bolster the tale that the pirates had not failed to take the women and dowry. A nearly crippled *Verdant Bough* would limp into the docks at Haarlem, at least two days north, and report that the pirate had last been seen heading north, but had also been on fire.

Ursula felt she had taken far more from the captain than she had given. His honor was essential to his survival, and it might not bear the disgrace of failing to deliver her to Jutland. She could not ask for his daughter, too. And so she had not asked. Autumn was a wild and free creature of the sea. At best Ursula could offer her a confined monastic life with little fresh air and adventure to break up the days.

Autumn . . . Autumn . . . How she had longed for freedom, then valued it so little when she knew it meant leaving Autumn behind. She had the freedom she had hoped for, ever since her foster father had told her of the marriage, and freedom brought her nothing but sorrow. Her journey's ending was but a beginning, and each step would be heavy with loss and fear. She had her friends to help her, but the burden was not theirs to carry. She could only leave Autumn now because their freedom brought them a chance at happiness and she could not shirk her responsibility.

~ ~ ~ ~ ~

There were no lanterns lit on the deck of the *Verdant Bough* for the fourth night in a row. Autumn thanked the merciful fog for hiding them from the full moon, but wished too that she could see Edrigo's face as he listened to the muted whispers of the crew who were helping their passengers steal ashore.

He had told her he didn't do it for her but for his own honor. He had incurred a potent debt to the Lady Ursula, to her and the three other women. His honor did not allow him to deliver her to a life she neither asked for nor wanted.

The value of the ordinary cargo they carried would be just enough to repair the gaping slash that Edrigo himself had cut, separating a half dozen brails from the heavy mainsail. It would not be enough to repair the burned decking and riggings. They dared not use the unmarked gold plate Ursula had left for them, the valuable but heavy plate she could not carry with her. They could sell it when they reached Italy, where there would be less chance of anyone wondering how the ransacked *Verdant Bough* had come by such wealth.

Their story of the Jut-speaking pirates might save Edrigo his reputation and might mean that Ursula and the others would not be pursued where they were headed. Let the Juts suspiciously look among themselves for the missing bride, Autumn thought, and wonder if she went to the bottom of the sea.

She contemplated such things to drown out the pain of her heart shredding in her breast. There was not enough light for it, but she swore she knew exactly where on the shore Ursula stood. She knew because something not her eyes could see in the dark and would always be able to see Ursula.

She stifled a sob and pretended interest in the stars. They were empty and cold where once they had been warm and loving, when she had lain among them with Ursula in her arms.

"I would tell you something." Edrigo spoke in a near whisper, his voice gruff.

She inclined her head to listen, not able to speak.

"You will be angry, but it must be said." When Autumn didn't answer, he sighed. "Tain wished it so, or I would not have lied to you. There was little I could refuse him. It made sense at the time, and once the lie was said it was hard to say otherwise."

Thoroughly confused, Autumn swallowed hard and whispered. "What is it?"

"You know that Tain was but sixteen when he came into my life, and I was twice his age. Though I loved him true, he had no money, no rank, and couldn't find the north star an' it was the only one shining."

Autumn nodded. She had heard all of this before.

"He had one thing of value, and he pledged me to care for it, because even as my bedmate, he felt he could not protect so precious a thing. No one feared him or what I might do on his behalf. There were many who saw him as little more than my catamite."

"Father," she said sharply. More quietly she added, "That is not true." Tain had not been on board the *Verdant Bough* merely to service her father's sexual pleasures.

"He felt all his vulnerability, in those early days. So I agreed to take his one thing of value, to call it my own, and protect it as I protected him."

Autumn's breath rattled in her throat, and she thought for a moment she might faint. Her fingers twitched as she recalled how easily Tain had taught her to palm dice and other tricks with coins. He had said she could be good at it, if only she would practice . . . gods.

Gods.

"It was him, then, who fathered me?" Autumn tried to make it sound as if she did not care, but she did care, she cared dreadfully.

"You do take after your mother, Tain said, but I see him in you, your hands, your quick wits, your fearlessness. Autumn," he said passionately, putting one hand on her arm. "I love you as my daughter. At first I protected you for his sake, but within a week I was your willing servant. And always shall be. But it is his blood in your veins."

She looked to the shore and felt an immense pang of disloyalty. That she should take this information and think less of her place by Edrigo's side — it was not fit.

"I tell you because I think that many will find it odd the pirates took them and not you as well. Pirates are pirates and women, especially beautiful, young ones, are valuable."

He was choking back tears as he spoke, giving her a reason both to no longer cling to his side and to excuse her eagerness to go.

Elspeth and the bundles they would carry were already lowered into the boat. Edrigo hissed a signal into the heavy night air, and the boat didn't push toward shore, not yet.

"Go quickly and think of me often."

She held him to her as she had the night Tain died. "I shall never forget you," she whispered, and she prayed that she would keep that promise.

She was blinded by tears and darkness, but could still walk the deck that had made up her world all these years. She made it to her cabin without a false step. Her bow and quiver were necessary, and a quick bundle made of more clothing and boots as well. From the back of a drawer she drew the only gown she owned, little more than a plain black robe, and she rolled it into the bundle. She kept the dagger and sheath in her right boot as always.

She did not know if Ursula wanted her to come with them. She had not asked. She would have to trust, then. Trust that when Ursula said it had meant everything to lie with her she had meant it.

There was a mournful whine at her door and Autumn let Scylla in. She hugged the half-dog, half-wolf and knew she would take Scylla with her. She had protected Ursula with selfless devotion and would be useful in ways Autumn could not even foresee.

From her cabin she slipped into what would be again Edrigo's cabin. The little box of coins and ivory cubes was in the chest under the bed. Tain's box of what he had laughingly called magic tricks was made of the same wood as her bow, painted black and covered with tiny runes and symbols. It was all she had of him, that and his blood in her veins.

She covered her bright hair with the hood of her heavy, oiled cloak and went back on deck with Scylla at her heels. Her last stop was at the crate of weapons. She selected four slender daggers in leather sheaths and knew Edrigo would not begrudge them.

"I am glad she goes with you," Edrigo said as Scylla nudged and licked his fingers. "Though I love her, she will protect you better than any man I would have sent."

"Father," Autumn breathed, and she meant the word in all its variations. "I will try to send word."

Edrigo said nothing more as Autumn clambered into the netting that would lower her to the waiting boat.

She heard whispered partings from the crew on deck, then gruff, choked encouragement to Scylla as she was lowered as well. She heard a fervent, "I'm going to miss you, girl," and did not know which of them it was meant for. It did not matter.

"I am glad," Elspeth whispered as the oars silently cut the water. "Your place is with us. I have known it all along. We reach our journey's end."

Autumn trusted Ursula knew it too.

Why did she hold on? Ursula clasped the hands that had broken through the darkness, the hands that came from shimmering light. She held on, but did not know why.

Her hair was in her eyes, an unfamiliar obstacle. She could not see, but she felt the chaos pressing in, wanting what sanity she had left. She felt the darkness caressing her mind, still exultant. It did not know about the hands throbbing with power that held tightly to hers, not yet.

The hands lifted her off her feet and she kicked at whatever pulled her back to the ground. Fly, she wanted to fly, to soar to the stars and be warm and safe, away from cold darkness, away from the endless bedlam of chaos.

She hung suspended by her hands, exhausted and unable to reason what was happening. Her personal gate was only a visualization, and yet it seemed to be a real portal now. It wasn't her mind, but her dirt-streaked body that slowly rose through it, all of her, even the masses of hair that were incomprehensibly unbound around her.

Journey's beginning — journey's end. She didn't know which it was, had never known, might never know.

:Beloved.: The syllables rang in her ears, cutting through the cacophony. The hands held her wrists now and pulled, stretching her to a new level of pain as a dead weight seized her ankles and the vicious darkness finally realized she had help from the light shimmering like daybreak.

She kicked weakly at what restrained her and heard a curse. She looked down. Kelly was holding her and would never let go of her own volition. *:You must trust me, yet again. I am sorry.:*

Kelly held her though she looked pale enough to faint. *:This can't be happening!:*

:You must let me go, completely. This is the last time I will ask you to prove you love me.:

Kelly's grip slipped and just as Taylor's hands would have joined her she let go, no longer an anchor. Her deeply wounded eyes were the last image Ursula remembered of her before she soared upward, her body like a rocket.

She felt as if no part of her was spared the biting hunger of the darkness that wanted her. She had endured pain beyond reckoning while her braid was undone, and it had opened her mind enough to see the hands that would save her. Now she felt talons of cruelty inside her mind as the darkness destroyed what it could not possess.

The hands lifted her higher and higher, through the chaos, past it, over a wasteland of salt, so far to the west.

The shimmer of light went out. There were no hands, only her shaking body trapped in a space so small she could not bend or turn.

Behind her she heard the snarl of the darkness.

The boat bearing Elspeth ran aground, and Killera helped her cousin to the shore while a crewman carefully carried the bundles of clothing and coin onto the wooded bank. Hilea whispered thanks and told one last bawdy joke to make the men snicker, then the boat pushed off, severing all their ties with their past.

The blowing fog thinned, for just a moment, and the brilliant light of the full moon shone down on a solitary figure wrapped in a dark cloak. For a moment Ursula thought one of the crew had been left behind by accident.

Joy pierced her when she realized the truth and she stumbled down the bank heedless of tree roots and cold seawater.

She stopped short of Autumn's open arms. "You should have stayed on the ship. It is safer."

"What do I need safety for?"

"I could not bear it if you were hurt because of me."

"I'm already wounded to my very heart. I could not stay."

"If I ordered you to?"

"Are you a goddess today? That is what it would take." Autumn's chin lifted, then the moonlight winked out. From the darkness she quavered, "Didn't it mean anything to you?"

It was so selfish, to love so much that she could not give Autumn up. Their safety was all on her now, and yet the journey ahead seemed like nothing. The prospect of hardship, hunger and blistered feet was invigorating.

Ursula said softly into the darkness, her voice carrying as inexorably as the tide swirling at their feet, "Beloved, it meant everything." Journey's beginning, again.

Autumn knew her hands were burning, but she also knew what she grasped and would not let go. An unsuspecting woman, uncooperative even, with forces trying to keep her where she was, or carry her to someplace new — Autumn would never let go.

Rueda's laughter had stopped, and now there was a sound like a hungry animal fighting for its meat. The ravenous snarl raised all of Autumn's hackles, and she grappled with the fear engendered by it. She fought to bring what she grasped to her side of the spiral because she was a magician and she was strong.

:In a garden of fruit, among the splendor of flowers, we feed among the lilies in a garden of fruit.: The words came easily to Autumn, and though she did not have Hilea's voice she knew the power of the spell. *:In a garden of fruit, among the splendor of flowers, we feed among the lilies in a garden of fruit. We join with Ursula.:*

Light rebounded behind her eyes as the howling darkness

seemed to reach for her. She fell back, smacking her shoulder and head on the hard stage floor. Her arms felt as if she would never be able to raise them again.

The door of the *Spiralig Tor* was closed, but the box vibrated with energy. The dark wood glowed with impossible light.

She heard Rueda's laughter again, the low, pleased sound of having. She could not let Rueda through the spiral and had no idea how to stop her. She prayed she would know what to do when she needed to do it and snatched open the door again.

Astonishing black eyes, a wild mass of red hair. Autumn could not take it in. She blinked, but the vision remained. Tear-streaked, filthy and naked, knees scraped and body shivering with distress . . . a divine goddess stood inside the *Spiralig Tor*. Autumn lost herself in those eyes, wanted to lose herself in the mouth, the hair.

She had never met this woman and knew her intimately. *Most beautiful sight, sweetest scent of desired delights, I long ever after you in tearful exile. When may I see you and be with you?* Now, her heart cried and she reached out with her scorched hands.

"What are you doing?" Ursula was backing into the still turning spiral.

"Beloved." It felt so good to say it.

"Who are you? Where are my clothes?"

Autumn felt as if she'd been punched, not once, but for a lifetime. How could Ursula not know? She was so lost in confusion that she did not see the face that materialized in the spiral, not right away. Eerie green light dancing on the dagger was what unparalyzed her, and she snatched Ursula onto the stage as the dagger seemed to whistle past their ears.

You are a magician, you are a woman, you are a warrior. She faced the dagger that had cut her open less than a month ago. She knew it for her own, could even feel the callus on her ankle where it had once rubbed in her boot, many lifetimes ago. She did not know how she had lost it to the darkness. She faced the hand that had wielded it and knew no fear.

"You shall have nothing else of me or her!"

Rueda's lips curved with cruel intent. "I always win."

Autumn looked through the open door and into the green-now-blue eyes. "This is my stage, my gate. I win here." She slammed the door of the *Spiralig Tor* and threw all her weight on her hands, leaning hard into the hot wood to keep the shuddering door firmly closed. The burning pain grew worse and worse as the box began to shimmy across the stage, dancing with the energy trapped in its confines. The burden of fire was upon her now and she did not let go.

That first night they walked along the great river, following animal tracks that Scylla seemed to find with ease. When they rested and shared out their meager provisions Scylla loped into the woods and returned a short while later looking sated. Autumn held Ursula's hand while they rested, and it was her only demand. Still, Autumn could feel Killera's resentment like salt water on a cut. Hilea seemed to welcome her, though she said nothing except to complain about the thorns and hidden mud holes. Elspeth had withdrawn again, looking wan in the infrequent moonlight.

At daybreak they settled in a tight copse of pines, snug in a thicket that had probably been home to a family of deer during winter. Autumn smiled to herself, remembering her earliest impression of pampered court women. They had all made themselves comfortable on the ground without a demur. The day was warm and Autumn knew she would have no trouble sleeping, especially with Scylla standing guard.

She spread her cloak for herself and lay down, resting her head on the bundle of clothing. She was nearly asleep when she felt Ursula snuggle to her back, one arm around her waist. Ursula spread her cloak over them both, and Autumn was not embarrassed by the happy tears that soaked her makeshift pillow.

Autumn knew she was asleep and yet she felt awake. She saw the woman on the other ship, her regal bearing, the dark light that sparkled around her. In her dream the arrow passed right through the woman, leaving her undamaged. The woman turned her gaze to Autumn's vulnerable position in the riggings and seemed to reach across the space between them to wrest Autumn's dagger from her boot. She saw the dagger arc toward her, green light dancing on the tip.

Autumn gasped awake and sat bolt upright. She was abruptly aware that the others had all done the same, including Ursula.

They looked to Ursula for an answer, though Autumn already knew.

"We are pursued."

She had labored more lifetimes than she knew to learn how to make the *Spiralig Tor*, but all Autumn could think about now was how to destroy it — without letting go.

She did not know what she had trapped inside, but she knew what it was capable of. She no longer had just herself to guard. Ursula was still sprawled on the stage and did not seem able to get up.

She did not know any words of power, at least not yet. If she failed this lifetime perhaps in the next she would know to learn some.

No, she thought. She had found Ursula, had saved her from this thing that gibbered inside the box. Failure was not an option.

She heard a sound of stirring behind her, and the distraction cost her dearly. The *Spiralig Tor* seemed almost alive as it thrust against her, burning her cheek. She was on her knees now, and her hands slipped once, then again.

A slender hand, streaked with dirt, touched the *Spiralig Tor,* and all its motion ceased. Autumn wanted to relax her trembling arms, but she did not trust that it was over.

A moment later the door almost burst open as the fury of the darkness slammed against it. Autumn heard the hinges creak, but they held for now.

"I can't, not again." Ursula slid to her knees, then all the way to the floor. Ursula knew how to fight this darkness, but was too far gone from some ordeal of her own. Autumn held the door closed because it was all she knew to do. She knew she could not do it forever.

Something not Ursula and not the darkness and not the river of chaos flickered in her awareness. Someone was coming into the club. Another distraction. Autumn slipped and had to put her shoulder and face against the door to keep it closed. The heat was intense and she felt a wash of memory from another fire, when she had been surrounded by angry, frightened people who cheered the flames.

"Get down!"

She ducked her head but would not let go. Something whistled just over her head and buried itself in the wood. The back of the ax bumped her forehead as Ed plucked it free.

She scrambled out of its path and Ed swung again, then again, and again. He did not stop when a blinding light poured out of the cracks in the *Spiralig Tor,* nor did he seem to hear the insane laughter and screams from inside. Autumn felt a gate open, not her own, not Ursula's, and then everything on the stage not nailed down sailed toward the gaping swirl. Autumn saw her cards spill into its depths, the stool, too, and then it began to pull her toward it.

The ax fell again, and chunks of black painted wood were sucked into the maelstrom. Ed seemed completely unaware of it as he raised his weapon one last time. With a great cry he buried the ax into the side of the *Spiralig Tor* and the box exploded, splinters of it flying in all directions.

The swirling gate was snapped shut and Autumn's ears rang with sudden cessation of noise. She was hurt but there was no pain, not yet, to tell her where.

Ed panted as he slowly sank down. "You didn't come home. Scylla woke me up and I swear — I swear she told me you needed an ax." He shook his head, all disbelief and worry. "An ax, so I got one and then" — Ed's eyes widened in shock — "Who . . .?"

Ursula had managed to get to her hands and knees. She was clad only by her lank and matted hair. "What . . . happened?"

Autumn slithered across the floor toward her, but only managed a few inches before pain immobilized her. She could not keep from bumping the three-inch splinter of wood that impaled her blistered left hand, nor the one almost as big in the back of her knee.

Ed said the most insane thing, just before Autumn fainted. "You're safe, my lady, safe for now."

Walking was not enough, not when what pursued them rode. They had planned to avoid the first few towns along the Rhine, but instead went boldly into the second they came to, using some of Ursula's dowry coins to buy horses for themselves. There were plenty of witnesses and a great deal of curiosity about the five women wanting horses. For a time it wasn't a sure thing the blacksmith would sell horses to unaccompanied women, but an unveiled Ursula persuaded him. It could not have been worse for their hopes of slipping deep into the countryside of Germania unnoticed.

Autumn did not know how to ride, and Ursula did not mind Autumn riding pillion behind her, not at all. She was afraid but in some ways had never been happier in her life. She loved and was loved.

Out of sight of the town they stopped by the river long enough to drink and change. Autumn's drab black gown was as suitable as Ursula's plain gray one for the guise of a nun and pilgrim.

Autumn shied away when Ursula offered a beaded necklace from which a silver cross dangled. Ursula quickly kissed it and said lowly, "There's nothing but love on this. It's not from the White Christ, but from me." It made her heart sing to see her gift gleaming on Autumn's breast. They had had no such moments before, and she did not know when they might again.

They rested when they could and went around as many villages and towns as the landscape would permit. They begged a night's stay as pilgrims at a small abbey near Arnhem and were on their way at daybreak.

It was Elspeth who first said that the pursuit had fallen far behind them and was perhaps gone for good.

"Why do you think so?" Killera was rubbing her horse's legs while it drank from one of the many cool streams that branched off the Rhine.

"That first day ashore, when we all woke up, I felt — I can't explain. Like something hungry, but more than that. I felt someone looking for us, and I haven't felt it all morning."

Ursula had the same feeling. "Maybe we could raise a circle and see what is there."

"I don't think that's a good idea," Autumn said sharply. Ursula forgave the tone because she knew that every part of Autumn's body ached from riding.

"What would you know about it?" Killera's simmering resentment was at the surface now.

"The first time I felt something like pursuit was the first time I worked with all of you, that night when we made the pirate ship turn back. It was after we'd raised a circle."

"Do you think that attracted someone's attention?" Ursula had never considered the possibility that the power of a circle could attract someone to it.

"If you'd been on the receiving end, would you have known? Wouldn't what we did have gotten your attention?"

"I suppose —"

"You don't know anything about it," Killera snapped at Autumn. "When we needed you most you pulled out of the circle. You have no idea the damage you caused."

"Killera!" Hilea's admonishment brought a dark flush to Killera's face. "We agreed not to speak of it."

Autumn looked chagrined but also defiant. "I did what I could to stop her, and —"

"Who?" Ursula and Hilea asked the question in unison.

"The woman — didn't you see her?"

"What woman?"

"On the other ship." Autumn looked beseechingly at Ursula.

Ursula had felt nothing but the darkness spilling through her gate. "You were higher than we were."

"She was not there at the beginning. When I noticed her she was surrounded by light, like you were when we . . ." Autumn blushed as she recalled what the light had witnessed. Ursula knew her own color was high as well. "When the pirates attacked, you had just surrounded me with the circle and stopped that fire arrow. Her light was dark, and it was like what I felt, being inside the circle with you at that moment. I was looking at her light, and it was behind my eyes, too. I don't know how to explain otherwise."

Hilea said with dread excitement, "I know what you mean. You were looking at the source of the darkness. We all heard a woman's scream, just before the attack stopped."

"That was Scylla and my arrow. I left the circle because I needed to concentrate on shooting."

Ursula knew Autumn was looking at her for reassurance. She had not talked to Autumn about how she'd left the circle during the battle, mostly because she had had other things to say when they would be so soon parted. "I understand why you did it." She held out one hand. "Show me what you saw, your thoughts. Like I showed you . . . that night."

Autumn's eyes were as murky as the ocean when it rained. She lifted her chin bravely, however, and put her hand in Ursula's.

:It is easy for us now.:

Autumn's reply was shaky, and Ursula did not understand why she was still afraid. *:This is what I saw.:*

The images came all in a rush because Autumn had had no practice at sharing. Ursula clearly saw the woman's green-blue eyes as well as the chestnut-blond hair coiled on her brow like a crown. She had not expected to recognize her and wasn't disappointed.

:You had no choice.:

:Ursula, I . . .: Autumn shuddered and shut her mind.

Ursula realized then, Autumn's reluctance to touch minds. Just before she ended their link Ursula had felt a surge of all the desire and love that she was keeping to herself, knowing it for a distraction.

:Beloved, don't go.: For one long moment Ursula wanted to release the flood of her own pent-up words and whisper her feelings into Autumn's ears. If she did that, she knew she would not stop. If a circle would attract attention, then the light that threatened to suffuse her as she felt Autumn's love so near might do the same. It would be unnecessarily dangerous. They slept together under one cloak, and it was all there could be, for all their sakes. Some day they would find a place to rest, just the two of them.

Hilea's knowing glance told Ursula that her feelings were no secret to the others. Ursula touched Autumn's hand to her lips before she let it go and then pushed all she felt down inside her, as far away as Aldtyme, as far away as the stars. They would have a later.

"I have no idea who it was." Ursula turned from Autumn's nearness and sat heavily on a rock. "But Autumn was right, that woman attacked me through my gate, and I guess it's possible she knew she could do that because we had raised our circle so vividly."

Another thought occurred to her, and she caught her breath.

"What is it?" Killera sat down beside her.

"He owed me nothing." Ursula did not know why the realization struck her so harshly. "I — we saved Autumn and she saved me. He need not have put us ashore."

Autumn knelt quickly before her. "He would not have seen it

that way. You saved me from the fire arrow, and no matter what happened after, he had a debt."

"What about my debt?"

"Your debt is to me." Autumn lips curved in an unwilling smile. "I shall demand recompense at another time."

Lightly said, but Ursula shivered as if Autumn had uttered prophecy. "I am not as sure as Elspeth that what pursues us has given up. So we'll go with haste and not use the circle to gather information, not yet."

They rode into the waning afternoon, not sure where they were, but always following the river. Ursula knew of a Benedictine abbey near Cologne that supported a women's house. They would at a minimum be able to rest there for a time. As for staying — she did not know. Her heart was with Autumn wherever she was. She did not see Autumn taking well to the religious life. She did not know where, in this impossibly large world, they could be safe and together.

"She's safe. Scylla is with her. Won't leave her side, in fact." Ed looked her up and down, then gently patted Autumn's head. Considering the wealth of bandages on her hands, half her face, her left knee and shoulder, the top of her head was a safe choice.

"Is she . . . okay?" Autumn had insisted that Ed leave her at the hospital and take Ursula home where, as he said, she knew Scylla would watch over her.

"She didn't say much beyond thank-you, but does listen. Wouldn't eat anything, though. She curled up on your bed and went to sleep, still wearing your jacket."

Ursula was unchanged, then. She had looked at Autumn as if she did not recognize her. The emptiness of her gaze was almost unbearable after seeing those black eyes dance with sunlight and glitter in the light they had made with their love.

She did not know where this Ursula had come from and her dreams told her nothing. She'd been asleep before Ed arrived, and her mind was murky with painkillers. Horses, a river, and the darkness she knew all too well coming behind them — that was all she remembered of what she'd dreamed. In those dreams, however, it had been very clear that the Ursula she knew was still with her companions.

Her dreams begged the question about exactly who Scylla was watching over. Autumn had thought that if she successfully brought Ursula to her that she would change the legend of Saint Ursula. But the past hadn't changed, and it hurt her head to puzzle over it. The only Ursula she knew still rode for an abbey near Cologne.

"I think you should stay here for today," Ed said.

"It's not as bad as it looks." Autumn had insisted on being discharged today and had listened to an endless droning lecture on the care of her burns. She was to take lots of cool baths with special goo dissolved in the water, exercise care air-drying the burned skin, and carefully apply layers of antibiotic ointment that promoted skin growth. She would rather do all that at home where she could at least look at Ursula. "The hand and knee are the worst of it, really, and they'd never let me stay overnight for either."

The doctors weren't sure she would get full dexterity of her fingers back in her left hand because it was impossible to tell how much muscle damage there had been. They'd compared the size of the wound to a small-caliber gunshot. The back of her knee wasn't nearly so bad, just tender as all get-out. She'd taken every prescription they'd written for painkillers and hoped there were refills.

Ed helped her up the stairs at home, and she was no longer afraid to lean on him. If she were to tell anyone she believed that she and Ed had known each other many, many times over many, many centuries they would think she was delusional.

She believed.

When she saw the dark tangle of Ursula's hair streaming over the edge of the bed, she believed.

When she saw the devotion in Scylla's eyes as she came through the door, she believed.

She soaked herself in cool water liberally laced with the burn goo and rubbed the ointment wherever she could reach. She carefully dried and bandaged her two puncture wounds and was ready to drop where she stood, but she found the energy to watch Ursula, for just a few minutes.

The delicate face was gaunt, and the fragile hands scraped and calloused. All the nails were broken, far from the white manicured beauty they had maintained on the ship. Her hair was tightly kinked in places, as if she had been in the act of unbraiding it when Autumn had taken her from wherever she had been.

All Autumn remembered of that place was the darkness she had had to traverse to reach it. The *Spiralig Tor* had given her the chance to reach Ursula first and take her from whatever place that had left her so vulnerable to Rueda's plans. All her pasts were quiet now, and whatever desperate acts she had committed in those pasts had been worth this moment.

A month ago she had felt nothing but distant contempt for everything, including herself. She had had no love or friendship or community, and precious little hope that it would ever be any different. She had love and friendship in abundance now, her soul finally released from an endless fixation. She still had questions, but answers could wait. She knew who Autumn was now. Over the long years she had been a sailor, a magician, a daughter, a gambler, a warrior, and always a woman in love. She was those things now and would never forget them again.

She watched Ursula's hands moving in her sleep and wondered what she dreamed. Eventually, when her eyes were sated, Autumn crept into bed next to her because it was the only place to sleep. She covered them both lightly with the sheet and contented herself with crossing one ankle under Ursula's.

The feel of this stranger's skin was familiar beyond words.

Fourteen

The five of them rode a journey of a week in four days, sparing neither their horses nor themselves. All feeling of pursuit was gone, but Ursula pressed them onward.

They slept in a woodsman's hut, in thickets, and the last night before they would reach Cologne in an orchard redolent with the heavy scent of oranges. The smell reminded Autumn of the day Ursula had stepped onto the deck of the *Verdant Bough*. She let it soothe her to sleep — no easy thing with most of her body an aching mass of muscle.

Scylla's growl snapped her awake, and she felt about for her dagger, bow and quiver. The moon was waning, but bright enough to see that they appeared to be alone. The horses were moving restlessly, however, and she heard Scylla's low growl again.

She was wearing her deck clothes to sleep in, sparing her fake nun's habit as much as possible. She was glad of it when she moved unhampered by a skirt. She wished for shoes when she stepped on something sharp.

Her dagger was warm in her hand. She was not afraid. Still, Ursula's methods might be more fruitful than a frontal assault on whatever was disturbing the horses. Human, not animal, she felt :*We're going to get caught.*:

There was a mumble of nervous voices. Two men, perhaps three. Horse thieves, Autumn thought. :*The camp is full of soldiers with bows and swords. They'll kill us.*:

She deliberately stepped on a fallen twig and heard a suppressed gasp. In as deep a voice as she could manage, she yelled, "Who goes?"

Scylla's deep bark and growl was all that was needed to send the men scurrying into the darkness like frightened rabbits.

She grinned and turned back to their camp where the other women were stirring. "Go back to slee—"

A heavy fist struck the side of her head, and she was knocked to the ground near Killera. The man fell on top of her, using his weight to his advantage as he grappled for her throat.

The other women were jolted awake by Autumn's cry and grunt of pain. Autumn tried to plant the image of a huge sword aimed at his neck, but her attacker was too far gone in anger and drink for either the trick to work or for him to care. Her hand with the dagger was trapped under her, and the weight on her was too heavy to get her hand free.

Killera was the first on her feet. The dagger Autumn had given her was in her hand. She looked at it in confusion, then dropped it to throw herself on the man's back. Autumn choked for air, then grunted from the extra weight as Hilea also tried to pull the man off of Autumn.

He snarled with rage when Scylla sunk her teeth into his calf. Autumn felt the pain radiate through him, then the combined effort of Killera and Hilea finally tipped him off of her. He rolled to his feet, knocking Hilea off of hers in the process, then shook off Killera's desperate grasp with a vicious punch to the side of her head. His screaming and Scylla's howls split the night, and one thing they did not need was more people wondering who they were and why they traveled this way.

Autumn's dagger flew true, a mere flick of her wrist. The screams of rage and pain were instantly silenced as the sharp blade buried itself in his throat.

Scylla's howls stopped almost as quickly and she backed shuddering against Autumn's legs. The only sound left was Elspeth being sick and Ursula's soothing whispers.

Once Elspeth could cling to Ursula's waist, they were on their way, leaving the body to tell its own story. Autumn rode Elspeth's horse because Ursula's bay was the only one that could carry double. The night was heavy on Autumn's skin, and it took all her concentration to stay in the unfamiliar saddle alone.

Killera guided her mare until she was level with Autumn. Autumn did not know what to expect. Although she'd explained why she had pulled out of the circle during the battle with the pirates, Killera had still not spoken directly to her since.

"I don't think I will ever call you friend," Killera said in a low voice. "You know why."

Autumn nodded. "I understand, I truly do." Were their positions reversed she would feel exactly as Killera did.

"But you have saved her twice now, and that is all that matters." She drew the dagger Autumn had given her from her boot. "When we settle, whenever that may be, I want you to teach me how to use this."

"I will," Autumn said lowly. "But I cannot teach you to kill."

"I understand. I would hope that necessity will teach me only what I must do and never that." She touched what Autumn knew must be a sizable bruise on the side of her head. "You were right to act, and so quickly."

They rode side by side for some time, more companionable than Autumn would have thought possible. She even hoped, just before daybreak shimmered in the fertile, rolling hills to the east, that they were leaving darkness behind at last. She would know, before the day ended, how foolish her thoughts had been.

Beyond the open door of the tiny bathroom, Ursula rose from the bathtub like Venus — Autumn could not help but make the comparison. She tried to hide how moved she was, how hungry and how full.

Ursula's nervous quickness to pull on Autumn's bathrobe told Autumn she had failed.

"I have some cereal, if you're hungry."

Ursula padded to the little table and shrugged her wet hair over her shoulder as if she did not know quite what to do with it. "Thank you."

They ate in silence while Autumn wondered why Ursula was so thin. She ate everything Autumn had given her, though, obviously not lacking for appetite. Autumn was glad to see a little color in her hollowed, pale cheeks.

"Why am I here?" Ursula had taken her dishes to the sink and now turned to face Autumn. If she was frightened, it didn't show.

Honesty was demanded. "I don't know."

"I know how I got here. You pulled me here. But . . . from where?"

"I don't know."

"Then why did you do it?"

Knowing that answering would take a very long time, Autumn parried with, "Tell me first who you are."

She shrugged. "I am Ursula."

"You don't know me, do you? Do you remember anything before yesterday?"

Ursula shook her head and there was a suspicion of tears in her eyes. Scylla padded across the floor to lean against Ursula's legs. Ursula tickled her ears absentmindedly, as if she'd done it so many times it required no thought.

Autumn wanted to hold her, but stayed where she was. "I know what that's like. I was that way for a long time. Then my past started coming back."

"What am I going to do?"

"Wait. Dream." It had, after all, worked for her. "You're safe here."

"I remember my dream from last night."

Autumn didn't ask. After a long, shared gaze, Ursula continued. "You were in it. We were traveling by horse . . . and you . . ."

"I killed someone. That was in my dream, too." A month ago

233

Autumn would not have believed she could do such a thing, but she believed now, that she would do it again if Ursula was in danger.

Ursula's swallow was audible. "I think I would like to rest now."

"Me too." Her painkillers were kicking in. "There's only the one bed, I'm sorry."

Ursula was stiff on the other side of the bed. Autumn wondered how to reassure her she was safe.

"I'll never take anything of you that you don't offer."

Her answer was very faint. "I know."

"Pleasant dreams, then . . ."

They made their way through Cologne's crowded streets, thankfully anonymous in the throngs at market. They left by the south gate and turned on the next road west. The abbey they sought was just beyond sight of the city.

Ursula felt her spirits lift as they enjoyed the midday sun. They'd stopped at a secluded stream before entering Cologne and bathed. It felt good to be clean. For the first time since leaving the *Verdant Bough* she enjoyed the lush surrounds. The forests, deep and old, teemed with life. The farms were healthy and productive, it seemed, with crops ripening to harvest. She knew the farmers in Aldtyme would already be counting their bushels and planning for the coming winter, but it was yet summer and the air was heavy with scent and the buzz of bees.

Hilea was singing about the garden of fruit and it was fit. Elspeth, still shaken by last night's events, hummed along as she swayed behind Ursula. Even Autumn and Killera seemed in harmony.

It was a beautiful day.

The abbey was nestled against hills to its north and east, with a flourishing orchard spreading to the southwest. Banners of noble guests snapped in the light breeze — a stag with eight-point horns leapt against green, and a white bear reared up on bright blue. The main buildings were small and made of thick stone. The grounds had no fortifications beyond a short fence designed more to keep livestock in and out than for any other purpose. The foregate was spacious and there were sufficient stables for guests.

The gates were open and why would they not be? Ursula slackened the reins, and her tired horse resumed a plodding walk. She went over in her mind what she would say to the abbot, how she would offer the heavy gold altar plate in her pack as dower for entrance into the women's community for the next few months.

There was no porter at the gate, so Ursula rode through, not yet surprised at the number of brown-frocked Benedictine brothers milling about. She halted in the center of the yard and looked about, wondering if someone would offer assistance or if she would have to be the first to speak.

She was facing the steps that led to the chapter house, where the abbot or prior might be expected to be. If this house was run like the one in Aldtyme, it was not yet time for sext and someone ought to be curious about the arrival of guests.

The door at the top of the steps opened and everything changed.

Autumn was last through the gate and furthest from the steps when the door opened. She stared in utter disbelief. She had seen her arrow find its mark and heard Scylla's attack. But it was the same woman, her cloak a bright blue. Today the cloak was trimmed with white bears at the hem. Her chestnut hair was coiled still, like a crown on her brow.

Autumn lacked the skill to back her horse, so she tried instead to circle toward escape, but hands seized the horse's bridle. She looked in surprise at the monk and saw the sleeve of the robe fall back to reveal hardened leather armor.

They were surrounded by soldiers, between half and a dozen. She tried to send Ursula a warning, mind to mind, but something heavy kept her thoughts in her own mind. She did not protest when her horse was brought level with Ursula's. If there was an escape it would have to be when the soldiers were dismissed. Not when, she told herself grimly, but if. They were neatly caught in a trap none of them had suspected.

"You are a long way from your wedding, and late besides." The woman's voice was husky and yet mellifluous. She stood proudly at the top of the steps, surveying everything as if she knew its price and had added it to her own accounts.

"We have come to seek sanctuary here, to enter this life as brides of Christ." Ursula played the only card she had. The words weren't out of her mouth before the woman laughed.

"A nun? You?" She raised one long hand and drew first one pin, then another from the coil of hair on her head. When she was done she shook it down and a braid, like the one Ursula wore, cascaded down her back. Autumn felt a chill and knew with certainty who this woman was. "We have so much in common that I'm certain how unpleasant you would find the monastic life. They ring the bell even in the middle of the night. I had to send Staghorn to stop it." She gestured at the soldier to her right.

He picked at his nails with his dagger, a cruel smile on his feral face. "The brothers have been uncommonly cooperative since, have they not?"

The woman's beautiful mouth curved in a smile that echoed the one on her lieutenant's face. "Indeed. But enough of the boredom of this place." She addressed herself to Ursula. "This place is not for you. Let us greet one another as we should. We shall soon be relatives."

Ursula did not move, and if she was surprised to be facing the daughter of her husband-to-be, it did not show. "I have no intention of marrying."

"My father is old. It would not be for long. After he dies what is his becomes mine."

The predatory tone sent a shiver down Autumn's spine. Scylla growled from under the horses.

"It will not be," Ursula said firmly.

Uda of Jutland's mouth lost its smile. She gestured with her head at Staghorn, who grinned. "It shall be."

Staghorn's heavy boots crunched across the courtyard as he surveyed the five women dispassionately. For his own reasons he settled on Elspeth and reached up to pull her from the back of Ursula's saddle.

"No!" Ursula turned her horse. "We are virgins seeking sanctuary. Does that mean nothing?"

Staghorn hesitated, but a coarse command from Uda set his mouth in a cruel line. He pulled Elspeth roughly from the horse's back, and she cried out as she fell.

Autumn watched helplessly as he propelled Elspeth to the foot of the steps.

"There are four excellent reasons for you to be more agreeable." Uda spoke as if to a small child. "Shall I demonstrate?"

"No!" It wasn't Ursula this time, but a new voice, forceful and unafraid. A veiled woman ran out from behind the chapter house, her gray robes held off the ground to keep from tripping. As she bolted across the courtyard her headdress came loose and a long, black braid, a match to Ursula's and Uda's, followed behind her as she ran. "You cannot profane our house! You've done enough! I will not let you kill again."

Autumn saw Uda's gaze narrow as if she recognized the threat the woman posed.

The newcomer interposed herself between Uda and Elspeth, her breast heaving. She was braver than the abbot, who cowered in the chapter house doorway behind Uda.

Uda came down one step. "Are you so eager to be a martyr? You've betrayed your past for this place, turned your back on true power for what — kneeling six times a day while men tell you all that is good comes from men and all that is evil is the fault of women? Defy me if you want to, but you've already sealed your destiny. I won't let her do it as well. A bride of the White Christ — a congregation of the lamb." She spat eloquently. "We serve the great goddess, the only goddess. You have betrayed her."

"I follow my heart as she guides me."

"The White Christ or the goddess, which is it, Abbess Claire? Are you a lamb or a she-bear?" She looked over the abbess's shoulder at Elspeth. "Lamb, definitely. She doesn't even know how to close her mind."

The abbess whirled around to face Elspeth, and in that instant Elspeth stood taller and more substantially than Autumn had ever seen. Her normally quiet voice rang with fervent certainty. "I knew I would find you."

The abbess seemed stunned and did not hear Uda's tread on the steps behind her until it was too late.

"I'm disappointed, Abbess Claire. You're a lamb at heart. Let's make you one for real."

Ursula screamed when Uda seized the abbess by her braid with one hand while the other slashed a dagger into the braid at the nape of the abbess's neck. Elspeth shrieked when lightning seemed to crackle around them. With a sound like a thunderclap, the braid was severed, the blade shattered. The abbess staggered into Elspeth's arms.

Uda cursed and tossed away both braid and the remains of her broken blade. "Now I'll make you a saint!" She waved an imperious hand at Staghorn. The sunlight, so bright and now deadly, glinted on the blade of his raised broadsword.

The two-handed blow caught both of them in the side, and they toppled while what monks there were fainted and Scylla howled. The horses plunged and reared, and they had all they could handle to keep their seats. Autumn felt a white-hot rage light inside her.

Ursula's second scream was more than grief and rage. She invoked something that built pressure behind Autumn's eyes. Autumn was off her horse before it could throw her, dagger in her teeth as she strung her bow. One arrow had been enough before and would be again. Scylla raced in a circle, snapping at anyone who moved closer to any of them. The horses jostled against each other with the whites of their eyes showing, but Hilea and Killera tried to keep their mounts in a flanking position on each side of Ursula's. For the moment, Ursula was guarded.

In the bedlam of it all, only Autumn and Uda were still. Uda was looking down with satisfaction at the lifeless bodies of the two entwined women. Rage was all there was in Autumn's mind as she pulled the first arrow from her quiver.

:Go, Autumn. Leave me. Go now!:

:No! Never!:

:You must!:

She fired at Uda's heart, then nocked another before she saw what damage the first had wrought. The second arrow she sent into Staghorn's exposed throat. He deserved death and she only made it quick so she could be certain he died. Tain had had a saying — the best revenge was revenge. Another arrow was on her string when she glanced back at Uda.

She only believed what she saw because it had happened to her. She fired the third arrow even though she knew it was hopeless.

Both arrows trembled a scant inch from Uda's chest. She plucked them from the air as if she was not surrounded by death and terror. She kissed them both and regarded Autumn across the courtyard.

Ursula was a blur of light as she stood in her stirrups, directing Autumn knew not what at the malevolence Uda exuded. Uda did not even notice. Only when Hilea's voice soared over the courtyard did she glance toward Ursula again.

:Go! I can't protect you and fight her. This fight is mine.:

What Autumn knew was that Killera would never leave and neither would she. She slung her bow over her back and drew her dagger. She crouched in front of Ursula's horse, ready for any opening.

Hilea's voice was focusing Ursula's energy, but Uda was smiling still. She nudged Staghorn's body with her toe before she stepped over it. "The lamb was not the one she loved in the stars." She regarded the three of them guarding Ursula, each in her own way. "Which of you loved her?"

Killera shouted, "I love her," and kicked her horse forward. The beast lunged toward Uda and she fell back.

It was the only opening she was likely to have. Autumn followed the raging horse and when the snorting beast shied to the left she ducked around it, her dagger raised in her right hand.

Uda sparkled with dark fire. The terrified horse succeeded in ridding itself of Killera, who thumped painfully to the ground nearby. Autumn had startled Uda, but it was not enough. A force like an iron manacle circled her right wrist, and she could not move her hand. But the dagger was no longer in that hand and Autumn threw it with her left.

It found its home in the black heart. Autumn's choked cry of victory was short-lived. Uda did not even blink when she pulled the dagger out of her chest. Her soldiers, who had made no move to protect her, split the air with a cry as if from a single throat. *Uda! Uda!*

Sick with dread, Autumn for the first time believed in the White Christ's devil. There was not a drop of blood on the dagger, and Uda considered it dispassionately. "It is a fine blade. I think I'll use it from now on. And thank you for these arrows. I'm well-armed now."

Killera had pulled herself out of the dirt and she wielded her own dagger. Her inexperience with it was pathetically obvious. "You'll not take her."

"But I will," Uda answered. "You love her, but you're not the one she loved the night I first saw her in the stars." Her gaze flicked over Autumn, whose right wrist was still caught in some immovable force. "That was you. I'll take that experience from you in just a moment."

Killera charged like an enraged bear protecting her loved ones. Autumn cried out that it was useless even as Killera stumbled and crashed to her knees, almost at Rueda's feet.

Rueda twisted Autumn's dagger where it had penetrated Killera's breast, then withdrew it slowly. She watched Killera's eyes all the while the life leaked out of them as if she fed on the knowledge of death.

Ursula was running toward them now, whatever she had been attempting with her powers gone all awry. Autumn was choking with inchoate rage. She had nothing left to protect Ursula with.

Uda continued to ignore Ursula as she turned her cold, dark gaze to Autumn. "I've never seen such power in the sky. You brought her to light. Show me how. Show me why she shone like a hundred stars."

The touch of a foreign mind, this way, was the worst sensation Autumn had ever experienced. It was only a moment, and then Uda had taken it all, the memory of Ursula's cries, the scent of her skin, the way she had tasted, how tightly she had grasped at Autumn's pleasuring fingers. All taken and made unclean.

"How delicious," Uda murmured.

Ursula was sobbing over Killera's closed eyes. "Forgive me," she pleaded. "Forgive me."

Tiny Hilea stood over Ursula, her lute clasped over her breast like a shield. She tried to sing, but her voice was hoarse and none of the melodies seemed right.

Autumn strained against the force that held her wrist. A handspan's distance was all she needed to be able to claw out those hateful eyes. "What have we done to you to deserve this? What do you want of us?"

"Everything, of course." Uda raised an eyebrow, as if surprised by Autumn's failure to understand.

"Never," Autumn promised. "All you'll ever have is what you can take. There are things within us you'll never find and we'll never give up."

"Not while you live." She snapped the necklace Ursula had given Autumn from around her neck.

Autumn did not know what terrified her more, Uda's seemingly unlimited power or her horrible nonchalance about the destruction and chaos she wreaked without regret.

Autumn never knew what Uda had planned for her. She raised her unbound hand to defend herself but a fierce bundle of gray and white fur, all intent and rage, surged past her.

Uda screamed in terror and Autumn was suddenly free. She yanked Ursula to her feet. "Run, it's the only chance we have."

Scylla had buried her teeth in something and soldiers were running to their mistress's aid.

"No! You must go, leave me. She wants me. She'll stop looking for you if she has me."

"I won't go!"

"Nor I." Hilea's voice had broken and she looked down at Killera's limp body with her face twisted in a rigor of grief. "I have no reason to go!"

"No matter which way we turned it was going to end like this. Let me at least know you're safe." Ursula spoke to both of them, but her words were for Autumn.

"I won't go —"

Uda's scream made them all glance at her horrific battle with the enraged Scylla. All at once she raised her hands and a spiraling gate, visible to eyes as well as minds, opened behind her. Chaos roiled in the spiral and Uda seemed to feed on it. Her hands shaped a dark ball of light and she held it high for a moment. Then she sent it spinning at Scylla.

Scylla yelped once and dropped where she had stood panting.

Ursula gasped and raised her hands to the spiral spinning behind Uda. "Here, it's here. All the power I need! Now go!"

Autumn was seized like a child's toy and lifted off her feet.

Hilea shouted, "Ursula, no! Don't do this!"

Ursula was on her hands and knees, her braid pooled in the dirt under her. "I didn't know it could be like this," Ursula gasped. "This is my choice, to try. I can endure anything if you are alive."

Autumn felt herself pushed and lifted, swaying in the wind almost like being in the crow's nest. Hilea clutched her lute as she was similarly lifted toward Ursula's gate. Then they were both pushed through and Autumn lost all sight of Hilea, of Ursula. There was only the tunnel protecting her from the chaos.

The tunnel dissolved abruptly, and she tumbled to her feet. She was halfway up the hillside above the abbey and there was no sign of Hilea. She could see the courtyard below, where Ursula still gasped on her hands and knees. *:Go now, you must.:*

:She wants more than your body, more than your love. She will take the goddess within you.:

:Then be quick, for me, for my love. Beloved, be quick.:

Autumn drew her bow, one last time. She had never aimed so far. She sighted along her best arrow, the tip deadly sharp. The power she had learned from Ursula strengthened her vision and she saw her target clearly.

She could even hear Uda's husky, laughing voice. "Do you come to me willing?"

"Yes," Ursula said. "If you spare them."

"Do you believe you can bargain with me?"

Autumn knew she could not miss.

Her cold, aching fingers would not release the string.

She could not do it.

Uda knelt to press her mouth to Ursula's, and in a heartbeat they were gone, the soldiers, Uda, Staghorn's body, all of them. And Ursula.

The arrow on her string was the only weapon Autumn had left. Her rage was gone and an unreasoning, inexorable tide of grief washed away all that had been. Ursula was gone because Autumn had failed her.

She fit the tip of the arrow into the notch where her ribs came together to protect her heart. She had no heart left.

She fell.

"What is truth?"

"You know the answer to that." Autumn looked across the unbroken horizon.

"I don't. I sometimes think I know. I feel it. The old ways are true and yet some of the new ways are true, too. Because they mean something to us. But what is truth to you?"

"The sea is truth. It is always there, always the same, the rules never change. Even the sun sets, but the sea is forever. It is the only thing I know of that is permanent. The only thing that can't ever be taken away from us."

"What about love?" Ursula's words were quietly said, but they brought a hot flush to Autumn's cheeks. She did not yet know the feel of Ursula in her arms and had therefore not yet forgotten the pleasure of it.

"Can love be that permanent? Here today, here in a hundred years, a thousand, here when empires fall and new gods are born, here like the sea?"

"I think so."

Autumn awoke to find Ursula weeping in her sleep, and she knew why. Her stitches ached along with the burns and wounds in her hand and knee. The past was powerful and it reached for them still.

Nothing she had done with the *Spiralig Tor* had changed the past. Ursula was gone to some horrible, unknown fate, and the rest of them had died trying to save her.

She eased her grief with memories from dreams, when they had sailed and argued, trying to dislike each other because they feared their feelings. She grieved because the past was destroyed and it reached for them still.

She rose quietly from the bed and pressed the play button on the CD player. Scylla padded across the floor to nuzzle her hand.

It was not Hilea's voice, but her words that soared into Autumn's soul. Words written more than nine hundred years ago, and seven hundred years after they were first sung to begin Ursula's journey.

Most beautiful sight,
sweetest scent of desired delights,
We long ever after you in tearful exile.
When may we see you and be with you?
We are alone and you are in my mind . . .

243

Redeal

"Child."

So much in a single word — admonition, understanding, a gentle reminder of who was who in this long journey they had shared.

Three voices called in love, wanting her to come back to them, come back to the way they had taught her. She did not know their names, nor the way to reach them.

The way had closed to her and she walked a new path. The three voices were all that reminded her that she had known something other than this small room and the ardent devotion of a woman with oceans-deep eyes and hands that coursed with magic.

She turned her dreams away from that place, as pleasant as the memories were of moors and oranges, festivals and unstinting love. The road she walked now was quiet but shadowed by a darkness she knew hungered for her. But she would not go into that place again. Never again.

She did the only thing she knew how to do. Soil broke in her hands, and she led bees to the nectar of the young orange tree Autumn had brought her. The flowers she did not know, nor the plants that prickled with spines, but she planted all that Autumn brought her because it was all she knew how to do. She called birds to their rightful feast on the tiny bugs that nibbled at the blooms. She stroked the new plants and the leaves reached for the sun.

A musician knelt in exhaustion, her fingers cramped from the notes she scrawled on paper marked with musical staves. Words spilled across the pages ... *gardens* ... *delight* ...... *exile* ... *kiss of peace* ... *lilies* ... *death* ... *blood*. The room was strewn with broken instruments — a violin, a lute, a cello and others. All that remained was the 20-string harp guitar with its tipped neck and coils of cable connecting the two tuning boards to a wild array of mixing boards and equalizers — and finally, to the amplifiers that dominated the small room.

"Not again," she whispered. "I can't, not again."

A farmer wept in the loneliness of her bed, too weak to sleep and too broken to care. Lovers tangled in the next room, taking what comfort they could from lives suddenly empty of power and purpose. The circle was shattered and would not come together again. Their gates were sealed against the darkness that had broken them. The darkness did not stop searching.

A magician spread her hands and invited anyone to "pick a card, any card." Her left hand moved less gracefully than her right, but she no longer practiced sleight of hand. She was a magician, a woman and a warrior.

She reached for her power. A torn card reassembled itself in the closed palm of her hand. Her power came from her gate, more easily as she learned to use it with confidence. Whenever she touched it she knew the darkness was beyond. It knew where she was and that she had what it wanted. But she was strong now.

Journey's beginning.

She would leave the little club to sleep next to a goddess who remembered nothing of her past but everything of her soul. When she awoke she would find the fire-haired woman in her landlord's barren backyard, coaxing life from dirt that had long baked under the glaring desert sun. Already an orange tree thrived and late summer blooms scented the hot nights. They would sit down together and tell each other of their dreams, side by side in a garden of fruits and a splendor of flowers.

The Tunnel of Light trilogy will continue with book two,
Seeds of Fire.

About the Author

Laura Adams is the alter ego of Karin Kallmaker. She is let loose on a regular basis to pen romantic fantasy, supernatural, and science fiction novels. Karin Kallmaker was born in 1960 and raised by her loving, middle-class parents in California's Central Valley. The physician's Statement of Live Birth plainly declares, "Sex: Female" and "Cry: Lusty." Both are still true. Her genealogically minded father recently informed her that she is descended from Lady Godiva.

From a normal childhood and equally unremarkable public-school adolescence, she went on to obtain an ordinary bachelor's degree from the California State University at Sacramento. At the age of sixteen, eyes wide open, she fell into the arms of her first and only sweetheart. Ten years later, after seeing the film *Desert Hearts*, her sweetheart descended on the Berkeley Public Library determined to find some of "those" books. "Rule, Jane" led to "Lesbianism—Fiction" and then on to book after self-affirming book by and about lesbians. These books were the encouragement Karin needed to forget the so-called mainstream and spin her first romance for lesbians. That manuscript became her first Naiad Press novel, *In Every Port. Sleight of Hand* is her first book for Bella Books.

Karin now lives in the San Francisco Bay Area with that very same sweetheart; she is a one-woman woman. The happily-ever-after couple became Mom and Moogie to Kelson James in 1995 and Eleanor Delenn in 1997. They celebrate their twenty-fourth anniversary in 2001.

Visit
Bella Books
at

www.bellabooks.com